FELONY REPORT

D0050929

As Elizabeth Linington:

FELONY REPORT
SKELETONS IN THE CLOSET
CONSEQUENCE OF CRIME
NO VILLAIN NEED BE
PERCHANCE OF DEATH
CRIME BY CHANCE
PRACTISE TO DECEIVE
POLICEMAN'S LOT
SOMETHING WRONG
DATE WITH DEATH
NO EVIL ANGEL
GREENMASK!
THE PROUD MAN
THE LONG WATCH
MONSIEUR JANVIER
THE KINGBREAKER
ELIZABETH I *(Ency. Brit.)*

As Egan O'Neill:

THE ANGLOPHILE

As Lesley Egan:

MOTIVE IN SHADOW
THE HUNTERS AND THE HUNTED
LOOK BACK ON DEATH
A DREAM APART
THE BLIND SEARCH
SCENES OF CRIME
PAPER CHASE
MALICIOUS MISCHIEF
IN THE DEATH OF A MAN
THE WINE OF VIOLENCE
A SERIOUS INVESTIGATION
THE NAMELESS ONES
SOME AVENGER, ARISE
DETECTIVE'S DUE
MY NAME IS DEATH
RUN TO EVIL
AGAINST THE EVIDENCE

THE BORROWED ALIBI
A CASE FOR APPEAL

As Dell Shannon:

DESTINY OF DEATH
EXPLOIT OF DEATH
CASE PENDING
THE ACE OF SPADES
EXTRA KILL
KNAVE OF HEARTS
DEATH OF A BUSYBODY
DOUBLE BLUFF
ROOT OF ALL EVIL
MARK OF MURDER
THE DEATH-BRINGERS
DEATH BY INCHES
COFFIN CORNER
WITH A VENGEANCE
CHANCE TO KILL
RAIN WITH VIOLENCE
KILL WITH KINDNESS
SCHOOLED TO KILL
CRIME ON THEIR HANDS
UNEXPECTED DEATH
WHIM TO KILL
THE RINGER
MURDER WITH LOVE
WITH INTENT TO KILL
NO HOLIDAY FOR CRIME
SPRING OF VIOLENCE
CRIME FILE
DEUCES WILD
STREETS OF DEATH
APPEARANCES OF DEATH
COLD TRAIL
FELONY AT RANDOM
FELONY FILE
MURDER MOST STRANGE
THE MOTIVE ON RECORD

FELONY REPORT

ELIZABETH LININGTON

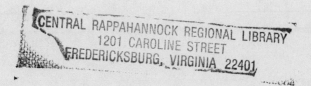

CENTRAL RAPPAHANNOCK REGIONAL LIBRARY
1201 CAROLINE STREET
FREDERICKSBURG, VIRGINIA 22401

PUBLISHED FOR THE CRIME CLUB BY
DOUBLEDAY & COMPANY, INC.
GARDEN CITY, NEW YORK
1984

M
C.2

All of the characters in this book
are fictitious, and any resemblance
to actual persons, living or dead,
is purely coincidental.

Library of Congress Cataloging in Publication Data
Linington, Elizabeth.
 Felony report.
 I. Title.
PS3562.I515F44   1984   813'.54
           ISBN: 0-385-19557-5
Library of Congress Catalog Card Number 84-4118
 Copyright © 1984 by Elizabeth Linington
       All Rights Reserved
 Printed in the United States of America
        First Edition

This one is for Elaine with love

"There's nowt so queer as folk."
—Old Lancashire proverb

God hath made men upright; but they
have sought out many inventions.
—Ecclesiastes 8:29

CHAPTER ONE

Maddox had just finished talking to one witness to last night's heist, and watched the man go out to the corridor glumly. He hadn't given them anything useful; it was a run-of-the-mill heist, nothing to tie it up to the several heist jobs over the last three months or so which were the work of the heister they had nicknamed Dapper Dan, or any of the other anonymous holdups they had on hand to work. This one, at a twenty-four-hour convenience store, was just another anonymous heist, a vague description of the man with the gun, the take fairly modest, and nowhere to look on it.

D'Arcy was still talking to the second witness; he probably wasn't getting anything more useful. Pool what they got, thought Maddox, and toss a coin for who should write the report. It was getting on for ten o'clock on this Tuesday morning of early March. He wondered if it was too early to call the coroner's office. They had asked for priority on those autopsies; six bodies at once was something unusual. Central beat downtown might be used to that sort of thing, but Hollywood division —as wild and woolly as Hollywood could sometimes get—wasn't. Maddox contemplated the meager notes he'd taken on this latest anonymous heist, and thought about those six bodies—the Babcocks and the Hogans.

George Ellis came into the communal detective office from his office down the hall, looked around, and asked, "Where is everybody? Have we heard anything from the coroner's office yet?"

"I was just about to call and ask," said Maddox. "Joe went out on a new burglary, and Rodriguez is out looking at a body—I don't know where everybody else is. There's no lead at all on this heist, just damn all. They don't give any kind of description, just a man with a gun."

Ellis hunched his beefy shoulders. "Bricks without straw. It's a thankless job."

D'Arcy's witness got up and ambled out to the corridor, and D'Arcy came over to Maddox's desk and said, "Nothing. No useful description, just a fellow maybe twenty-five with a big gun. Nothing to go anywhere on."

Neither Maddox nor Ellis said anything; there wasn't anything to say. Maddox sat back and lit a cigarette and said, "I suppose Bergner'd bite my head off if I called him. They always take their time."

"Well, I suppose all the scientific analyses take time," said Ellis vaguely. And then he said under his breath, "Oh, my God, I'd forgotten about those damn Germans, and here they are. Damn."

Maddox followed his glance to the door of the big communal detective office. He'd forgotten the Germans too; they'd been briefed about them from the chief's office last week. A group of West German journalists on a tour of a lot of Western nations doing research on police techniques and methods; they had evidently visited most European nations and were now visiting a good many American cities before heading for the Far East. The little crowd of people at the door of the big office could be nothing else than the Germans, shepherded by a tall, dark, urbane man who herded them over to Ellis and made introductions. "Lieutenant Ellis—" And he mentioned names, Miller, Keller, Erickson—there were four men and a woman, a buxom fortyish blonde, Mrs. Grunsky.

"Sergeant Maddox," responded Ellis politely, "Detective D'Arcy." It was necessary to be polite. The man with them was a Captain Devereaux from the chief's office at Headquarters. The Germans were polite in turn, looking around the office, at thin dark Maddox, lanky D'Arcy, bulky-shouldered Ellis. They had already had a look at the Communications room. "Perhaps you'd like to see our laboratory," said Ellis. "Of course any detailed analytical work is sent down to the main laboratory at Central Headquarters, but we're equipped to process fingerprints and so on—"

The buxom blonde gave them a toothy smile. "It is all so very interesting," she said earnestly, in excellent if guttural English, "learning of all these so excellent new scientific methods for combating evil." She trailed obediently after the others as Ellis led them out toward the lab.

Devereaux sat down at Rodriguez' desk next to Maddox's and offered him a cigarette. "Evil," he said thoughtfully, lighting his own. "Not quite the word for it, is it? It's a while since I've been out on the street, but it's not quite the word."

D'Arcy thrust out his long lanky legs, slumping in his desk chair, and said, "When you come to think of it, real evil is damn rare, you know."

"That's right," said Maddox. "The thankless job isn't dealing with evil—that's too big a word. What we're seeing and coping with, for our sins, is the foolishness—you could say the foolishness of fallible man."

"Nice phrase," said Devereaux.

"It's the stupidity—the laziness and greed and mindless violence and the egotism and the impulse. The goddamned foolishness. It gets tiresome."

"I believe you," said Devereaux. "I'm thankful to be in administration these days. You boys can cope with the louts on the street."

"And the victims," said Maddox tiredly.

The little party of journalists came back from the lab and Devereaux stabbed out his cigarette and got up. "They had a tour of Headquarters yesterday—we're visiting all the divisions today. Captain Flagg at Hollenbeck is taking us all out to lunch—at the chief's expense."

He had just shepherded the group out when Rodriguez came in, looking disgruntled, and said, "Just more paperwork. An old wino dead on a bus-stop bench out on Sunset. No ID. See if anybody has got his prints, but the city will have to bury him. Looks like natural causes, he was probably in his seventies and not a mark on him." He sat down at his desk, brushing his neat moustache, and didn't immediately start to type a report.

Ellis came back and asked, "Have we got anything from the coroner's office yet on those bodies?"

"I was just about to call," said Maddox. He took a last drag on his cigarette and thought idly, in addition to all the stupidity, the foolishness—the real evil, a thing they didn't see once in a blue moon—there was also the occasional lunacy, and that wasn't the individual's fault either. He reached for the phone, and it shrilled at him.

"Sergeant Maddox."

"Well, we got this and that for you," said Dr. Bergner at the coroner's office.

"I was just going to call you."

"It was meperidine," said Bergner. "An OD of meperidine, all six bodies."

"I'll be damned," said Maddox mildly. "Well, it looked like an OD of some kind. How did they get it?"

"That's your business," said Bergner. "But it looks fairly offbeat,

Maddox. It wasn't injected—there's not a mark on any of them—so it was orally ingested. There are a number of prescription tablets and capsules on the market, might have been any one of them—we're still completing analyses and we'll pin it down for you eventually. All I can say is, I can't think of any of those that come any stronger than about fifty milligrams—it's a narcotic analgesic similar to morphine—and the usual dose is one to two every four hours. All of these people had a massive overdose, call it something like twelve to fifteen tablets or capsules. As I say, we're still working on it, probably be able to tell you more later, but to go on with, the four Babcocks died anywhere between ten and midnight on Saturday night, the Hogans about the same time. They'd all had a meal sometime about six o'clock. The damn thing is, if they'd been found and treated, they could all have been saved, you know—pump the stomachs, administer an antidote, and they'd have lived."

"Yes," said Maddox. "You can't say how they got it?"

"Just, it was ingested orally," said Bergner irritably. "I'm not going out on a limb—I don't know. I will say that judging by the times—the time it would have taken them to die of the OD—they probably ingested it about the time they had the meal. Call it five to six P.M."

"Symptoms?" asked Maddox.

"They'd have come on fairly rapidly, with that much of an OD. Light-headedness, dizziness, weakness—in medical terms respiratory depression, depression of the central nervous system, eventual coma—the first symptoms would have come on within thirty to forty-five minutes. If any of them had been able to call for help—but apparently they weren't. It's a damned queer thing, Maddox. Was there any connection between them?"

"Not that we know. Queer isn't the word for it. That's all you can tell us so far?"

"We'll have an analysis of stomach contents for you by tomorrow, if that's going to say anything. And we'll be able to pin down just what prescription brand it was, but as I say, there are several on the market —some of them prescribed as tranquilizers too."

"Well, thanks very much," said Maddox. "Whatever else you can tell us we'll appreciate."

"I'll get back to you when we've got anything else," said Bergner.

Maddox relayed that to D'Arcy and Rodriguez.

"But that doesn't make much sense," said Rodriguez. "All six of them? They didn't know each other, by what we've heard. A suicide pact is just damn ridiculous—the Babcocks a nice, normal, happy family, and the Hogans—I haven't seen any lab reports, but damn it, Ivor, we were on the Babcocks and there wasn't any prescription medication in the place. My God, and the two little kids—it doesn't make sense."

"Not much," agreed Maddox. "We want to talk to the Durands again and the Bryant woman. Bergner isn't committing himself, but it sounds to me as if they could all have gotten it with the meal they'd had, about five to six, he said. The times seem to be right."

"That's crazy," said D'Arcy. "Somebody sneaking in and spiking the soup? Two ordinary, quiet, humdrum families? Why and how?"

"God knows," said Maddox. "We'll have to go around on it, that's all, and hope to get some more detail from Bergner eventually. D'Arcy, you see if you can get hold of the Bryant woman." He looked up the number in his notebook and reached for the phone to call Mrs. Durand.

She was at home and said yes, of course they'd tell the police whatever they could, it still didn't seem possible and they couldn't understand it. Yes, she'd call her husband and they'd be expecting him.

Maddox went out to the corridor and met Sue and Daisy Hoffman just coming back to their little office across from the communal detective office. Sue said, "I can't say I'll be sorry to get out of this rat race for a while."

"And I'll be just as happy to have you sitting quiet at home," said Maddox. "Minding the baby." The baby was due at the end of July; Sue would be starting maternity leave in six weeks, and could take six months off the job without losing seniority. "You all right?"

"Just a little fed up," said Sue. "We've wasted a couple of hours."

"What do you expect of people?" asked Daisy robustly. Slim, blond Daisy didn't look at all like a grandmother, but she was. "Kids."

"What was it?" asked Maddox.

"Probably attempted molestation, but we'll never know unless we catch up to him another time. Little girl playing in her own front yard tells mama a funny-looking man tried to get her to go somewhere in his car. She can't give us a description of him or the car, just says he was funny-looking and she was scared of him. What can you expect? She's only six."

"And the next thing we'll hear," said Sue, "is that the same character succeeded in coaxing another little girl into his car."

"Take it as it comes," said Daisy. "Something new down?"

"Just the autopsy findings on those bodies," said Maddox. "OD of meperidine, probably Demerol, and there's something damned funny about it. At the moment it just doesn't seem to make much sense."

As he went out to the parking lot for the Maserati—and one of these days he was going to have to think about another car, the old girl was probably on her last legs, needing various new parts—he was thinking about what Bergner had said, and trying to fit the few things they knew into the picture. He and Rodriguez had gone out on the Babcocks, D'Arcy on the Hogans, but the two pictures were oddly similar.

Charles and Linda Durand lived in a small attractive house on Laurel Street in West Hollywood. Linda Durand had been Betty Babcock's sister, and her husband worked for a large insurance firm, as had Edward Babcock; the men's friendship had been cemented through marrying sisters. They had both been transferred to California by the firm a couple of years ago, from Chicago, and the Babcocks had been buying a house not far from the Durands on Hayworth Street. The Durands had a three-year-old girl; the Babcocks had had an eight-year-old, Steve, and a six-year-old, Eileen.

Linda Durand had called her husband and he was there; they looked at Maddox and heard what he had to tell them, and Linda said incredulously, "Demerol? But that's just impossible—there wasn't anything like that in the house! None of them was on medication of any kind, and Betty had a sort of thing about not taking medicine of any sort—about the only thing there'd have been there was aspirin—but we told you that then, on Sunday, when you said it looked like an overdose—Demerol—it just isn't possible. You don't mean you think it was suicide, that they wanted to die—and to kill the children too—that just isn't possible!"

"We don't know, Mrs. Durand," said Maddox. "All we know is that's what killed them. Do you know if they knew a Mr. and Mrs. Hogan, on Oxford Avenue?"

They looked at him blankly. They were a nice-looking couple, Durand tall and well-built with a blunt-featured face, friendly eyes, she small and blond and pretty. "Hogan?" said Durand. "No, I'm sure they didn't. We all knew most of the same people, you know. And that's right, what Linda says, it's just impossible that they—that they did it themselves—and the children—"

She uttered a little sob. "Just not possible they're gone—we told you how it was on Sunday. It was their tenth wedding anniversary and we were going to have dinner together. I said I'd make an apple pie, it was Ed's favorite. We were supposed to be there at one o'clock, and we couldn't get any answer at the door, and the back door was unlocked and we went in and found them—all of them dead. And I just don't understand it. There wasn't any reason, they were in love with each other and crazy about the kids—" She broke down crying, and Durand put his arm around her, obviously distressed and upset. He just said miserably, "That's so. There just wasn't any reason for it."

Maddox thought it didn't make much sense either, but thinking of what Bergner had said, he asked, "Could you tell me about what time they usually had dinner?"

Linda clutched her handkerchief in a little ball. "Dinner? Well, Ed usually got home around six or a little before and Betty always had dinner ready. The way I do. Why? Do you think somebody *murdered* them? But how? There's nobody—everybody liked Betty and Ed! I don't understand it!"

How indeed, thought Maddox, and why? An ordinary, harmless, well-liked young couple? With a pair of nice, normal kids. It would, in early March, be dark by five or so, but it was hard to imagine some nameless, motiveless villain sneaking into the little suburban house and adding Demerol to the dinner keeping warm in the oven. And, thinking of what Bergner had said, he thought back to that scene last Sunday afternoon. The attractive, well-kept little house on a quiet residential street. The Durands standing by stunned and shocked, and the stolid uniformed man who had answered the first call. Just a few things obvious: that it had been an OD, poisoning of some sort, judging by the bodies; that it had probably happened the previous night. Babcock had been in a big armchair in the living room, the evening *Herald* in his lap. The TV had been on, in the tiny den down the hall, and the kids had been there. An eight- and six-year-old, probably their bedtimes would have been eight, eight-thirty; so they'd been unconscious before that. Betty Babcock had been in the kitchen, and you could deduce that she had realized something was wrong, for she had been trying to call for help. She had been sprawled on the floor just below the wall phone, and the phone was dangling off the hook. Bergner said, lightheadedness, dizziness, respiratory failure, coma. Had she called her husband, found him already unconscious, been trying to call the paramedics? And passing out before she could do so, dying quietly on the kitchen floor while the others died elsewhere?

Dinner. He asked Linda, "Did your sister usually clean up the kitchen as soon as dinner was over?" She had that night, at any rate; the dishwasher had been full of clean dishes, the kitchen counters polished.

"Yes, she always did, she didn't like to leave things. But how could it have happened?"

Maddox wished he knew. He hadn't seen a lab report yet as to whether there had been any extraneous latent prints in the place. Before he had left the office he had called the lab and told Baker to get a sample of everything edible at the Laurel Street house for analysis, and eventually that might tell them something. They had, of course, looked through the house, and as Linda said there was no prescription medication anywhere, only a bottle of aspirin and an antacid remedy.

Marking time, he got the name of the only doctor the Babcocks had gone to here. "Betty didn't like doctors much, she took Stevie to this one only when he had an ear infection last year." A Dr. Bauer on Melrose Avenue, a pediatrician. And a pediatrician wouldn't have been handing out a prescription for Demerol, and even if Betty Babcock had had a fit of some kind and decided to do away with herself and her family—or if Ed Babcock had—what had become of the container? Where had the Demerol come from? They had searched all the wastebaskets, the refuse can in the garage, and nothing had shown up. They hadn't taken the garbage disposal apart; maybe they'd better do that, just in case. But where could the Hogans fit in a scene like that?

Maddox sighed and tried to think of any more intelligent questions to ask.

* * *

At about the same time, D'Arcy was getting much the same thing from Marlene Bryant. She was a plump, rather pretty woman in her forties; she lived in an old apartment building on Vermont, with a husband who drove a delivery truck for Sears Roebuck. Their three children were all grown and married. She worked at a dress shop on Western, but told D'Arcy she just hadn't felt up to going to work yesterday or today. "After finding Mom and Dad like that, you know. I can't get over it, it was terrible. Just terrible. And now you're telling me they were poisoned some way—Demerol? That's some kind of medicine, isn't it? They weren't taking any medicine regular, either of them —and they were both just fine. They weren't young, Mom was seventy-one and Dad seventy-three—but they were just fine! Just like I told you Sunday, I usually went to see them on the weekend, and they didn't go out much, just to the market or once in a while to play cards with the neighbors, and when nobody opened the door, well, I had a key, of course, in case of emergency, and I went in—and found them. Oh! I tried to keep my head, I called my husband and he called an ambulance —but how could they have gotten poisoned? With this medicine? There wasn't any medicine around, they'd both been just fine—"

Hogan had worked for the Parks and Recreation Department, been retired for eight years. They had owned the modest little house on Oxford Street and by the daughter's account had been a humdrum, harmless, elderly couple with no enemies and not many friends. They had stayed home and watched television. There certainly hadn't been any prescription medicine in the place.

Thinking of what Bergner had said, D'Arcy asked her what time they had usually had dinner. "Oh, between five and six, I guess. Maybe earlier on Saturday, there were some shows on TV that night they liked. But how could they have gotten poisoned? Mom was always careful about keeping the refrigerator clean—but you said it was this medicine—"

"Do you know if they knew anyone named Babcock?"

She stared at him bewilderedly. "Why, no—I never heard the name —and I'd know everybody they knew—no, they didn't."

D'Arcy couldn't think what else to ask her. There would be a lab man at the Hogans' house now, collecting everything from the refrigerator, the medicine chest; probably whatever they got on this would be from the lab. And they did sometimes get the offbeat ones; but this was the queerest one they had had in a while.

He went back to the office and met Maddox just driving into the parking lot. They compared notes and Maddox said, "It's so damn shapeless. Why these people? And the two poor kids?"

"Just ordinary people," agreed D'Arcy. "No rhyme or reason. Maybe when Bergner gives us something else it'll begin to make sense, but I don't see how."

"The lab ought to know something about prints by now." Maddox called and got an irritable-sounding Franks.

"Listen, there are only twenty-four hours in a day, Maddox. With all these heists and burglaries—I've been out most of the day dusting for prints, and probably it's a damn waste of time, and the householders pawing over everything, now I've got all the comparisons to make. Talk about going through the motions! Oh, those homicides—well, Baker was doing a report before you chased him out again—just a minute." After a hiatus he came back and said, "Short and sweet. The Babcock house, the only prints we picked up were theirs and some of the relatives'—the Durand couple. The Hogan place, only theirs anywhere."

"That's a big help," said Maddox.

"Well, you can't make bricks without straw," said Franks.

"So where do we go from here?" said Maddox to D'Arcy.

"Wait and see what more Bergner and his boys come up with. If they can tell us what the Demerol was in, or whether they just took capsules—but all six people?" said D'Arcy doubtfully. "And look, Ivor, just as we said—neither of those houses is very big. Can we see somebody getting in and adding the Demerol to the soup or something? The Bryant woman says her parents didn't go out much, and there was no sign of a break-in—"

"Or at the Babcocks'. And Mrs. Babcock was a homebody too," said Maddox. "We can't hope to hear from Bergner until tomorrow at least —I just hope to God they can give us some lead."

Joe Feinman ambled in looking tired, sat down at his desk, and pulled his tie loose. "You doing any good at anything?"

Maddox told him about the Demerol, and he grunted in surprise. "All up in the air. Same with all these burglaries. Frustrating."

"Which burglaries in particular?" asked D'Arcy. The burglaries were just one of the ongoing problems, and in spite of the man-hours and lab work spent, it was rare that they caught up to any of the burglars, or retrieved any of the loot for the outraged householders.

"Five of them," said Feinman, shutting his eyes and slumping down in the desk chair. "I don't count any of the rest still on the books—just run-of-the-mill break-ins, no leads, no prints, nothing. But these five— the fifth one was last night—I think it's the same joker, and we only know one thing about him. It sort of came together when I looked at this one today. I went back over the other reports and it adds up. The first couple, Nolan and Dowling were on. The couple I looked at I put down to juveniles at first, and nowhere to look for those. But then I looked at that damned dog door this morning and a little bell rang."

"He got in the dog door?" Maddox was amused.

"That's right." Feinman's dark, intellectual face wore a small, unamused grin. "And the addresses—all fairly big, nice places off Laurel Canyon, and nice pieces of loot." Places up there might contain the loot; it was not a newly fashionable residential area, but old, solid, and good. "I took a look back at the reports, and it adds. He, whoever, got in a bathroom window about eighteen inches square—a couple of closet windows not much bigger—and now this damned dog door. The dog's dead, so he wasn't there to bark. The first couple I put down to juveniles, the kids are starting younger and younger—but when you take a look at the loot, they were all very pro jobs, pretty slick. All of those places had good security too, good locks and bars on the most inviting windows and so on. And he's taken a nice haul—radios, cameras, tape recorders, a couple of fur coats, jewelry, cash, a coin collection. It's got to be one man—he hasn't gone for any big stuff like TVs, and the only thing we can guess about him, he's a little guy, to get in all those small spaces."

"See what Records might have to offer," suggested D'Arcy.

Feinman sat up and lit a cigarette. "Bill's downtown asking them now. If we've got any midget burglars in the files the computers will turn them up, and then we can go looking for them. It should have dawned on me before—I'd seen two of those break-ins, and none of the loot has turned up, so he knows a tame fence, which says he's an experienced pro."

They all sat silent for a few minutes, ruminating on the various cases on hand to work. "That heist," said Maddox. "Nowhere to go on it."

"Nope," said D'Arcy. "Just a heist. No decent description. But it wasn't Dapper Dan. This one—they both told us—needed a shave and smelled dirty. Let's see, Dapper hasn't hit in a couple of weeks."

"Him," said Feinman, shutting his eyes again. The heister they had nicknamed Dapper Dan had been around town for about three months. Comparing notes with other divisions, they had belatedly found out that he had probably pulled a few heists in the valley area and Hollenbeck's territory as well as Hollywood's. He specialized in liquor stores, usually hit just before closing time, and was fast and professional. Various victims had described him in much the same terms—anywhere between thirty and forty, a white man, medium coloring—he always wore a hat so nobody could say what color his hair was—and he was well-dressed, neat, and clean in good-looking sports clothes, usually brown or gray. One store owner, an ex-Marine, had claimed the gun was a .38 Colt, but that was no use in looking for him. To date, the detectives in all three divisions had gotten the names of known heisters from Records, who conformed to the rather vague description; some they had found and questioned, with no results, some they were still looking for, but that one was all up in the air too.

"He's about due to hit again," said Maddox. It was getting on to the end of shift, and this had been a largely unproductive day. Tuesday, the middle of the week—nothing much might show up for the night watch; on the other hand you never knew. At least, as usual in March, the weather was nice, not too hot.

Sue looked in from the corridor and said, "I'm taking off early. All the paperwork's up to date for once and Daisy's got a date to baby-sit the grandchildren."

"Take care on the freeway," said Maddox automatically. She waved at him and went out.

"You decided on names for baby?" asked Feinman, yawning again.

"Nothing to decide," said Maddox. "She won't hear of anything but John or Mary. Nice, simple names."

"I'll say amen to that," said D'Arcy, and they both grinned at him. D'Arcy's life had been complicated by his very peculiar first name; he had them all trained never to use it. He stood up and settled his tie. "I think I'll take off early too. Tomorrow's another day, and I've got some homework to do."

"Going back to school at your age yet," said Feinman. "What I say is, let 'em speak English."

With the ever-increasing Hispanic population frustrating the simplest interrogation, D'Arcy was improving his detective techniques with evening classes in Spanish. "You wait," he said to Feinman, "until someday you've got a hot homicide suspect who no spicka de English, and you'll come to me and say pretty please help us out. And maybe I'll make sergeant quicker too."

Rodriguez came in, marched over to his desk, and picked up his cigarette lighter. "I knew I'd left it somewhere. I'm getting out of this place before anything else goes down. Did anybody tell you another body turned up? Nothing to work—another damn fool kid on the H, an OD, on a junior high campus. At least I could rope Ambrose in on it, and he's doing the report." The detectives in the Narco office down the hall came in on anything involving drugs.

There was a general exodus: nothing more to do on any of the current cases today, and tomorrow would tell if any new leads on anything would show.

On his way home, Maddox ruminated fruitlessly on those six bodies; he should have learned long ago to leave business at the office. If they got anywhere on that, it would be on the lab evidence, and you couldn't hurry those boys. Traffic was thick as usual on the freeway, and he turned up Verdugo Road with relief. The old Maserati needed a tune-up; he had a date to take it in on Thursday, his day off. When he came to Starview Terrace and the rambling big house at its dead end, he felt the usual warmth in his heart; they were so lucky, he and Sue— they had each other, and now the baby to come, and Margaret. He hadn't had a home for quite a while, until he and Sue were married; it was nice to have a home to come back to.

As he came in the back door a single polite bass woof uttered welcome, and he bent to pat the big brindle Akita, Tama. Margaret Carstairs was slicing tomatoes at the sink and he kissed her cheek. Sue was going to look exactly like her mother in about twenty years' time, which was fine with him. Margaret smiled at him. "Sue's relaxing over sherry, you'd better join her, Ivor. You look as if you need a drink."

"Not sherry," said Maddox, and got out the bottle of bourbon.

"Dinner in half an hour."

Dinner—and dammit, there he was thinking about the Babcocks and the Hogans again. Who had gotten the OD of Demerol about the time they had dinner. He carried his drink down to the living room where Sue was lying back in an armchair. She looked up at him, his darling Sue, her dark hair a little ruffled and the baby definitely showing now, and she said, "It's silly. Bringing the office home. But Daisy and I both worried about it, you know. That man trying to coax the little girl into his car—and no way to start looking for him."

"It's a thankless, dirty job, love," said Maddox. And he thought, evil. Too big a word. The stupidities, the lust and greed and laziness and mindless impulse. And tomorrow was another day.

* * *

The night watch came on at Hollywood division, and waited for what might show up. They were all on, on Tuesday night—Dick Brougham, Ken Donaldson, Roger Stacey. As usual, Stacey had some new snapshots to show; he was a camera buff like D'Arcy, and proud of his six kids; he must have a thousand snapshots of them, and they were nice-looking kids, and his wife was a very pretty blonde.

They didn't get a call until just before ten o'clock; Brougham and Stacey went out on it. It was a heist, at a liquor store out on Sunset nearly to the Strip; and they hadn't listened to the owner for five minutes before Stacey said succinctly, "Dapper Dan. It was about time for him to hit again." The owner, Robert Kuykendall, had been alone in the place, getting ready to close up. He told them the heister had been maybe thirty-five, a white man with a big gun, kind of medium coloring, he had a hat on and he was pretty sharply dressed in brown slacks and jacket, a beige shirt. "He wasn't in here three minutes, see, he puts the gun on me and just says, all the cash, buddy, make it snappy. So I handed it over—Jesus, I couldn't say how much, the register tab will say, but it'd been a fairly good day, call it four-fifty, five hundred bucks. Some of it was checks, of course, and he didn't take those—maybe four hundred cash—and Jesus, you know what? He thanked me! He stashed it in his inside breast pocket and then he said, 'Thanks, buddy, I appreciate this'—and out he went."

"Dapper Dan," said Brougham. That was an earmark, besides the description; on every heist he pulled he had said that. "Could you give us a better description? Do you think you could describe him to a police artist, to get a sketch?"

"Jesus, no," said the owner. "He wasn't here three minutes. I was sort of shook, if you get me. That's all I can tell you," and he repeated the description again.

It didn't give them anywhere to go, and all it told them was that that had been Dapper Dan again; but of course a report had to be written on it. They went back to the office and flipped a coin; Brougham lost and began to type the report.

At five minutes to midnight they got another call, to an address on Lexington Avenue. Donaldson went out on it with Stacey. When they got there, they found the uniformed man, Johnny McCrea, talking to a nice-looking young couple who were obviously in a state of shock. There were also two dead bodies, both young women.

"Look," said McCrea, who was a big dark handsome young fellow, "all I know is I got chased up here, and here's the bodies, and these people had just found them. They'd just gotten home from a date—the girl, Brenda Cobb, lives with these other two girls—I've got the names for you, Doris Adler and Deborah Carlson. The guy's name is Eric

Emmons. They'd been out on a date, went to dinner and a movie, and he brought her home about forty minutes ago and they found the other two girls dead. It looks like some kind of OD to me."

It did to Donaldson and Stacey too. They looked at the bodies, two young women in their mid-twenties. One was on the couch in the living room, the other on one of the twin beds in the second bedroom. They were both fairly recently dead, both still warm.

"But I don't understand it!" sobbed Brenda Cobb. "How could they be dead? Ricky picked me up at six—they were both fine then, just as usual—they were going to have dinner and watch an old movie on TV —a rerun of an old Astaire–Rogers musical. What are you saying, it looks like an overdose of drugs? None of us takes drugs, there's nothing like that in the place, we're not that kind of people—" She was crying harder now. "They were my best friends."

Stacey and Donaldson had seen Maddox's report on what the coroner's office had said about those other homicides. This one looked peculiarly similar, at least.

They got a few facts. Brenda Cobb worked as a receptionist at a doctor's office. Doris Adler had been a waitress at a well-known restaurant, Deborah Carlson had been a file clerk at a savings and loan company. Emmons was a bookkeeper in the office of a local department store. They all looked like respectable, honest people.

The paramedics were standing by then. The bodies would end up in the coroner's office, and it would remain to be seen what the doctor said about them.

CHAPTER TWO

Kuykendall would be coming in to make a statement, but of course he wouldn't give them anything useful. They were still looking for several possible suspects out of Records, with the suggestive pedigrees for the heists and burglaries, and the word was out to the street informants, not that it would probably be of any use. The cash was unidentifiable, and it was doubtful that any of the victims could identify the heister definitely.

They were all more interested in the two new bodies that had turned up overnight, Doris Adler and Deborah Carlson. "By God," said Maddox, "it fits the pattern, and just what the hell is this? By what Stacey says, ordinary girls working ordinary jobs, three girls sharing an apartment, one out on a date, and she says the other two were just getting dinner when she left. Going to watch an old movie on TV!" He had already been onto the coroner's office to ask priority on those autopsies. "I'll lay you any money it's the Demerol again, it's the same damn pattern." Nobody had been in the lab when he called ten minutes ago; now he tried again, and got Garcia, told him to chase up to that apartment and go over it, get samples of all the food left, and dust for prints. The third girl, Brenda Cobb, worked at a doctor's office, but when he called she wasn't there; he and Rodriguez went up to the apartment on Lexington Avenue and found her there. She was a nice-looking dark-haired girl, about twenty-six, and she was looking pale and sick. She was still in a nightgown and robe. She said she had spent the night at the apartment across the hall, where a couple of other girls they had known lived. "I just couldn't sleep, it's like a nightmare, I can't believe it. Dorrie and Deb dead. We'd lived together nearly three years, they were my best friends, Dorrie and I had known each other forever, we'd been in school together."

Garcia arrived, lugging his big lab kit, and Maddox explained to her what they would be doing, the scientific examination. "All right," she said, "whatever you have to do to find out what happened. I just don't understand it, it's like a nightmare, Dorrie and Deb dead. They were both just twenty-five. And somebody's got to tell their families, and I don't know how to do it—I don't know what to say—Deb was from Iowa, her family has a big farm there, and I guess they'd want to, you know, bring her back for a funeral there, but there's been this awful drought and I guess money's been pretty tight with them." She bowed her head onto her folded hands. "I just don't know, Dorrie's mother lives in Sherman Oaks, she's divorced, I've got to call and tell her—I just don't know how. I don't know how to tell them."

All she had to tell them wasn't any more enlightening than what the Durands or Mrs. Bryant had said. She was an ordinary girl, in the old-fashioned word respectable, and that was the picture that emerged on the other two cases. Holding ordinary jobs, living ordinary lives. Doris Adler had had a steady boy friend—"Oh, I've got to call Jim too, he was crazy about her and I guess they'd have gotten married—" The Carlson girl had dated a couple of young men but it hadn't been anything serious. When Brenda had left with her date last night the other two had just been starting to get dinner. And none of them had been taking any prescription medicine. "Dorrie had some codeine tablets from when she had that abscessed tooth out last month, but there were only a couple left—" Garcia looked, and after he had printed the bottle and raised nothing but smudges, he said, "Three tablets—not enough to kill anybody."

"Drugs?" said Brenda. "Poison of some kind? None of us took any dope—we're not that kind of people." She sobbed and hiccuped. "And I just don't know how to tell their families—I just don't understand how it could have happened!"

"Damn it," said Maddox, "with what Bergner gives us on the other two, it looks as if they must have gotten it with the meal, about six P.M. And if they'd been able to call for help, if somebody had found them, they could've been brought back. We want an analysis of everything left in the refrigerator." Frustratingly, there were no dirty dishes to look at; evidently the girls had been neat, clean housekeepers and popped all those into the dishwasher as soon as they had finished the meal.

"What were they having for dinner?" asked Rodriguez.

Brenda put a hand to her forehead. "Could something have gotten poisoned accidentally?" she asked dully. "I don't see how. Food poisoning—it makes you sick, doesn't it, and they hadn't been—they were just sitting on the couch and the TV on where they'd been watching that old movie—Dorrie was fixing hamburgers and french fries and Deb was making a salad—Dorrie and I had done the week's shopping the night before, we sort of took turns at it, you know, and split the bill —it was the easiest thing to do. We'd gotten a chocolate cake, but Deb wouldn't have had that, she was always trying to lose weight—"

They got her to look at the refrigerator, where Garcia was taking various samples. "I don't know what I can tell you," she said drearily. "We got two packages of hamburger, Dorrie opened the little one for dinner last night." There wasn't any of the salad left; the frozen chocolate cake had about one slice missing. Garcia had come across the remains of the package of hamburger in the wastebasket, the usual cardboard carton with its Pliofilm cover. The blurred red stamping showed a date of three days ago and a weight of three quarters of a pound, which would be about right for two ground-beef patties. There were two fat tomatoes left, half a head of lettuce, and the cake, and aside from that the refrigerator held only a full jar of mayonnaise, half a pound of butter, a six-pack of orange juice, and a half gallon of milk. "Well, have a look at everything," said Maddox.

None of the girls had known anyone named Babcock or Hogan.

"But how the hell did they get it?" said Rodriguez. "It's the pattern, sure—same as the other two cases—but what the hell was it in and how did it get there, for God's sake?"

Maddox said ruminatively, "What I'm remembering, César, is that case back east. Where some lunatic tampered with a nonprescription painkiller and killed a handful of people. All they got on that, he'd abstracted the bottles off the store shelves, added the cyanide, and put them back. This wasn't cyanide, but it's the same principle maybe. There was a bottle of aspirin at the Babcocks' and the Hogans'—get the lab to analyze that pronto."

"But you can't walk into a drugstore and buy Demerol over the counter," said Rodriguez. "And by what Bergner gives us, it was one hell of an overdose. And how the hell could it have gotten into the food or the aspirin? None of these people knew each other, there's no connection. Ordinary honest people, for God's sake."

"I know, I know," said Maddox irritably. "At least we can tell the doctors what to look for first, on Adler and Carlson, and I'll lay you any money it's the Demerol."

They went back to the office and Maddox talked to Baker at the lab, sent him to pick up those other bottles of aspirin at the Babcocks' and Hogans'. Then he called Bergner at the coroner's office, who was interested to hear about the two new bodies. Maddox said, "You're just a ghoul. Evidently they were two nice girls. What's occurred to me now, that case back east—"

"Oh, yes," said Bergner, "the lunatic spiking the nonprescription stuff. Well, we'll have a look for the Demerol in the two new ones right away, it could be a copycat case in a sense—but Demerol, you can't just walk in anywhere and buy it, Maddox, you realize that. Well, I've got a little more for you, if it says anything. The stomach contents. All the Babcocks had had a meal consisting of ground beef, potatoes, lettuce and tomatoes, green beans, and tapioca pudding. The adults had had coffee, the children milk. The Hogans had had ground beef, potatoes, cauliflower, and blueberry pie."

"Well," said Maddox, "ordinary meals. Could the damn stuff have been in any of the food?" But it was hard to see how.

"Possible," said Bergner. "We're still running tests. Probably pin down the exact type of Demerol, and we'll get to the new bodies right away. If this is a wholesale lunatic killer, we'd like to know."

"So we would," said Maddox. "You get on it, doctor."

The office was humming along at the usual rate. D'Arcy was talking to Kuykendall and taking notes. Bill Nolan was typing a report, Feinman on the phone looking exasperated about something, Lee Dowling just towing in a thin little man for questioning; he lifted a hand to Feinman, who put down the phone and trailed them toward the interrogation rooms down the hall.

Maddox said, "And we won't get anything from the lab in a hurry, damn it."

Rodriguez said cynically, "Do we ever?"

* * *

Records downtown had obediently used their computers to look for any known undersized burglars, and had come up with three names for Feinman—Rodney Abel, James Leach, and Walter Decker. Abel was still on parole from his second term in Susanville, and his P.A. officer supplied an address. Dowling had picked him up at his job, at a gas station out on Beverly, and he and Feinman talked to him in the cramped interrogation room with expectable results. Abel was a little fellow about five-three with a narrow pale face and a nervous Adam's apple. He said, "I'm clean, I've been straight ever since I got out, you got nothing on me."

"At least while you're on P.A.," said Feinman, "that's about the size of it, isn't it?" He had applied for a search warrant for Abel's apartment, but that would probably be a futile gesture; Abel was a pro burglar, and would know the fences, wouldn't keep any loot around long. If he'd been the one to get in the dog door last Monday night, and through those other small spaces on the other jobs, there wouldn't be any way to prove it unless he admitted it. He would have taken some nice loot on that last job, too, another fur coat, jewelry, an expensive camera.

"Listen," Abel said nervously, "I'm real clean and I'm gonna stay that way, I'm not about to go back to the joint. I got a nice girl and we're gonna get married, see. You can't put nothing on me." He went on saying it and they wasted some time talking to him, finally let him go. When the warrant came through they went over to his apartment on Las Palmas Avenue and got the manager to let them in, but of course came up empty. There was nothing there but his few shabby belongings.

So Feinman went looking for James Leach and Dowling for Decker; they had old addresses for both of them. Leach had been out, and off parole, from his second term in at San Luis Men's Colony, for a couple of years. He was still living at the address Records had, an apartment on Whitely Way above Hollywood Boulevard. There wasn't a manager on the premises but the one neighbor at home told Feinman she didn't know where Leach worked but his wife had a job at a discount chain store in Burbank. Feinman stopped for a quick lunch, looked up the address, and found her behind one of the cash registers, a sharp-faced, dark young woman who looked at the badge impassively and answered him in reluctant monosyllables. Leach was a clerk at a men's store in Hollywood, and he'd been clean, sure, he'd been home last Monday night, she could swear to that. Feinman drove back to Hollywood and had a look at Leach, and he liked him a hell of a lot better than Abel. Leach was a nattily dressed little fellow, no more than about five-two, a hundred and ten pounds, slim and neat, with handsome regular features, and he was cool and cocky. He smirked at Feinman and said, "I've been straight ever since I got out, nobody can pin nothing on me. You damned fuzz just like to lean on anybody been in a little trouble before." "Little trouble" was the word for it; he'd served two terms for burglary in California, which probably meant that he had pulled forty or fifty jobs or more he had never been dropped on for, and he had a record with the Feds for burglary of post offices in Pennsylvania.

"Monday night?" he said jauntily. "Hell, you go ask my wife, I was home like a good little boy all night. Watching TV."

And of course the wife backed him up. The apartment on Whitely wasn't the classiest in town, but it would rent for around four hundred and fifty and evidently they both had cars. Just for curiosity, when Feinman got back to the office, he ran a make with the DMV in Sacramento, and was interested to find that Leach was driving a two-year-old Buick and his wife a year-old Chevy. That would run into a piece of change, and neither of them would be earning top money at those jobs. But again, there was just no evidence; Leach would know the fences and the loot would be turned over to one or the other of them within hours of the burglary, the cash in hand paid over. None of it would go through a bank; they would be using their legitimate earnings for the rent and car payments, keep the cash to live it up with all the extras. No evidence at all: but they would keep Leach in mind.

Dowling hadn't come back when Baker called from the lab and said the only prints they'd picked up on that job belonged to the householders. That was expectable too. And half an hour later Dowling came in and said, "We can forget about Decker. I found him, he's living with his brother and the brother's wife, and I wouldn't put it past either of them to give him a fake alibi, but he doesn't need one. He got clobbered by a hit-run driver last Thursday night, and he's in the Good Samaritan Hospital with a leg in traction."

"Oh, hell," said Feinman. "And there'll be more than three pint-sized pro burglars around town, whether they're in Records or not, but I'd have a small bet our boy is Leach. He smells right for it—he looks right for it. He's too damned pleased with himself—cocky."

Dowling heard about Leach, running a thoughtful hand through his sandy hair, and agreed. "But we'll never get the evidence on any of these jobs." That was occasionally the frustrating thing about even the burglaries, usually anonymous; as in other kinds of jobs, sometimes they were morally sure of who X was, and couldn't prove it.

Feinman said moodily, "We'll just keep him in mind."

Dowling started to fill his ancient briar pipe. "That's right," he said amiably.

* * *

Sue had gotten past the morning sickness a few months ago, but she'd been feeling lackadaisical and uninterested in the job the last couple of weeks; she'd be glad to stay home for a while, before and after the baby came.

She and Daisy had both come in late this morning, Daisy looking rather bleary-eyed; she said she hadn't gotten to bed until after one, her daughter and son-in-law out later than they had promised. None of the other detectives was in when the dispatcher relayed a call to a junior high school campus. They both leaped to the same conclusion, something to do with drugs, so they collected Sergeant Ambrose of the Narco office and went to see what it was.

Ambrose took one look and said disgustedly, "These damn punks."
"Oh, my dear Lord," said Daisy. "What a mess!"

It was a mess all right, and there was nothing anybody could do about it but clean it up. The punks, and there had probably been several of them, had smashed a big window at the rear of the administration building and proceeded to wreak havoc—the destruction for its own sake. Desks were overturned and hacked to pieces, blackboards smashed, typewriters hammered to bits, more windows broken, the tile flooring gouged, in the teachers' lounge the carpet ripped into shreds, and they had gotten into the school cafeteria and thrown food from the refrigerators all over the damaged classrooms. The kids were all milling around by then, distracted teachers trying to shoo them into the halls and bring some order. At least half the classrooms couldn't be used until a lot of cleaning up was done, and in the end the principal sent all the kids home. There wasn't anything for the police to do about it. The juveniles couldn't be fingerprinted. A number of the teachers might make some shrewd guesses about the kids responsible, but there wasn't any evidence. It was just the kind of mindless destruction the aimless, violent punks went in for. "Satan finding work for idle hands," said Ambrose.

They left the teachers mournfully surveying the mess and awaiting a clean-up crew, and went back to the office. Ambrose said there had been some dope floating around that campus, but there was dope on any public school campus these days. Daisy looked into the juvenile office to brief Sergeant Ralston on it, and Sue typed up a report, which would get filed away and forgotten.

It was George Ellis' day off. All the other detectives were apparently out on the legwork. They had just heard briefly about the two new homicides from Maddox, and talked about that desultorily for a while. Then a woman came in, sent up by the desk, to report a purse snatching. That happened at least a dozen times a day in most divisions, and there was never anything to do about it, just more reports to type. This victim's name was Ruth Greer and she was in a fine rage about it. "What things are coming to these days, all these worthless kids on dope, and right in broad daylight on a main street—" She was a middle-aged woman, fat and dowdy. Sue asked her, "Could you give us any description?"

"Just one of these dirty, worthless kids, he came up behind me—I was just looking into the window at the Broadway, I was thinking about my husband's birthday, there were some slippers on sale in the window, and he came up behind me and shoved me real hard, I nearly fell down, and just grabbed my bag and ran off—by the time I turned around I just had a glimpse of him running off toward the corner of Vine—and there were people all around, some men too, but nobody did anything or tried to stop him—and I didn't know what to do, we live way down on Genesee and I couldn't walk that far, I'd taken the bus up town, only about five minutes later a police car came along and I stopped it and the officer drove me up here."

"How much money were you carrying?" asked Daisy. "Any credit cards?"

"I had about twenty dollars, Harry keeps all our credit cards, but there were all the snapshots of the children in my billfold, and my keys —what the world's coming to—and how I'm going to get home, or get in when I get there—" They offered her the phone to call her husband, and he came to take her home.

Sue said, "There'll be an address in your billfold, I suppose you carried ID—and the keys in your bag—it might be a good idea to have your locks changed, Mr. Greer."

He said querulously, "Listen, you have any idea how much lock-smiths charge these days? Goddamn it, I don't know why you damned cops can't get off your asses and catch some of these goddamned criminals and stash 'em away! Crime rate higher every day, and when an honest woman can't walk down the boulevard in broad daylight without getting robbed, well, it's a hell of a thing, all I can say."

Sue and Daisy just looked at each other as they went out. And that was another report to type; Daisy uncovered her typewriter resignedly.

They went out to lunch together, to the little coffee shop down the block on Fountain. They had just gotten back at one-thirty when the desk sent up another woman with a complaint. She came in and looked at them rather belligerently. "Is this where I'm supposed to come? That sergeant said, the little office across from the big one. Are you detectives?"

"I'm Sergeant Hoffman," said Daisy equably. "Detective Maddox. What can we do for you, Mrs. . . . ?"

She sat down in the chair between their desks. She was a woman in her forties, with a hard-looking, square-jawed face, sharp dark eyes, bleached strawberry blond hair in a sleek professional coiffure. She had a trim figure showed to advantage in a well-cut navy suit, a crisp white blouse. "I'm just as glad to talk to women police," she said. "I want to lay a complaint, if that's the way you put it. About a man molesting my daughter. My daughter Jill. My name is Enid Fenton, by the way."

Sue got out her notebook. "Yes, Mrs. Fenton. What happened and when? Have you had a doctor examine your daughter? And where is she now?"

"That's just it," said Enid Fenton. "She's in school, and this man, he's one of her teachers, and that's not right, it shouldn't be allowed, a teacher making up to a girl in his class, isn't there a law about that?"

"There certainly is," said Daisy grimly. "What did your daughter tell you about it? Do you know his name? What school is it?"

"His name's Ronald Davenport. But you wouldn't get anything from Jill," said Enid Fenton flatly. "She likes it, she's a silly stupid kid and she won't listen to a word I say. But I thought, because he's a teacher—there's got to be some law about a teacher making up to one of the school kids, it's not right, and the police could do something about it. Get him fired maybe."

Sue asked, "What do you mean, your daughter likes it? Exactly how has he molested her—did she tell you about it? What happened?"

"Well, of course she told me about it, how else would I know? She's just being stupid and stubborn, and after all the money I've spent on her and the way I've worked making contacts and planning out everything—and when she won't listen to me, she won't listen to Al Bernstein either—he's her agent—and I'm not going to stand for it. I'll be damned if I see her throw away her whole future just because she's a silly romantic kid. A teacher, my God—he's got no business interfering with her."

Daisy asked, "Just how old is your daughter, Mrs. Fenton?"

She was still flushed with anger. "She won't be eighteen till May. Just a stupid kid. Talking about being in love and getting married! She's got a lot of time for that, and she'll get somebody better than a damn fool teacher, with a hundred times as much money—and I thought, there's got to be a law about teachers interfering with pupils, and you could get him to leave her alone. Can't you?"

Sue had put down her notebook. "Mrs. Fenton, your daughter will be of age in a couple of months. Has this Davenport actually raped her, attacked her physically?"

"Well, no. I wish to God he had, then you could put him in jail and maybe she'd forget all about him. Saying they're engaged! He's not even very good-looking—and I can usually talk her into whatever's best for her, but she's acting so stubborn about the whole ridiculous thing—and I'm not standing for it! She's got a great career in show business ahead of her, Al Bernstein's just set up a screen test with Devlin Productions, and I haven't wasted all these years paying for the acting lessons and dancing lessons and singing lessons, not to mention the orthodontic work, to see her throw it all away! To marry a damn fool teacher, who can't see a yard without glasses and makes about fifteen thousand a year! It's just stupid."

"Mrs. Fenton," said Daisy gently, "we seem to be talking about two consenting adults here. This teacher hasn't harmed your daughter, in fact he's just asked her to marry him. They're planning to get married?"

"It's ridiculous," said Enid Fenton. "About fifteen thousand a year —wasting everything she's got going for her—she could be a big star— and I'm not going to stand for it—" She looked at them in blind frustrated fury. "You aren't going to do anything about it? I thought there was some sort of law—"

Sue said, "Your daughter is nearly of age. I'm afraid there isn't anything the police can do about people falling in love."

She stood up abruptly. "That damned silly little fool. When I think what she's throwing away—after everything I've done for her—never thinking about me—I'm damned if I'll stand for it—"

"There doesn't seem to be much you can do either, Mrs. Fenton," said Daisy, amused.

Enid Fenton just gave them a furious look and marched out of the office.

"People," said Sue. "But the girl must have some guts, to stand up to one like that."

"And the teacher too," said Daisy. "The female of the species."

Nothing else went down for the next hour, and none of the other detectives had come back yet. About three o'clock Maddox looked in and asked, "Has anybody from the coroner's office called?"

"Not that I know of," said Sue.

"Well, I didn't really expect it," said Maddox. "But damn it, the lab ought to have something by now."

* * *

In the big detective office Rodriguez was hunched over his type-writer, writing a report on something; the paperwork was the worst part of this job. Maddox got the lab on the phone, and Garcia said, "Look, these things take time. I've just gotten to the aspirin from the girls' apartment, and it's just aspirin. And look, Maddox, what the doctor said, nobody could mistake these Demerol tablets or capsules or what-ever for aspirin, and didn't they say the corpses must have had about fifteen pills apiece?"

"Yes," said Maddox, "I thought of that too. What about the food in all those places?"

"Nothing much yet. There was a big beef roast in the Babcocks' refrigerator but it hadn't been cooked yet." The anniversary dinner, thought Maddox. "Some leftovers, tapioca pudding, string beans—as far as we've got, all perfectly okay. Have you heard about the girls yet?"

"I hope we'll know today," said Maddox. Everybody else was evi-dently out on the legwork; there were still a lot of possible suspects to look for on the heists and burglaries. He lit a cigarette and decided it would be a waste of time to call Bergner; Bergner would call as soon as he had any news. "Anything new down?" he asked Rodriguez.

"There will be," said Rodriguez, and the words weren't out of his mouth before the dispatcher rang Maddox.

"You've got a new burglary. Pinehurst Road, the squad just called in."

"Oh, hell," said Maddox, and relayed that. "I suppose we'd better go look at it. God, I wish they'd send us a few more lab men—now we'll have to get somebody out to dust for prints, and ninety-nine times out of a hundred that's no damn use anyway, but we have to go by the rules."

Rodriguez abandoned the report without regret and they took his car. The address on Pinehurst Road was a single house, tan stucco, in that old but good residential area up in the Hollywood Hills. The squad had gone back on tour, and the householder was waiting for them, a paunchy middle-aged man, Roy Kramer. He was mad as hell, the usual reaction. He said, "I wasn't gone half an hour, dammit! Not half an hour! I'm on vacation this week, I work at Paramount Studios—in the commissary—my wife works at Robinson's and she's not off so we didn't go anywhere. Damn it, I just went up to the market for a six-pack of beer and cigarettes, and when I came back there was this mess, and the side door broken open—"

It had been a hasty crude break-in, the door forced with a chisel or something similar, and the burglar had left the usual mess, drawers dumped, cushions out of chairs. "Not a very pro job," said Rodriguez, looking around. "Can you give us any idea of what's missing?"

"I've been looking, there wasn't any cash in the house, but he got my tape recorder, the radio in the bedroom, the portable TV from the kitchen. And some of Mae's jewelry, I guess. Her jewelry box is dumped on the bed—not much of that's very valuable, I guess, but sentimental value—" Of course he didn't know the serial numbers of the appliances, and said they would have to get a description of the jewelry from his wife. He kept saying indignantly, "I wasn't gone half an hour!" He thought he could identify the tape recorder by a crack in the plastic lid.

It was on the cards this one had been an amateur, snatching in a hurry. There had been a spate of the daylight burglaries lately; with so many wives working, a good many houses were empty all day, which anybody could discover by ringing the doorbell. They would add the description of the haul to the hot list sent to all pawnbrokers, where the amateur's loot usually ended up, but it wasn't very likely that any of it would ever be identified. And somebody would have to write a report on this.

It wasn't far off the end of shift. Neither Maddox nor Rodriguez felt inclined to start the report now. Both Maddox and Sue were off tomorrow, and Maddox wanted a heart-to-heart talk with the head mechanic at the garage about the Maserati. If it was going to cost an arm and a leg for new parts, he'd be better off to get rid of it and find something newer in decent condition. And one of these days Sue's old Chrysler would be giving up the ghost. At least, by the grace of God, the house was paid for.

Feinman was talking with Dowling and broke off to say, "D'Arcy and Bill picked up a couple of heist suspects but one of them had an alibi. They're talking to the other one now, not that it'll come to anything."

"You're just a little ray of sunshine, Joe."

"I just know the damn job," said Feinman. Ten minutes later D'Arcy and Nolan came in from an interrogation room, the suspect scurrying ahead of them. He went out in a hurry without saying good-bye, and Rodriguez said lazily, "No good?"

"Need you ask?" D'Arcy draped his long lean length on a corner of

Maddox's desk. "He could be, he couldn't be—nothing to say but the vague description. I think I'll take myself out to a decent restaurant instead of warming up a TV dinner. I've got a class tonight."

The phone rang on Maddox's desk and he reached for it, hoping devoutly that it wasn't a new call. "Well," said Bergner, "you win your bet. We've just finished those two girls—we went for the Demerol right off, and that's what it was. It looks exactly the same setup as the first bodies."

"The pattern," said Maddox. "The times?"

"The same pattern all right. They'd had a meal about six hours prior to death—same as the rest. Dammit, if they'd had time to call for help —" Maddox thought about Brenda Cobb, late home from her night out. If she'd gotten home even a couple of hours earlier—"Dammit," said Bergner, "both pretty girls. And, incidentally, both virgins, if you're interested."

"Nice girls," said Maddox. "So it begins to look for pretty sure they all got the OD along with the meals."

"That's right, but how the hell? I told you they'd pass out within about forty minutes, that massive an overdose, and it's not too surprising they didn't have time to call for help—the onset of the symptoms would be quite rapid."

"Yes." Deborah Carlson and Doris Adler had been side by side on the living-room couch, facing the TV, which had been on. Watching the old Astaire-Rogers musical. Evidently one of them, feeling the symptoms, had gone to lie down in the bedroom and died there. "But how the hell indeed? What could it have been in, and how did it get there? We're running analyses on all the leftover food, something may show up, but that doesn't answer the main question."

"Well, we'll do what we can for you. One thing I can say pretty definitely, it was tablets and not capsules. But what good it is to tell you the brand, God knows. Have you found out if there was any connection among these people?"

"Not a smell," said Maddox.

"I'll get back to you with anything else we turn up."

Maddox shared that information and they kicked it around a little. "It's a lunatic," said Rodriguez with conviction. "However and who-ever, it's just senseless killing." He shot open the bottom drawer of his desk and took out the *County Guide*. "Look at it—the Babcocks way out in West Hollywood, a couple of miles or more from the Hogans—

the three girls on Lexington, another couple of miles off. And while, by what we've turned up, they were all respectable citizens, they weren't the same kind of people, Ivor."

"That's a point," said Maddox. "Hogan probably the diamond in the rough—Parks and Recreation. Babcock, the young junior executive. The girls in little jobs, marking time until they got married. And no remote reason for anybody to want any of them dead. An eight-year-old and a six-year-old, for God's sake."

"A lunatic," said Rodriguez. "Let's just hope we find out who's doing it and how before he kills anybody else."

"That's a nice thought," said Maddox. He stood up. "If anything breaks somebody give me a call—this is the funniest one we've had in a while."

* * *

The middle of the week was usually slow. The squad-car men would be dealing with the drunks and bar brawls, the occasional mugging, the stolen cars, but the detectives on night watch didn't get a call until nearly ten o'clock, and by what the dispatcher told Brougham they guessed what it was all about, so all three of them rolled on it.

This little gang had gotten tagged as the pillowcase heisters, and this would make the ninth time they had hit in the last three months. The detectives had heard a lot about them, but nothing that was very helpful in locating them. Sometimes three men were involved, sometimes four, and they were, by all accounts, as businesslike and cool as the lone heister they'd nicknamed Dapper Dan, and as specific. Where he hit the liquor stores exclusively, they hit bars, and bars of a certain quality. In the last twenty years, Central Hollywood had lost most of its glamour and turned into just another part of the big city, sleazy and dirty, with porn movie houses and bookstores scattered around, the main drags haunted by the cheap hookers and pimps. But there were still, toward West Hollywood on the way to Beverly Hills, a few high-class bars. The pillowcase heisters had hit that kind, and a couple somewhat less high-class in the same general area.

This one was called the Black Cat Bar and Grill, it was on Melrose just this side of West Hollywood, and there were about thirty witnesses. Listening to them, Stacey, Donaldson, and Brougham heard the same old story they had listened to before. There had been four of them on this job, all with guns. All four were Negroes, two of them light-colored, one very tall, the others nondescript; no good descriptions offered. As in all the other cases, everybody had been scared and confused. The heisters had come in quick and smooth, spread out to cover all the bar patrons, and one of them had gone to everybody in the place holding an open pillowcase. Only one of them had issued instructions —"Just the cash, folks, put it in the kitty when it comes around—" And they'd been in the place only about ten minutes.

The bartender and a couple of the victims told them something they already knew. "That tall guy," said the bartender, who was a bull-necked fat man named Casey, "man, he was a real handsome dude. Could have been a movie star, you know? Little thin moustache, and real light skin."

They took only cash, and by what all the victims came up with, the haul had been nearly five hundred bucks; as usual they had cleaned out the cash register too.

"And not one damned thing to give us any lead," said Stacey, annoyed. "Why the hell can't people use their eyes? These damn punks were in there at least ten minutes—"

"They were all looking at the guns," said Brougham wryly.

The cash, of course, wasn't identifiable. When the gang had first shown up, they had asked Records downtown about the MO, but it was evidently a new caper; Records didn't have anything to tell them.

It was just something else to write a report on. And, the paperwork going on forever, they'd have to take the statements from the witnesses.

* * *

The garage mechanic said, "Well, I won't lie to you, Mr. Maddox. She's been a damn good car in her day, but it'd cost you more to fix her up than she's worth. Sure, I can keep her running awhile, but—" He shrugged.

"That's about what I thought," said Maddox. He looked at the Maserati regretfully; he had liked that car. But good things came to an end, and while the damn thing was still running and worth something, he'd better trade it.

He spent the afternoon wandering around car lots, and finally made a deal for a sedate two-door Pontiac that looked like a fairly good bet, only thirty thousand miles on it. But he had liked the old Maserati.

* * *

Feinman was the only one in at five o'clock on Thursday afternoon when the dispatcher relayed a call. "I don't know what it's about, but he says he wants detectives, it sounds like an attempted homicide, it's a doctor, I didn't catch his name."

Feinman answered inattentively; he was thinking about the diminutive burglar. Those jobs, damn it, had been pulled by Leach, but whether there would ever be any way to prove it—"Sergeant Feinman," he said.

"This is Dr. Bauman. I dislike having to call the police but I must report a most puzzling case—an apparent deliberate poisoning, an overdose of Demerol, but I had not prescribed it and I simply do not understand how the patient ingested it. The circumstances are very peculiar and I thought the police had better be informed—"

Feinman snapped to attention. "Yes, doctor? What's the name? We'll want to talk to you. Is the patient dead?"

"No, no, she's recovering quite well, but I have no idea how she could have ingested the overdose."

CHAPTER THREE

Feinman and Rodriguez went out on that in a hurry. It was a big old house on a side street off Laurel Canyon Boulevard, and the doctor was there and a woman he introduced as the housekeeper, Mrs. Rose Mackey. Bauman was an elderly man with a fussy pedantic manner, old-fashioned pince-nez, but he seemed to be on the ball and to know what he was doing. The housekeeper was slightly more forthright. She was a stout, round-faced, sensible-looking woman in her fifties, and she said, "It's just a mystery to me and the doctor knows that, neither of us can make it out at all, and I just thank God Mrs. Seaton's going to be all right. I've been with her more than twenty years, since before Mr. Seaton died—he was a stockbroker downtown and left her a lot of money—I think as much of her as I do my own mother, she's a wonderful woman and she's been awfully good to me, I'd do anything for her. I just can't make this out, and the doctor was quite right to call the police, but what I say is it's got to have been an accident of some kind, because it's just silly to say anybody tried to murder her. There's not been another soul in the house for weeks."

"Mrs. Seaton was taken ill after lunch, you said?" asked Feinman.

"Yes, and I called the doctor right away, he's been her doctor for years, not that she ever had much the matter with her—she'd gone upstairs again after lunch to have her nap just as usual, and I was in the kitchen mixing up a cake when I heard her call me, she did look queer, she was on the landing and she said, I do feel so dizzy, Florrie, she said —and she fell down before I got to her, and I thought maybe she was having a stroke, I was scared, I called the doctor right away and he sent an ambulance, she was unconscious then—and I went to the hospital with her—"

Bauman said, "Of course she's an elderly woman, seventy-six, and my first thought was a heart attack or stroke, but it was obvious almost at once that it was a drug overdose, and we took all the indicated measures. I didn't understand it because she wasn't on any medication that could cause such a reaction—we pumped out the stomach and I sent the contents for immediate analysis—and meanwhile we administered the standard antidotes for an overdose of narcotic. And she responded very well, she's conscious and alert, but we'll keep her under observation for another day. She's not a young woman."

"And thank God she's all right," said Mrs. Mackey, "but what it could have been, that's what neither the doctor nor I can make out."

Bauman said testily, "Well, the analysis told us what it was—it was some form of Demerol, one of the morphine-type synthetics, and I'd certainly never prescribed such a thing for her, she's basically a very healthy woman for her age, she's never required sleeping aids, and it was very puzzling. When she was out of danger of course I questioned Mrs. Mackey." He was polishing the old-fashioned glasses with his handkerchief. "Mrs. Seaton is an old and valued patient, I've known her for twenty-five years—"

The housekeeper said shortly, "And I hope you know nobody in this world would want to harm her. I admit you got me riled up, asking what I'd given her, and if she could have meant to kill herself—the last thing in the world Mrs. Seaton would do, and how could she have anyway? There's nothing stronger than aspirin in the house, after all the poking around you've done you know that—"

"Quite right," said Bauman stiffly, "but naturally I had to look and be sure."

"She was taken ill after lunch, you said?" Rodriguez asked the housekeeper again. "What did she have?"

"She always likes a good lunch, she'll only take orange juice and coffee first thing, no reason for her to get up early and usually she's not up till around ten. Then she wants a pretty good lunch. I broiled a hamburger patty for her, and fixed a salad, cottage cheese and canned pears, and she had some of the peach preserves on toast."

"I've taken samples of everything for analysis," said Bauman, "but I'm quite at a loss to understand how a prescription medication could have gotten into any of the food—"

"I think you can leave the analysis to us, doctor," said Feinman. "Was there anything left over?"

Mrs. Mackey said bluntly, "Well, I can't understand it either, it was all perfectly fresh food, I had some of the cottage cheese and pears myself, and I'm all right, the loaf was fresh from the bakery yesterday, and the hamburger I got at the same time when I was out to the market yesterday afternoon. No, I didn't have any of that, I always have a pretty good breakfast and don't take much for lunch. But how any poison could have been in the food—it's just silly to say anybody wanted to poison her. Mrs. Seaton!"

"Nobody's accusing you, Mrs. Mackey," said the doctor fretfully.

She bristled at him, "Well, I should certainly hope not, I love her like my own mother, she's a wonderful old lady and still enjoys life. You could say she's been lucky some ways and unlucky others, Mr. Seaton leaving her plenty of money and all, but they never had any family and that was a grief to her, she hasn't a chick nor child, her two sisters gone too, no relations left except her niece back in New York, she always looks forward to her letters."

"Yes, yes," said Bauman, "but the question is just what happened. There's certainly no Demerol in the house, and I'm quite at a loss—"

Rodriguez said thoughtfully, "Hamburger. I seem to remember— what Bergner said about the stomach contents—at least some of them had had hamburger. Let's get a lab man up here, Joe." And it was the end of the shift, but once in a while they had to do overtime. Mrs. Mackey said yes, there was some of the hamburger left. Feinman got on the phone to the lab, and Franks cussed him but came out in one of the mobile vans. He parceled up samples of the leftovers, the hamburger and cottage cheese and pears, the loaf of bread, the butter, and carted them off back to the lab. Rodriguez asked the doctor, "What does the old lady say herself? I suppose you talked to her when she was conscious."

"Well, of course, I asked her if she'd taken anything—with, a—er—suicidal intent, not that I really suspected that—"

"And if I know her, she took you down a peg," said Mrs. Mackey tartly. "The last thing she'd ever do—"

"Yes, indeed, she was quite annoyed at me for suggesting it—but I can't understand how it happened. However, it does amount to attempted homicide and I thought the police should be informed—"

Rodriguez said briskly, "Quite right, doctor. We'll see what we can find out."

They got back to the office an hour after the official end of shift, and prodded Franks into doing the overtime. He said bitterly, "You catch me five minutes before I'm about to leave, and my wife's mad at me, we're having company for dinner. All right, all right. At least as long as I know what I'm looking for, it'll only mean running one test."

Rodriguez said, "Have a look at the hamburger first, will you? I've just got a small hunch—"

*   *   *

On Friday morning when Maddox came in five minutes late, he found everybody else clustered around his desk. Feinman thrust a lab report at him. "So now we know," he said tersely. "It was in the hamburger."

"But how the hell did it get there?" asked D'Arcy blankly.

Maddox scanned the report rapidly, while Feinman gave him a brief breakdown on Mrs. Seaton. In the sample of raw hamburger from the Seaton house, there had been a massive dose of crushed Demerol tablets mixed into the ground beef. "This time," said Feinman grimly, "nobody got killed. They pumped her stomach and she's all right. But didn't Bergner say all the rest of them had had hamburger, and it looked as if they'd gotten the OD with a meal—it could have been in the hamburger every time. But my God, what a queer thing—hamburger, yet!"

"By God," said Maddox softly, "but it looks possible but impossible, when you think about it. Prepackaged hamburger—it's wild." But there the results of the analysis were. He called the coroner's office, finally tracked down Bergner, and told him about it.

"For God's sake," said Bergner, "that's the wild blue yonder all right. The hamburger—but it's got to be the answer, they'd all had ground beef—at least, we haven't got to the stomach contents of the two girls yet—"

"I can tell you that," said Maddox. "They had too, the Cobb girl told us that. They were broiling hamburgers when she left on her date."

"So there you are," said Bergner. "My good God, what a queer—" And then he uttered a little growl. "But that gives us a shortcut on something else. I can tell you what brand it probably was. I said it was tablets, not capsules, and I think this tells us which. Demerol APAP, it's a brand of meperidine, pretty commonly prescribed as an analgesic. Reason I leap to the conclusion, they're a pretty pink color. You could crush them up and mix them into the raw hamburger and it'd never be noticed, they're about the same color. I will be goddamned. But how in hell could it have been done? The meat is all prepackaged these days."

"Yes, it's a teaser, but at least now we know part of the answer." Maddox passed that on and they thought about it.

"But look, Ivor," said D'Arcy, "what César was saying, these people lived in different parts of town, all over the place, it isn't likely they all bought groceries at the same market. So, say there's a lunatic butcher mixing the lethal dose of Demerol in the hamburger—there can't be more than one, for God's sake."

"How does the hamburger get to the markets?" Feinman asked reasonably. "I don't know—is it packaged at a warehouse somewhere?"

"I don't know either," said Maddox, "but we'll find out." The night watch had left them a new one yesterday, another hit by those pillowcase heisters, and as usual they had a list of the possible suspects on heists and burglaries to find and lean on, but this one now had top priority. A lunatic, Rodriguez had said, and if this was what it began to look like, how right he was. The lunatic, somehow adding the OD of Demerol to the hamburger, when and where and how?

D'Arcy said, "Prescription tablets. Somebody at a pharmacy or at a pharmaceutical supply place—but that's wide open because—"

They all saw that; it offered too many possibilities. In every case, where the heisters hit the pharmacies, they were after drugs as well as the cash; even when the heisters weren't users themselves the uppers and downers were as good as cash for street sale; and there was a big black market in all that, the stuff smuggled from here to there all across the country as well as locally. The lunatic could have gotten hold of the Demerol rather easily.

"The lunatic," said Feinman, "just spiking the hamburger at random, not aiming at anybody in particular? My God, that's what it looks like—"

"And a few things to do about it," said Maddox, "to keep us busy for a while." And then he said suddenly, "My good Christ, that Cobb girl had bought a second package—" He clawed open his notebook and found her number, got her at the doctor's office where she worked.

"The hamburger?" she said blankly. "What do you mean? That other package—no, I haven't opened it, I haven't felt much like cooking, it's in the freezer. But—"

"Good," said Maddox. "Somebody'll be up to collect it for analysis."

"You mean there was something wrong with the hamburger—but how?"

"We're looking into it. Tell me, what market did you generally go to?"

"What market—well, we generally went to the Lucky on Santa Monica, it's the handiest, but why on earth? The hamburger—yes, Dorrie and I had just done the week's shopping the night before—I told you we got two packages of hamburger, and Dorrie had opened the small one that night. But why—"

They roped Sue and Daisy in to do some of the telephoning and the legwork.

Mrs. Bryant said, "What market Mom and Dad went to? Well, usually Ralph's up on Third Street, or the Safeway on Beverly. The closest ones. Why do you want to know? Dad was still driving, you know, but his eyes were starting to give him trouble and he didn't like to drive too far. Have you found out any more about how they got poisoned? And you said about arranging the funeral, someone would let us know—about the bodies—"

"Yes," D'Arcy told her, "you can claim the bodies at the coroner's office. Thanks very much."

Mrs. Durand said, "Why on earth do you want to know that? Well, of course Betty had her own car, she went to different markets, but mostly to the Lucky on Melrose or the Safeway on Sunset. Do you know any more about it yet? Why are you asking about markets?"

Maddox didn't tell her; he reflected that everybody was going to know about it in short order. If this thing was what it looked like they would want plenty of publicity on it. All together there were a number of possible markets, and now he came to think about it, he didn't know much about how the various commodities got onto the market shelves. Warehouses around, and he thought the different market chains had their own, but possibly not for everything. Hamburger, he thought dismally: about the commonest kind of meat sold, most people buying hamburger every week because it was usually the cheapest meat, and all those damn markets—my God, there could be lethal packages of hamburger waiting for unsuspecting shoppers at any of them, any market anywhere in town, and even just in Central Hollywood that would mean dozens of markets—and how to be sure, how to work this damn thing—they had just so much manpower. But they had to go and ask the questions.

*   *   *

The manager at the Safeway on Hollywood Boulevard where Mrs. Mackey had done her shopping on Wednesday afternoon was an affable young man by the name of Moffat, anxious to be helpful to the police, if puzzled. "Oh, it's all ground right here," he told Maddox. "All the market chains handle it that way. The various cuts of meat are delivered from our warehouse downtown almost daily, and the hamburger's all ground and packaged by the butchers at the individual stores. Why are you asking?" He looked surprised. "You aren't going to tell me there's been a complaint? All our meats are top quality, we pride ourselves on the quality of our meats." Maddox had to tell him about the probable lunatic, and he was outraged and alarmed. "But that's impossible!" he said. "It's just impossible that it could have happened here, Sergeant. I don't see how it can have happened at all, it's impossible—you can see for yourself, nobody could have done such a thing—"

Maddox surveyed the big open room behind the refrigerated meat counter and talked to the butchers, who told him the same thing. There were four of them, and by what they said none of them was ever there alone; they took different lunch periods, two by two. They all seemed to be ordinary honest citizens, and he heard all about their routine. "See," said the biggest one, a heavy-shouldered middle-aged man named Kelly, "this is a big market, we've got quite a turnover. We get deliveries from the warehouse truck four times a week, Saturday to Thursday. We grind the hamburger fresh every day, before the store opens—well, nearly every day. Sometimes there'll be a few packages left over from the day before, but not much. You got to judge pretty sharp, know what the turnover's going to be, see. The store says all meat absolutely fresh, that's what it's got to be." He was openly scornful of the idea that any tampering with the hamburger could have happened here. "Even if any of us wanted to do such a crazy thing like that, how could we?" He gestured around the big room, with its huge refrigerated safe at the rear. "One of the guys'd notice, see? And we're usually busy. People think we haven't much to do, account of all the packaged meat, but who does the packaging? The hamburger, well, it's not all just hamburger, you know, we make it up in different grades, plain hamburger without the fat removed, lean and leanest, there's a difference in price." Maddox said he knew that. "You got to judge how much you're gonna sell of which, see. And some days are different too, middle of the week not so many people in, weekends are busiest. Like today, we got the hamburger case full when we opened this morning, and in about an hour I'll check it, see how much is gone, and probably have to package up some more. You try to tell me somebody put poison in our hamburger, right here? That's just crazy, nobody could."

"Possibly," said Maddox, "at some other markets too." They were all incredulous and said so volubly. And it certainly didn't look very feasible. This was all wide-open space, and the glass windows between the butchers' workroom and the long meat case, and as they said they worked together, the same hours, nine to six. The market was open from ten to nine most days, and the butchers would replenish the meat case before they left.

Maddox went out with the manager to look at that, and the manager pointed out that it would be impossible for anyone to tamper with the packages there. The layout of this market was similar to that of most big markets; the meat case was across half the rear of the store, arranged in orderly fashion with fowl and fish in the left trays, the various cuts of beef and pork and lamb on up to the right. He surveyed the packages of hamburger in the tray of the long refrigerated case, the three different grades of hamburger—and probably Mrs. Mackey had bought the leanest for the well-endowed Mrs. Seaton; conceivably the

Hogans had bought the cheapest grade. The packages were all different sizes, each neatly parceled up in the cardboard trays, covered with the transparent Pliofilm, and on each package a little label under the Pliofilm with the market name, weight of the contents, and the price stamped in red.

He reflected that Betty Babcock would probably have bought a package weighing a little under two pounds, enough for the four of them, and there hadn't been any left over. The Hogans would have bought just enough for the two of them, and no leftovers there either. Betty Babcock had probably shopped frequently, the Hogans not so often. He looked at the packages in the tray and wondered if any of that hamburger was spiked with Demerol, for God's sake: Bergner said, the pretty pink pills. It was worse than offbeat. And he thought, all these different markets, and thousands of innocent people wandering around them, and he felt suddenly helpless. The whole LAPD had just so much manpower, they couldn't station even one man at every market in town—to look for what?

* * *

D'Arcy and Feinman landed back at the office about three-thirty, just after Maddox had come in, and they compared notes. They'd all shopped at the big markets often enough and had known they all had much the same layout; now they knew more about how the meat got into the refrigerated cases, and there didn't seem to be any difference to that among all the chains. Feinman and D'Arcy had gotten the same story at Lucky's and Ralph's as Maddox had at the Safeway. The hamburger was all ground on the premises, nearly every day, from wholesale big cuts of beef deliveries from the warehouses. There were anywhere from two to four butchers on duty every day, in sight of each other.

"It reminds me of a magic trick," said D'Arcy. "The stuff all packaged before it gets out onto the shelf. And come to think, it'd take a little time to mix all those tablets into it, what did Bergner say, about twelve or fifteen pills each, my God. That'd be—"

"For the Babcocks, call it forty-five or fifty," said Maddox. "I suppose Babcock had the lion's share of the hamburger—yes, indeedy, it couldn't be done in a hurry, you'd have to crush those tablets up thoroughly and mix the powder all through the ground beef. A little conjuring trick all right. I'm bound to say I don't see offhand just how it was done, D'Arcy."

Sue and Daisy trailed in looking tired and pulled up chairs. Daisy accepted a cigarette from Feinman and said, "Of course all these places are laid out the same. Seem to go by the same general regulations. And big markets, usually a lot of people around. The different chains—" She blew a thoughtful cloud of smoke. "We can read it that the lethal hamburger came from at least three different chain markets, but that doesn't say much."

"Why don't you think so?" asked Maddox.

"And," she added, "we're going to create one grand uproar if we tell all the markets to stop selling hamburger—and I don't think we could anyway—"

"But how in hell was it done?" fumed Feinman. "There are lunatics all over the place, God knows, and no way to start looking for this one, but how the hell did he do it?"

Sue bent to Maddox's lighter, and said sweetly, "Come on, Joe, you've been shopping with your wife. That's an easy one, Daisy and I saw that right away. It's why it doesn't matter which market it is. Haven't you ever seen your wife pick up one package of meat and then decide on another and put the first one back?"

"Oh, my God, yes," said Maddox, sitting up abruptly. "My God, that should have occurred to me—that's got to be how it was done."

"That Pliofilm," said Sue, "peels off in one piece, and you can fold it back over the package again easily, it sticks to itself. All he'd have to do would be to buy the package of hamburger, take it home, mix the Demerol in at his leisure, and take it back to the market the next day. In his coat pocket, say. And put it back in the case. If he picked a slack time, there wouldn't be anybody nearby to notice, and if anybody did see him—if he put the package in his shopping cart—he'd just decided the package was too big or too little and was changing it for another."

"By God, of course," said D'Arcy. "The only way it could have been done. But, my God, it could be anybody walking around, there's no handle to it at all, no way to look for him."

"Well, it just does occur to me," said Daisy, "that the public ought to be warned."

"There is that," agreed Maddox. "We'd better contact the newspapers and TV stations."

"And what a howl that'll raise," said Feinman, suddenly aghast. "We'll have all the market chains suing us for saying they're selling poisoned hamburger. No, I guess they couldn't do that, but can you imagine the trouble they'll be in if everybody stops buying hamburger? But I see that, we've got to warn people about the danger. The lunatic —eight people yet—" He rubbed his lantern jaw. "But nowhere to begin to look—all those markets will have regular customers the check-out clerks would know, but it's not likely he'd be one of them, and all of them have the casual one-time customers too, in and out all the time."

"And," said Maddox, "when there's no reason, no motive except an insane one, no way to look for him."

"Or her," said Daisy.

"And that could be too. We just don't know."

"Just a nut," said D'Arcy dismally, "wanting to kill people and not giving a damn who. For some lunatic reason. And you know, it could be," he added suddenly, "now he has killed somebody—eight somebodys—he's feeling satisfied, and he'll just fade into the woodwork and we'll never hear of him again. Maybe all the packages of ham-burger everywhere in town are perfectly innocent, just hamburger."

"And maybe not," said Maddox rather savagely. "I think we deduce one other thing, which isn't a hell of a lot of help. He planted the packages last weekend. Mrs. Babcock shopped on Saturday, the Bryant woman tells us her parents usually shopped on Saturday too. And Brenda Cobb went to the market on Monday night, so that package of hamburger had been left over in the case from Saturday or Sunday."

"Which takes us nowhere," said D'Arcy. "We haven't got the man-power to station a guard at every market in town, even just on week-ends."

"Hardly," said Maddox wearily. "It's too late to get it into the papers today, but we'd better talk to them, get it in tomorrow's editions, and on the TV news."

They divided up the people to talk to, and that was going to take the rest of the shift. Maddox had just looked up the number of the *Times-Mirror* building downtown and reached for the phone when it shrilled at him.

"Say," said Rodriguez, "I've been trying to raise somebody there." It had, of course, been his day off. "You've been busy, I take it. I'm just curious, did my little hunch about the hamburger work out?"

"Oh, my God," said Maddox, "wait till you hear. We're busy at the moment, I'll call you from home later and tell you about it."

He had just finished talking to an editor at the *Times,* who asked a lot of interested questions that couldn't be answered, when Garcia called from the lab. He said that package of hamburger from Brenda Cobb's freezer was just hamburger, nothing lethal added to it.

Maddox sat back and thought, three packages of hamburger. That they knew about. Planted in three different markets, probably last Saturday. And freezers—a lot of busy people didn't shop every week, bought things ahead and stashed them in freezers. There was no way to guess how many packages of doctored hamburger the nut could have planted, now tucked away in freezers. No guarantee, weekend be damned, that he hadn't been busy in the last couple of days planting more. And more innocent people about to die—

But he thought about Mrs. Seaton. The eight innocent people who had died had been unlucky; they hadn't been found in time, been able to call for help. Betty Babcock, realizing there was something wrong, had been trying to call somebody on the phone, hadn't quite made it. If Brenda Cobb had come home earlier from her date last Tuesday night, those two girls might not have died. It crossed his mind to wonder whether the nut, whatever kind of nut he might be, really intended death, or just—mischief. Just general deviltry.

* * *

All the local networks carried it as a public service, using the careful wording to avoid the possible libel suits from the markets. The warning went out on the six o'clock and eleven o'clock news. There would be articles on the front pages of the *Times* and *Herald* tomorrow. But not everybody read the papers or even listened to the news on TV. The people who did would be talking about it, of course, which would be of some help.

And of course D'Arcy could be right—about the nuts you never knew. This one might now be satisfied with having brought about the violent deaths—or not having intended that, have taken fright—and would fade away and never do it again. But that they couldn't count on.

And what all the public warnings would do to the sale of hamburger was something for the market managers to worry about.

* * *

Maddox had left the night watch a note about it, and that gave Stacey and Brougham something to talk about; it was Donaldson's night off. "But what a hell of a crazy thing," said Stacey, "and kids too —a homicidal maniac. They do come along every so often."

At least one thing about being on night watch, they got out of most of the necessary wasted time in court: generally they just saw the starts of things. There would be formal inquests coming up on all those bodies, and the day men would have to cover them. There were a few arraignments and indictments scheduled too, on a couple of heisters and one of the rarely caught burglars from a few weeks ago. They had a call at a little after nine, and it was another burglary; another anonymous one they would probably never catch up to. The burglary rate was way up. It was a single house on Waverly Place, and the householders were a couple named Appleby. They had gone out to dinner, gotten home about eight-thirty to find the usual mess. They contributed a rather incoherent list of what had been taken, a portable TV, a little jewelry—probably unidentifiable—a radio, two cameras. Surprisingly, Appleby had records of the serial numbers. It could have been an amateur, in which case the loot might show up at a pawnshop.

"I thought we had good secure locks," said Appleby mournfully. "Dead bolts all around."

"If they're bound to get in they will," Brougham told him. The burglar had broken the glass pane of the outside door to the service porch, just reached in and unfastened the bolt. Just going through the motions, they told the Applebys not to touch the door, there would be somebody up in the morning to dust for prints.

They had just gotten back to the office at eleven o'clock when a new call went down. It had been a slow night, but with the weekend coming up the next two nights might be a lot busier. The call was to an address on Melborne Street, a little side street the other side of Hillhurst, and when they got there Stoner was waiting for them beside the squad, parked behind another car in front of an old two-story apartment building. He had a civilian beside him, a tall lanky young fellow smoking a cigarette, head bent.

"You've got a homicide," said Stoner laconically. "In the car ahead. This is Mr. Bert Peterson, he can tell you something about it. He says she shot herself, he just found her."

In the pale light of the one streetlamp along here behind the squad, Peterson was looking wan and a little sick. He was about twenty-five, with narrow nondescript features, sandy hair, and he was wearing pajamas and an old gray bathrobe. He just nodded at the detectives.

They went to look in the other car; it was an old two-door Ford, and the passenger's door was hanging open. A woman's body had slumped from behind the wheel across the bench seat. Stoner came up behind them with his flashlight. "The gun's on the floor." He knew better than to have touched anything. The gun was a little one, probably a .22, and it looked as if it had fallen from her right hand as she fell across the seat. They couldn't see her face, but in the wavering light of the flash her general figure showed up as slender and curved. She was wearing a dark dress and a beige coat, all they could make out.

"He says her name's Sandra Allway, they'd had a fight and she shot herself. The gun was hers. He lives right here in one of the front apartments."

"All right," said Stacey, "we'd better see if there's anybody still at the lab and get some pictures at least before we call the morgue wagon." They went back to talk to Peterson. "So what's the story, Mr. Peterson?"

He was chain-smoking, by the butts on the sidewalk around. He said drearily, "I feel so damned bad about this, she's a nice girl, Sandra—I never imagined she'd do a thing like that. We weren't engaged or anything, but we'd dated some—we both work at the same place, the Blue Max Restaurant on La Cienega, I'm in the bar and she was one of the waitresses. Jesus, she was only about twenty-three—I never imagined she'd do anything like this—I just can't get over it. See, we both had Fridays off and that's when we usually had a date, I don't mean every Friday but maybe a couple of times a month. Or in the afternoon, neither of us was on till four. Only I'd been dating another girl a few times lately, and she got to know about it. She didn't have any call to be mad, like I say we weren't engaged or anything, but anyway—" He swallowed nervously, and lit a fresh cigarette from the stub of the old one. "We went out to dinner tonight, we were going to a movie, only she started arguing about the other girl—she got mad about it—and we had a fight. I mean, she had a fight with me. I mean, just arguing, you know."

"Is that your car?" asked Brougham, nodding at the Ford.

"No, it's hers. She was driving, my car's on the fritz, I'm supposed to get it back tomorrow. So she picked me up and brought me home, she was still arguing at me then, and I said if that's the way she felt we'd just call it quits, I was sorry, but I wasn't her personal property. I went up to the apartment, naturally I thought she'd gone off, I guess that

was about nine o'clock. It wasn't until about half an hour ago, I was
getting ready for bed and I just happened to look out the window and
saw her car was still here, and it seemed funny so I came down to have
a look, and, well, there she was. She was dead—and I saw the gun—I
couldn't believe it at first, but she'd shot herself."

Brougham said, "The gun. It was hers—you knew she had it?"

He nodded. "Sure. She had to drive home late alone, she always
carried it in the glove compartment. She said her father had given it to
her. For protection. You know how many creeps there are around.
She'd showed it to me once, but I don't know much about guns."

They couldn't raise anybody at the lab, and it didn't look like anything very abstruse. Stacey slid the little gun into an evidence bag, to
drop off at the lab, and Brougham used the radio in the squad to call
the morgue wagon, called the garage to tow the car in.

"Do you know anything about her family?" asked Stacey.

"They live in Monrovia, I don't know where. Her apartment's on
Courtney Place. My God," said Peterson, "I never thought she'd do a
thing like that—"

After the morgue wagon came and the car was towed away, they
went over to Courtney Place and found the apartment; they had keys
from the handbag, which had only held anonymous odds and ends,
cosmetics, handkerchief, billfold with her driver's license, and a couple
of credit cards. It was a sterile little place; it didn't look as if she'd spent
much time there, just a place to sleep. There was an address beside the
telephone, and only one phone number had the Monrovia prefix; that
would be the family. Let the day watch break the bad news and take it
from here. It looked run-of-the-mill. It was a queer thing. But the
suicides often were the young people with, apparently, everything to
live for. And a lot of suicides did it on a moment's impulse, in a fit of
sudden desperation or depression. The nondescript Peterson didn't
look much like a lover to kill yourself over, but maybe Sandra Allway
had felt different about it.

*   *   *

On Saturday morning, with Feinman off, Maddox growled over the
new homicide report left by the night watch and passed it on to D'Arcy
and Rodriguez. "On top of everything else," he said. "Not that it looks
like much to work. The coroner's office will have sense enough to send

the slug up to the lab. And there'll be some paperwork. This Peterson is supposed to come in this morning to make a statement."

"And this goddamned nut—" Rodriguez swore, fingering his neat moustache. "Nowhere to start looking—"

D'Arcy looked up from Stacey's report and said absently, "Somebody'll have to call this Allway girl's family, break the bad news. Well, maybe a place to look. Just a first place. Ask about any of the crazies who just got let out of Atascadero or Camarillo. They didn't use to let them out of Atascadero very quick or easy"—that was the state institution for the criminally insane—"but I understand these days they're pretty crowded for space up there and let the tamer ones out. But if you ask me, none of the damned head doctors knows much about which of 'em is harmless or not."

"It's a place to start asking," said Maddox moodily. "The same thought occurred to me. There'd be addresses, relatives' and doctors' names—they wouldn't just turn them loose and wave good-bye."

"And then," said Rodriguez, "go find them and look at them. One thing I will say, the nuts usually come apart without much prodding. A lot of the time they like to boast about whatever they've been up to." They didn't have to deal with the nuts often, but now and then they showed up, whether they were the dangerous ones or just erratic; any cop had had a few dealings with them.

The phone rang on Maddox's desk and they all looked at it with foreboding. There was quite enough work without anything new turning up. There were still about ten witnesses due to come in to make statements about the latest caper of the pillowcase heisters, and on the more anonymous heists and burglaries the possible suspects out of Records to locate. The phone rang again and Maddox picked it up.

"Sergeant Maddox."

"Well," said the dispatcher down in Communications, "you got another one for the books, Sergeant. This is a thing about the hamburger, isn't it? I heard it on the late news and my wife put the package she'd just gotten down the garbage disposal. You've now got a new homicide. At least, part of one, by what the squad reports. Part of a dismembered body." Maddox uttered a very rude word. "The refuse collectors just came across it. It's in an alley down from Santa Monica just the other side of Colinga."

"My God, what next?" said Maddox, and took down the address and passed on the news.

"It never rains but it pours," said Rodriguez.

"Come on, César, we'd better go look at it."

They left D'Arcy dialing the Monrovia phone number to break the bad news. After that he'd get on to Atascadero. He and Dowling and Nolan were staying in to cope with all the witnesses.

The squad-car man was Ramon Gonzales, tall and dark and urbane as usual; he was waiting for them at the mouth of the little alley, which cut down behind Santa Monica Boulevard, narrow and dirty, a convenience for the city trash collectors. He said, "It's all yours. I've seen all I want to."

There was a big city refuse truck halfway down the alley, and the two refuse collectors, probably not among the more sensitive citizens, were looking queasy. One of them said, "You more cops? Jesus, what a hell of a thing, I nearly had a heart attack—I'd just took the lid off this can to dump it, see, when my God, I see a human foot sticking out of this plastic sack—Jesus, what a thing—"

Maddox and Rodriguez had a look, without touching anything; on one like this the careful lab work usually offered the only good evidence. The alley backed up to a block of stores and shops along the main drag, at this point hardly the classiest section of central Hollywood. The big metal refuse can had letters stenciled on it, Rudolph's Music. On top of whatever else it contained was the plastic sack, gaping open at the top, and visible inside was a human leg, foot uppermost. The sack wasn't big enough to hold a whole body, even cut up.

They took the refuse collectors' names and sent them on their way, and called the lab from the squad. Garcia and Franks came out in a mobile van and after a few expletives got to work while Maddox and Rodriguez watched. Photographs taken, they eased out the sack and carefully extracted the contents, which proved to be two human legs roughly hacked off at the thigh, and the lower half of a male torso.

"¡Santa María!" said Rodriguez.

The body parts were all naked, and there wasn't anything else in the sack, which was just an ordinary plastic sack of the kind used for refuse or yard clippings, about two and a half feet by three. But the lab could work some miracles with the microscopes and forensic tests.

The morgue wagon came eventually and carted off the remains, which looked fairly fresh, and the lab men went away to start looking through the microscopes. Maddox looked up and down the alley. "I know," said Rodriguez helpfully, "whoever it was, he could have been killed in Burbank and the parts dumped here just by chance."

"We don't even know he was killed," said Maddox. "Whoever he was, he could have died of a heart attack."

"And the relatives decided to get out of the funeral expenses. I suppose it's possible," said Rodriguez amusedly. "But we have to start where we are."

They started, naturally, with the place called Rudolph's Music. It was a hole-in-the-wall place, dingy and looking unprosperous, with racks of LP records, a few stereo supplies. It had just opened for business, and the proprietor didn't look very hopeful of getting any. He was a man about forty, thin and gray-haired with myopic eyes behind large glasses, and he told them he ran the business alone, and business was bad, he didn't know how he was going to make the rent this month. Times were terrible. The refuse can, he said vaguely, well, there wasn't much to put in it, he hadn't been able to add to the stock for the last couple of months. He was a bachelor who lived in a small apartment on Harold Way, and he didn't look like a candidate for cutting up an inconvenient corpse.

The other places that backed up to the alley were a woman's dress shop, a phone-answering service, a sleazy-looking coffee shop, a shoe-repair shop, and a cut-rate drugstore on the corner. The occupants all seemed to be ordinary citizens, not that you could always judge.

"Nobody in his right mind," said Rodriguez, "would leave parts of a cut-up corpse on his own doorstep, Ivor."

"Well, we have to look." It didn't, of course, take them anywhere. About one o'clock they came back to the office, and Maddox called the coroner's office and talked to a Dr. Farbstein. "Has anybody had a look at that partial body? I realize it's early to ask you for any conclusions, but—"

"Oh, yes," said Farbstein interestedly. "I had a glance when it came in, we haven't made any detailed examination yet, of course. And I've heard about the hamburger from Bergner—now that is quite something, isn't it? The homicidal maniac—they do exist."

"What about the corpse?" asked Maddox patiently.

"The partial corpse. Well, there's not much we can say, with only these parts of it. Bergner thinks the man was fairly young, but I wouldn't even pin it down to that. Unless he was poisoned—we'll have a look inside—there's nothing to say how he died. Of course if you ever find the rest of him—the head and hands—somebody may have his prints, and we could tell you more about him."

"Thank you so much," said Maddox; but it was only what he had expected.

CHAPTER FOUR

Sue and Daisy had been helping out on the paperwork, taking the statements from all those witnesses, a crowd of witnesses on the bar heist a couple of nights ago, and it was all going to add up to a handful of nothing. They'd heard the vague descriptions before, the four Negroes, two of them light-colored, the tall one very good-looking, the pillowcase, the terse demand for the cash only. On that, it could be any four heisters out of Records, or a bunch of amateurs never previously caught up with, and an endless job to work. The witnesses stopped drifting in about three o'clock, and Sue sat back with a long sigh and lit a cigarette.

"Talk about a waste of time," said Daisy, and then looked up at the door. "Can we help you?"

There was a young couple in the doorway, a tall broad-shouldered young man, with a pleasantly blunt-featured face, and a younger girl. He was soberly dressed in a dark business suit, a white shirt. He said in a deep soft voice, "I guess you'd be the two policewomen Mrs. Fenton saw, she said something about it." He sounded apologetic. "Is that right?"

"Fenton," said Sue. "Oh, yes."

"Well, we thought we'd better come in and see you about it," he said. "In case anybody got the wrong idea about anything."

The girl said, "I was so embarrassed about her going to the police—of course it was just silly, but she shouldn't have done that—"

"Come in and sit down," invited Daisy. "You'll be Miss Fenton?"

"That's right," the girl nodded.

They took chairs and the man said, "Silly is the word for it all right. But she's gotten so used to Jill doing whatever she tells her to, she won't realize that this time she's not going to." He had a good solid jaw and steady blue eyes.

The girl said in a distressed voice, "I've always just hated it." She was a rather startlingly beautiful girl, with a mass of dark auburn hair, a lovely complexion, classic regular features, a slim, curved figure. She was dressed modestly in a brown suit, beige blouse, low-heeled shoes. "If we're not taking too much of your time, we thought we'd like to explain—I was afraid Ronald would get into trouble on his job, if you got the wrong idea—"

"I see," said Daisy. "Your mother seemed to think we could make some trouble for him. This will be Mr. Davenport?"

"That's right," he said. "I wasn't afraid of that."

The girl said, "It's his first year of teaching, he hasn't got tenure yet." She was young and a little shy, but her voice and eyes were firm. "You see, Mother's a film cutter at Paramount and all she can ever see is the show business, the way to make money and be somebody—the way she sees it—the way she thinks of it. And just because I'm, well, a little prettier than some girls"— he gave her a loving, amused look— "she's always been bound and determined I'm going to be a big star, and I've always just hated it, I'm no good at acting or singing or dancing, any of the rest of it, I hate getting up in front of people, but she made me take all the lessons—and that fat Bernstein patting my hand and saying I'm going to make all their fortunes. I hated it, and now there's this awful screen test—" She was twisting her hands together.

"Take it easy," said Davenport. "It's not going to happen. If we have to we can go over to Vegas and get married before you're of age."

"That's just it," she said. "I never wanted any part of it, all I ever had any ambition to do was get married and have a family—and I'd sort of planned out what I'd do, I was scared when I thought about it, but I was going to, I'll graduate from Hollywood High in June, and I was going to get a job—any kind of job I could, and get away from Mother. Just tell her once and for all I didn't want any part of her ideas for me, I'd tried to tell her that often enough before but she just said I was a silly girl who didn't know what was best for myself. But then

Ronald and I"—she was blushing faintly—"well, we fell in love right off, when I got into his history class last September—"

He said bluntly, "I could guess what she tried to tell you about me, but you can see it's all on the level. Jill may be a little young, but she knows her own mind and so do I. I don't know if she'd ever have been able to get away from that woman on her own, but she won't have to try. She's got me to stand up for her now, and it'll be just fine with me if we never laid eyes on that woman again. It seems the devil of a thing to say, her own mother, but she's pushed and pulled Jill around all her life, like a damned tyrant, and she's not going to do it any longer."

"Good for you," said Sue. "Both of you."

The girl said, "She divorced Daddy when I was ten, I guess it's just that I'm more like him really—all I remember is, he was awfully quiet and called me 'Baby' and I loved him. But he lost his job and she was always nagging him and then he just went away and she divorced him, we never saw him again—"

"It's going to be all right, honey," said Davenport. "So long as the police don't have any wrong ideas about us."

"We really didn't, Mr. Davenport," said Daisy. "Good luck to both of you."

"We're going to get married as soon as the semester is ended in June, and," he said forcefully, "that'll be the end of Mrs. Enid Fenton and all her grandiose ideas about a career in show business." He stood up. "Come on, beautiful, we mustn't waste the ladies' time." Jill gave them a timid smile and went out ahead of him.

"Nice people," said Daisy. "They'll probably be very happy, and Ronald's just the buffer she needs to fend off that greedy bitch."

"Honestly, some women—" said Sue. "Well, you can see her reasoning, Jill's certainly a beautiful little piece. But there's more to her than that, maybe she's just as determined as her mother in her own way."

Typing up all the statements, they had been immured in the office all day, and it wasn't until the end of shift when they were getting ready to leave that they heard about the cut-up corpse. Maddox was still swearing about it.

"No kind of description even to ask Missing Persons about," he said.

"Did anybody get anywhere with Atascadero and Camarillo?" asked Sue.

D'Arcy said glumly, "I had a talk with the chief head-doctor at Atascadero. They haven't released any of the nuts in the last six

months or so, and of course he wasn't any help. Our nut may never
have been tucked away at all. The latest one they let go from anywhere
around here was one named Rodney Engel, he's got a little record of
child molestation, he's a schizo, he was about five years in, and the
doctor says the therapy and shock treatment were very beneficial. Ha!
How do they know? Anyway, I got an address, he's living with his
parents in Flintridge, supposed to be seeing a head-doctor there. And
speaking of parents, Ivor, I never did get hold of the Allway girl's
family, we'll have to try again tomorrow. Or leave a note for the night
watch."

"Saturday night, they may be busy," said Maddox. He looked at Sue.
"You're looking a little bushed."

"All the typing," said Sue. "I'll be glad to get home."

"I wish you could start staying home sooner."

They drove home separately, to the big old house on the quiet street,
and Margaret had dinner nearly ready; it was good to relax from the rat
race at least overnight.

* * *

Saturday night, the night watch was busy. There was a mugging in a
parking lot at a little after eight, a lawyer leaving his office late. He had
been knocked unconscious and he wasn't looking too good, not a young
man, and they called an ambulance for him under protest. "You might
have a little concussion, sir," said Donaldson.

"Nonsense, I'm just shaken up a bit, and my wife'll be worrying."
He'd been found by a couple parking on the way to a movie who'd
called the police. There had been about forty dollars in his wallet, and
credit cards, and the mugger was long gone—there wasn't any usable
description. Nothing to do on it but write the report.

They had just gotten back to the office when they were sent out
again, to a bar down on Melrose, where there had been a knifing. It was
a Mexican place, and the bartender about the only one there who
claimed to speak much English. The man who had gotten knifed in a
little brawl wasn't hurt badly but they sent him off to Emergency and
struggled to question the knifer. About all they got was his name,
Eduardo Vasquez.

"I don't know why the hell I picked this damned job," said Stacey
disgustedly, dropping the knife into an evidence bag. "This kind of
thing is just futile, a waste of everybody's time. There'll be a charge of

assault and all the damn paperwork on it, and he'll waste the court's time too, and get a suspended sentence. And I can see D'Arcy's point about the language."

"Yep," said Donaldson. "It used to be they had to pick up some English, but no more. I wonder how he's doing at night school."

"It's supposed to be an easy language to learn, but I was never any good at that kind of thing."

They went back to the office and Brougham typed the report while Stacey's portable radio muttered police frequency in the background. A good many calls were coming in that weren't their business, accidents, drunks, traffic violations. A squad car came across a dead body at ten-thirty, and Stacey went out to look at it. It was the body of an elderly man on a side street off Third, and there wasn't any ID on him. It looked like another derelict dead of natural causes.

He got back to the station to find Donaldson and Brougham just leaving on a call to a burglary.

The house was on Electra Drive off Laurel Canyon Boulevard, and after one look Donaldson said, "The midget burglar again." There were all the earmarks of that one. The owners, a Mr. and Mrs. Rosen, had been visiting their daughter in Pasadena and got home half an hour ago to discover the place ransacked. It was, as expectable in this area, an old house, big and sprawling; this was one of the more affluent sections of the area where the pint-sized burglar had been hitting, houses where he would expect to find the valuable hauls. Equally, people up here were conscious of security, and the Rosen house was well provided with good dead-bolt locks, bars on vulnerable windows. It hadn't looked necessary to put bars on one rear closet window, it was only about a foot and a half square, and only the midget burglar could have gotten through it after smashing it. And on all these jobs there had been no prints picked up; he was a slick pro.

The Rosens were lamenting, finally pulled themselves together to tell the detectives what was missing—this time he'd gotten quite a useful haul, a lot of diamond jewelry, a mink coat, two portable TVs, an expensive camera. Mrs. Rosen said, "I was going to take the mink in for summer storage next week." Rosen said devoutly, "At least, thank God, they didn't break into the safe, there's twenty thousand bucks worth of silver bullion there."

"My God," said Brougham. "We'll want a description of the jewelry, Mr. Rosen. If you can come into the station tomorrow and make a statement—" Rosen had the serial numbers, but that wasn't going to matter here, the midget burglar a pro who knew the fences; none of this would ever show up at a pawnshop.

*   *   *

And on Sunday morning Feinman said forcefully, "I swear to God it's that Leach! He's got the right record for those jobs, and he's just too damned cocky, he knows we've got no damn evidence here at all! But maybe we'll turn lucky this time, my God—if he pulled this one sometime in the middle of the evening last night, he's only had about ten hours to get to the fence—"

He went over to that apartment on Whitely in a hurry, and had to push the doorbell three times before James Leach opened the door. He squinted up at Feinman and a small grin stretched his mouth.

"Well, well," he said. "The fuzz again. What do you want now?"

Feinman said, "Just some questions, Leach. I suppose you'll tell me you've been home all night."

"Sure," said Leach. "Both of us, the wife can tell you, we stayed in all day. We were watching TV last night. You wanna talk to Jean? Come right in." He opened the door wider. Feinman went in to a small neat living room. Leach was in pajamas and bathrobe. The sharp-faced woman was in an inner doorway, fastening a housecoat over a nightgown.

"You coming to bother us again," she said angrily.

Feinman was already feeling resigned. He had asked D'Arcy to apply for the search warrant and told Traffic to dispatch a squad car up here to stand by until the warrant came through. All the correct moves to make, and he knew it was going to be a waste of time. Leach the very slick pro, none of the neighbors would have seen him come and go, the woman backed up his alibi, and after all ten hours was time enough to drop off the loot to the fence. But they'd go through the motions.

He didn't talk to the Leaches long; he left the uniformed man in the hall outside the apartment. The warrant came through at eleven o'clock, and he went back there with Rodriguez and they had a good look all through the place, and of course it was clean—nothing there but their clothes and furniture, nothing in the way of suspicious valuables—the Leaches would be too smart to spend the ill-gotten gains on the kind of possessions they shouldn't be able to afford on their humble wages.

"Just picking on us," she grumbled, "because Jim's been in a little trouble before."

"Now, honey," said Leach smugly, "they got to do their job. They've got no way to know I'm going real straight these days." He gave Feinman a sunny smile, and Feinman nearly snarled at him.

* * *

Rosen had come in while Feinman and Rodriguez were out with the warrant, talked to Maddox, and given him a precise description of all the jewelry. There were some custom pieces which would ordinarily be identifiable, but the fence would see that all those were broken up, none of it would ever be seen again. Sue typed up the list for transmission to all the pawnbrokers, an empty gesture.

Nothing new had gone down this morning, and there wasn't much to do about the cases on hand, except the perennial heisters and burglars. It would probably be an empty gesture too, but there was the nut released from Atascadero, Rodney Engel. Find him and talk to him, just in case he could be the nut spiking the hamburger. It was a very long shot, but one place to look. There wasn't anything to do about the partial corpse, unless the doctors could tell them something more. There were still possible heisters out of Records to lean on. Dowling had just brought one in, and Nolan was out looking for another. D'Arcy had been out on something, and came back as Maddox was starting out reluctantly on the legwork. He sat down on his desk and said thoughtfully, "I've got a kind of funny feeling, Ivor, about this suicide. The Allway girl. I finally got hold of the parents, they'd been out all day yesterday, and I've just taken the father down to the morgue for the formal identification. The little we've got on her, this boy friend, what's his name, Peterson, he says they'd broken up after a fight and later on he found she'd shot herself in her car."

"That's right," said Maddox. "What's the funny feeling?"

"Well, both the parents say they never heard of a boy friend named Peterson. And they talked with her on the phone all the time, the girl told them everything she was doing, who she was going out with and so on."

Maddox considered, massaging his jaw absently. "Nothing much in that. They might just have thought she told them everything."

"I suppose," said D'Arcy, "but it just struck me as funny. The morgue sent the slug over to the lab, and they'll get to the autopsy sometime."

"And we'd better go looking for some more possible heisters," said Maddox.

D'Arcy yawned. "Dammit, sometime I'd like to have Sundays off like a normal citizen. I was out on a late date last night."

Maddox eyed him with covert curiosity. D'Arcy went from girl to girl, and the rest of them had it figured out that it was on account of his funny name. He couldn't expect a girl to call him "Hey-you" and as soon as they found out his name they got to kidding him about it, or laughing, and he got turned off. It was something of a damn shame, because D'Arcy was a very nice fellow, he ought to settle down and marry some nice girl. He was a lonely sort, D'Arcy, no family left, and what his parents had been thinking about to saddle him with such a queer moniker—

"Nice girl?" ventured Maddox, and D'Arcy looked a little embarrassed.

"Well, teacher," he said. "My Spanish teacher. Her name's Rita Warren, she's a sweet girl all right. She's going to USC to get her master's, just teaching the adult course for extra money—only reason she knows Spanish, her father was in our embassy in Argentina. Well, who are we still looking for?" He got up.

Maddox didn't ask any more questions. The Spanish teacher of all women, he thought. Teachers. Sue telling him about that Fenton girl and the high school teacher. People were funny in a lot of ways, but usually interesting.

* * *

Everybody was in at three-thirty, Dowling and Nolan questioning one suspect in an interrogation room, Feinman and Rodriguez questioning another. Sue and Daisy had gone out on something. Maddox had just come in from an abortive hunt for another possible heister when the desk relayed a call to him, and a heavy bass voice said, "You one of the boys on this doped hamburger thing? That's really one for the books. This is Sergeant Carmody, Valley division. You've got us in on it now, we've had a little mayhem out here this afternoon. Five more people got the spiked hamburger. No, nobody's dead—the paramedics had heard about it on the news and as soon as they heard the victims had been eating hamburger, they told the doctors what to look for."

"For God's sake," said Maddox. "What happened?"

Carmody said, "Big party at a place in Van Nuys. Cookout in a classy backyard, the host grilling hamburgers, and five people passing out. It's our baby, but it seems to be all one case and we thought you ought to hear about it."

"My God, yes—we'll be out—where?" Carmody told him.

He collected Rodriguez and they drove out to Van Nuys. It was a big expensive-looking house on the outskirts of town, and it had a big manicured backyard with an outsized pool. All the equipment for the cookout was there, an electric grill, the picnic tables, comfortable lawn furniture. The owner, Robert Boyd, his wife, and the remaining guests matched the house. Boyd owned a big sporting-goods store and was obviously doing all right, a man about fifty, in a gaudy Hawaiian shirt and shorts. Everybody there was still agitated and upset.

"My God," said Boyd, "like I told the other cops, sure we'd heard about that poisoned hamburger, on the TV news, but that was way over in Hollywood, how could we know there'd be any right around here? The party just sort of grew, it's getting to be nice weather for an outdoor party, we'd asked the Colemans and Betty and Bob Kowalski, some other old friends, and then this morning Helen DeVore called and said they had some unexpected company, some old neighbors from up north, and of course I said fine, bring 'em along, the more the merrier, and so Myra says to me, with five more people we'd need some more hamburger, so I went out and got another package, a couple of pounds—"

"Where?" asked Maddox.

"Why, the nearest market, the Safeway over on Roscoe Boulevard. That was about ten o'clock. My God, all I can think of is, thank God Linda wasn't here—they were supposed to come, Linda and Bill, but Bill's picked up a flu bug and so they didn't. Linda's our daughter, she's expecting a baby—and people started coming about twelve-thirty. I'd gotten the charcoal started in the grill by the pool and I made some drinks—the women were getting out the salad and all the other fixings. It was all just informal, you know, and I started grilling the hamburgers the way people liked them, rare or medium or whatever—there was quite a little crowd—and all of a sudden Helen said, she'd come up to get some more salad, she said, my God, I'm dizzy as a fool, and I only had one drink. And my God, she passed out cold, nearly went into the pool, and my God, people started dropping like flies—it was terrible!"

Carmody, who had turned out to be a big blond fellow, interrupted the flow. "So Mr. Boyd called the paramedics and when they heard about the hamburger they told the doctors in Emergency. You'll want the rest of the hamburger for analysis, Hollywood seems to be handling the case. Just before I called you we had the word from the Emergency ward, it was the Demerol again, in the hamburger."

"Just terrible!" said Boyd. "It must have been the second package I bought this morning." He was mopping his brow, still shaken. The eight or ten guests still there were standing around silent, listening. "Thank God they're all going to be okay, but how in God's name this lunatic could be putting the stuff into hamburger—and it said on the news, Central Hollywood—we never gave it a thought—"

"By this, it could be anywhere," said Carmody. "And I suppose you've got no idea where to look for him. I don't envy you boys on this one. But I guess you'll want cooperation—if there's anything we can do—"

"How right you are, Sergeant," said Rodriguez. "We'd better get the media to spell it out, it could be anywhere."

"At least," said Carmody, "this time nobody got killed, but who knows about next time?"

There wasn't much point in talking to the victims, and they wouldn't be feeling very happy after the stomach pumping. Maddox got their names and addresses for the record and they went up to the Emergency ward at St. Joseph's Hospital and talked to the doctors. The paperwork was piling up on this.

It was long past the end of shift by then, and Sue out somewhere when he had left, but she wasn't a worrier. He dropped Rodriguez in the parking lot of the station and started home. He was starving. And he thought about all those markets, hundreds of them all over this great sprawling metropolis, and all the neat packages of hamburger in the refrigerated cases—it was too late to get the renewed warning on TV tonight, though Rodriguez had said he would try to get the eleven o'clock newscaster.

*   *   *

All the men had been out when a new call went down about three o'clock, an attempted assault and robbery, and Sue and Daisy had gone out on it. The address was Chula Vista above Hollywood Boulevard, and it was an old California bungalow beyond a neat strip of lawn. The uniformed man was plump, balding Cassidy, and he was looking concerned. "I thought maybe I ought to call an ambulance, the old lady took quite a knock on the head, but she wouldn't let me, says she's okay now. Her name's Mrs. Erwin, Mrs. Beatrice Erwin."

"All right," said Daisy, "we'll take it from here, you can get back on tour."

The front door was open and they went in, introduced themselves to two women in the neat well-furnished living room. Mrs. Erwin was looking pale and shaken and had a little cut on one temple which had bled some; she was holding a wet towel to it. She was a thin small woman probably in her seventies, with sparse white hair. The other woman was a Mrs. McMahon, who lived across the street, middle-aged and fat and anxious. "Oh, dear, oh, dear, what an upset, all these criminals everywhere these days, and this has always been such a quiet street. I'm the one called the police, I never had such a fright in my life, I'd been out to the post office to mail a letter to my husband—he's back East settling up his mother's estate—and just as I drove up I saw Mrs. Erwin lying on her front porch—I thought she'd had a stroke or heart attack or something—and I ran over to see—and then she came to and told me—"

Mrs. Erwin sat up and said forthrightly, "My heart's perfectly sound. It was the screen door. Because it's not there, I mean. The old one just rotted off its hinges and that dratted man I got to look at it said he'd put a new one on yesterday, but he never turned up, and he'd taken the old one away. Usually I'd have had the screen door hooked, so that fellow couldn't have gotten in. And don't I know what Dorothy's going to say about this."

"What happened, Mrs. Erwin?" asked Daisy.

"I didn't know they'd send women police out." She looked at them curiously. "Well, I was sitting here crocheting, when the doorbell rang, and I went to answer it—and like I say, no screen door—and it was a young colored man on the porch, he asked if I needed any yard work done, and I told him no, I had a regular gardener—and then, it was so unexpected, he'd acted polite, he gave me a real hard shove, shoved me back into the living room and knocked me down against the coffee table, and I must have passed right out, I don't know how long, but when I came to he was gone—and I guess I was confused, of course I ought to have called the police, but all I could think of was shutting the front door—and I must have fallen again on the porch—"

"Gave me the fright of my life," said Mrs. McMahon.

"Have you had a chance to look around, see if anything's been taken?" asked Sue.

She nodded. "While we were waiting for the officer, I looked around. He took my portable radio and everything out of my jewelry case and all the cash out of my handbag on the bed, there was about forty-five dollars in it."

"Could you describe him?" asked Daisy.

"Well, he was just a young fellow, not very black, kind of thin, kind of a long face. He had on jeans and a sweat shirt. That's all I could say."

"What about the jewelry?" asked Sue. "Can you give us a description of it?"

"There wasn't much," she said tiredly. "My grandmother's cameo pin, and three old garnet rings, one of those old-fashioned wide gold bracelets—and my engagement ring, I don't wear that much now, it's just a little diamond, all Fred could afford when we got married. And my mother's wedding set. That's kind of old-fashioned too, it's white gold and the diamond in the engagement ring is in what they call a Tiffany setting, you know, raised. And there are initials inside it, J.R. and M.B."

That would be readily identifiable, and this had been the crude thing, probably by an amateur on impulse.

Mrs. Erwin put the towel in her lap. "I'm all right, but I can just hear what Dorothy'll say about this. On at me about how I'm not competent to live alone and ought to go into a retirement home! Not while I've got my strength!" She looked at Sue. "You're going to have a baby, my dear."

"July," said Sue, smiling at her.

Mrs. Erwin sighed. "Well, I just hope it'll be a joy to you, but you never know. Fred and I—he's been gone five years and I still miss him, you know—we'd have liked to have had several children, but we only had the one. Dorothy. And from the time she was a little thing, she was just exactly like Fred's sister, Vina—greedy, never satisfied with what she had, always wanting more. She and that husband of hers, they just can't wait for me to die or go into a nursing home so they can lay their hands on my house—with real estate prices up it's worth something, and they're just itching to get hold of what I've got. And the grandchildren just spoiled brats, no pleasure to be around and they don't think anything of me. Life does some queer things to a person."

"Are you sure you're all right, Mrs. Erwin?"

"I'm fine," she said sturdily. "I'll be fine."

Back at the station Sue typed up a list of the jewelry, to pass on to the hot sheet to the pawnbrokers. She felt sorry for old Mrs. Erwin, whose family didn't care a damn about her.

It was nearly six o'clock, everybody was drifting out, and nobody seemed to know where Ivor was. Sue covered her typewriter and said good night to Daisy. But as she went out to the parking lot she was still thinking about Mrs. Erwin, who seemed like a nice old lady who deserved a loving family. And then suddenly she was thinking about her mother.

She started up Fountain for the nearest on ramp to the freeway, caught the light at Gower, and as she waited for it to change her eye caught the sign on a corner shop. On impulse she found a slot for the Chrysler half a block up, and walked back to the florist and bought a great sheaf of hothouse chrysanthemums, gold and amber and lovely.

It was full dark when she turned into the drive of the house on Starview Terrace and went in the back door to Tama's welcoming woof.

"Well, for heaven's sake, what's this for? It's not my birthday," said her mother. She took the flowers. "They're beautiful, Sue, but what's the occasion?"

"Just to let you know that we appreciate you very, very much, darling." Sue kissed her. "And evidently Ivor is going to be late."

* * *

On Monday both Daisy and D'Arcy were off. The autopsy report came in on that body found in the street last week. Maddox glanced at it: there was nothing to it, he had died of acute alcoholism. There hadn't been any identity on him: the city would pay for the funeral. Another one like that had turned up a few nights ago, he remembered.

Rodriguez came in just after that, towing a suspect on one of the heists, and Maddox sat in on the unproductive questioning. In the end they let him go; they always seemed to be trying to make bricks without straw.

They went out to lunch with Sue. For once, surprisingly for a Sunday, the night watch hadn't left them anything new to look at. Rodriguez had managed to reach the network newscaster yesterday evening, and the repeated warning had gone out on the eleven o'clock news.

Maddox told them about D'Arcy's new girl, and they were interested and amused. "The Spanish teacher!" said Sue, laughing. "How funny. It'd be a good thing for him if he settled down and got married. He's not really the natural girl chaser like our César."

Rodriguez brushed his moustache. "I just like to be independent," he said, grinning.

When they got back to the office Dowling told them there had been another daylight burglary, Feinman had gone out on it. "Joe's really ticked off about that Leach," said Rodriguez, "and I don't blame him. Ten to one he's our boy all right, on all those slick jobs, but how to pin it on him is something else."

Baker called Maddox five minutes later. "Just passing on the word, you'll get a report sometime. The morgue sent that slug over, from the body Friday night, and it matches the gun okay. The gun's a nearly new Colt .22."

"Thanks," said Maddox absently. That thing at least was straightforward, posing no mystery.

He was still sitting there smoking, disinclined for the legwork, half an hour later when Sue looked in. "I've got something you'll want to hear about," she told him.

"Oh?" He followed her back across the hall to the little office. She said, "This is Miss Alice Green. Sergeant Maddox. I'd like you to tell the sergeant what you've been telling me, Miss Green."

She was a shabbily dressed, dumpy old woman with thin gray hair, a big nose, work-worn gnarled hands folded in her lap. She said in a hoarse voice, "All I had. Everything. All my savings. Just gone, like that. You said, describe him, but how could I do that? I hardly saw him."

"Miss Green," said Sue, "has had her purse snatched." Maddox just looked at her, and she gave him her sweetest smile. "Go on, Miss Green. You were on your way home about an hour ago—"

"That's right. Like I said. I live on Orange Avenue, the block down from Santa Monica, I'd been out to the market. I don't have a car, never did, I've always been a good walker, even if I am seventy-two and retired on the Social Security. I never been married, and all my family's gone, but I worked hard all my life and saved up, and I been pretty smart about investments too." Her voice was dull. "I was just walking along with my bag of groceries, I'd just turned onto Orange, when he come up behind me, I never heard him coming, and he grabbed my purse, I had the strap over my arm and he pulled me right over, I fell down and dropped the groceries, and all the eggs got busted. I don't usually buy a whole dozen at once, they're awful high. And before I could get my breath he got the strap off my arm and run off with my purse, back toward the boulevard. He was just a young fellow by the one look I got of him, from behind. I never saw his face, I couldn't say what he looked like."

"Tell the sergeant what was in your purse," said Sue gently.

"Well, I can tell him that all right, just like I told you. There was the rest of the Social Security money in my wallet, sixty-two dollars and forty-five cents—I'd paid the rent on the first, and that had to last the rest of the month—and there was all my life's savings in the zipper compartment. Eighty-nine thousand and eight hundred dollars."

"What?" said Maddox sharply.

She repeated the figure precisely. "It's mostly in thousand-dollar bills and hundreds. Everything I had in the world."

"But, my God," said Maddox, "why did you have it in your handbag instead of in the bank?"

"I don't trust none of them banks," said Miss Green darkly. "They go broke and you lose all your money. I always carry everything I've got right with me, it's the safest way. I never leave it at home in case of fire when I'm out. I always keep everything in my purse, then I know right where it is and it's safe."

"My good God," said Maddox.

"And now it's gone, and I don't suppose there's anything you can do about getting it back. I figured the police ought to know, and I walked all the way up here, but I don't suppose there's anything you can do about it."

"Well, I doubt whether there is, Miss Green."

Compassionately Sue called up a squad car to drive her home. "The snatcher got a little surprise," she said gravely. "The things people do!"

"To say the least. My God. Eighty-nine thousand—my God. People indeed. The foolishness and stupidity and ignorance. I wonder where the hell it all came from."

"Investments," said Sue. "And don't call her ignorant, darling. She's smart. While she had it in cash in the handbag, she wasn't paying over half of it in taxes to Uncle Sam."

Maddox sat back and laughed. "Too true. I'd like to have seen the snatcher's face when he opened the bag and found it. But of course, he's going to run into trouble trying to cash those thousand-dollar bills. Banks can be inquisitive. Good God almighty—but of course the silly old fool's only got herself to thank."

* * *

The night watch had an unexpectedly busy shift, just a lot of little things. A waitress on her way home from the late shift was mugged and robbed in a parking lot on Beverly, and badly enough hurt that they called an ambulance. A couple coming out of an early movie were held up on the street; it had been dark along there and they couldn't give any useful description, just what the detectives had expected: "He was a young guy, I think, by his voice and the way he moved." He'd only gotten about ten bucks. There was a hit-run on Beverly with a young woman carted off to Emergency, but she didn't look bad. That was about ten-thirty, and there hadn't been many people on the street, and the two witnesses who had seen it gave vague answers about the car, unsure of its size or color or make.

"I hope she's got insurance," said Stacey.

Just before the end of shift there was a heist at a twenty-four-hour fast-food place on Wilshire, and they got nothing there either. The night clerk was young and scared; he couldn't say what the man had looked like, just that he had a big gun and talked tough. "The manager always tells all of us, don't act brave, if you get held up, hand it over, we're insured. So I did. I never got held up before. I didn't mind the night work at first, but I've had it now, God, that gun scared the bejesus out of me." The day watch would have to get a statement from him, but it wouldn't be worth a damn.

And it wasn't any of the LAPD's business—the highway patrol had jurisdiction over the freeways—but the radio had told them about a monumental pileup on the Golden State, a big cross-country semi-trailer out of control and smashing head on into a lot of cars in the slow lane. The last they had heard before the heist, there were at least six people dead and more carted off to Emergency.

"When you stop to think about it," said Dick Brougham seriously, "this nut poisoning the hamburger we'd like to catch up to, but when you think of the people killed in accidents every day—"

"Yeah," said Donaldson. "He's a piker. Only eight people so far."

"And I suppose a lot of people have stopped buying hamburger."

* * *

Late on Tuesday morning Maddox had just gotten back from a fruitless hunt for one of the suspects from Records when he got a call from the dispatcher. "You've got some more of that cut-up body, Sergeant. At least we can presume it's the same body, this can be kind of a hairy town these days but we don't get the dismembered bodies just that often. The squad just called in. It, or they, are at the old Hollywood cemetery."

"For God's sake. Well, they ended up in the right place, didn't they? All right, we're on it." Rodriguez was typing a report at the next desk. "Come on, César, we've got some more body parts to look at."

The squad, with Gonzales beside it, was waiting for them at the entrance gates of that old cemetery fronting on Santa Monica Boulevard. "Why does it have to be me who gets sent to look at these damned things?" said Gonzales plaintively. "First the legs and now the arms. My God. It's over at the side wall to the left, one of the maintenance men found it."

They sent him back on tour and went in past the gate, spotted the maintenance man waiting for them along one of the graveled paths. He was a big heavy man with a brown beard, and he said, "You're the front-office dicks. Jesus, I never ran into a thing like this before. This is a nice quiet place to work, you know? I mean, you know there are bodies all around, but you don't think about it, and they're all decently buried. Jesus. It's over here," and he led the way. "In there under the hedge."

The hedge was against the front wall, and halfway obscured by it, they could see the body parts, two arms and part of a torso. No clothes, no plastic sack. "It's not worth getting the lab out," said Rodriguez, bending to look. "Somebody just tossed them over the wall. They could have been here a couple of days."

"Don't ask me," said the maintenance man. "I wouldn't know. I hadn't trimmed that hedge in a couple of weeks. As soon as I saw what it was I called in. Jesus. You guys and the undertakers, you get paid to deal with corpses." That definition hadn't occurred to Maddox before, but in a sense it was true.

And, of course, the doctors. It wasn't worth calling a lab man out. They got the morgue wagon up and followed it down to the coroner's office, went in and asked for Bergner. He was busy in the autopsy room, but after a while Dr. Whitman appeared and was interested to hear that more of the corpse had showed up. "Let's take a look," he said cheerfully. "They probably took it right down to the cold room." In the end, they wound up in one of the autopsy labs with the body parts laid out neatly on the dissecting table. There was an upper torso and the two arms. The hands were missing.

Whitman looked at them with a professional eye. "Well, of course it's got to be part of the same corpse. Whoever cut it up hadn't any anatomical knowledge at all. Look at those cuts"—he sounded disapproving—"the hands just hacked off with a saw or something, and the torso cut in half probably the same way. A very crude job."

"I believe you," said Maddox, averting his eyes from the table, "but can you tell us anything more about the man?"

"I think Bergner was going to have a look at the stomach," said Whitman. "I was interested, because I don't remember ever having a dismembered body through here in my time. I had a look at the rest of it with Bergner. We could make some educated guesses by measurements. He was a fairly big man, probably around six feet, say a hundred and eighty pounds. It's possible that he was Hispanic, you notice the skin is olive-colored, and the hair on the arms is dark—as was the pubic hair. We can deduce that the hands were removed so the police couldn't take fingerprints."

"Yes, doctor," said Rodriguez. "We had deduced that."

"And no tattoo marks or scars," said Whitman regretfully. "Of course, if the head turns up, or the hands—There aren't any marks on the body, that is, gunshot wounds or knife wounds—but at least we can say, it was a very crude job of dismemberment."

"And there are ten thousand males just in the inner city who'd conform to that description," said Rodriguez, taking a grateful breath of fresh air on the front steps. "*Paciencia.* The rest of him may show up sometime."

"Looking just as anonymous," said Maddox pessimistically. They went back to base and he called the lab. "Those body parts," he said to

Garcia, "did you turn up anything under the microscopes from that plastic sack?"

"Oh, that," said Garcia. "Somebody should have sent you a report. Not much. There was some blood—type A, which isn't all that common. If you ever get a hint who he was, it could help to identify him."

"We're some way from that," said Maddox. "No hands, and no head." He sat back and lit a cigarette, and now he was thinking about the hamburger again. The lunatic. They hadn't yet chased up that one released from Atascadero, Rodney Engel. They ought to talk to him. But, while this nut was a nut—aiming at random—not every bona fide nut had ever been identified as such and tucked away.

He was vaguely aware of a uniformed man coming in and going over to D'Arcy's desk. D'Arcy said in an uninterested tone, "Another autopsy report." He slit the manila envelope and started to look at it. And then he said, "Well, now isn't that interesting. Isn't that interesting indeed. Listen to this, Ivor. This is the autopsy on that Allway girl, the supposed suicide last Friday night."

"Mmmm?" said Maddox lazily.

"I had a funny feeling about it," said D'Arcy. "And how right I was. She was shot by that gun, all right, we heard that from the lab, but she couldn't have done it herself. There weren't any powder burns on her clothes and no residue on her hands. She was shot from at least three feet away or more."

"Well, I will be damned," said Maddox. "That looked like an open and shut case. You said something about the boy friend—"

"What's his name, Bert Peterson? I think we go and talk to him," said D'Arcy. And the phone rang on Maddox's desk and he picked it up.

"Sergeant Maddox."

It was the desk relaying a call. "Look," said a nervous male voice, "am I talking to a detective? Well, look, I just think this looks very damn funny, I thought I'd better tell you fellows. I'm Willard Dillon, Dillon Foreign Imports, Beverly Boulevard. I've got a guy in here trying to buy a Mercedes sports model, and for God's sake there's something not very kosher about it, he's offering us cash—twenty-four thousand bucks cash—I ask you, thousand-dollar bills—he's just a punk kid, nineteen by his driver's license, and it looks damn funny. I don't really know if it's anything for the police, but it's so damn offbeat, I thought —well, he's still here, I gave him some excuse about making out papers, and I don't know there's anything wrong but I just thought—I mean, all that cash—"

Maddox sat back and laughed. "The snatcher! I said he'd run into trouble—but what a damn stupid thing. All right, Mr. Dillon, keep him quiet and we'll be with you."

CHAPTER FIVE

Dillon Foreign Imports was a high-class agency out on Beverly, with the shiny sleek new models in a big showroom, more of the equally polished used cars on a lot next door. Willard Dillon was waiting for them at the door of the showroom. He looked at Maddox's badge and said, "I just thought it was funny, my God, I never saw so much cash before in my life, and he's just a young kid. His name's Antonio Dominguez. You think there's something funny about it too?"

"In spades," said Maddox. "He's still here?"

"Yeah, he's in my office. I told him it'd take a while to make out the papers."

In Dillon's office the young punk was sitting in the chair beside the desk. He was a tall thin young fellow with girlish features, a weak sloping chin.

"Who are you?" he asked nervously, and Maddox showed him the badge and he shied back.

"We don't have to ask you where you came by all the nice cash," said Maddox, "because we know. It must have been quite a surprise when you found it in the handbag you snatched from the old lady yesterday. Expecting to find ten or twenty bucks, and coming across that wad."

Dominguez said weakly, "I—I—I won it at a poker place."

"Now look," said D'Arcy, "let's not waste time, boy." The money was in a neat stack on the desk; Maddox fanned out the greenbacks, and there were thousand-dollar bills, still crisp.

"They don't hand these out at the poker palaces, Dominguez," he said. "The old lady probably has the serial numbers on these."

Dominguez said sullenly, resignedly, "Oh, hell, I mighta known there's something wrong about it. They're fake bills, is that it?"

"Not at all," said Maddox, "just not very common. But that's where you came by them, isn't it? From the handbag you snatched from the old lady. Where's the rest of it? What did you do with the handbag?"

Dominguez said, "I mighta known. Nothing ever goes right for me. So I suppose you guys go and look, and find it." He might have a Hispanic name, but obviously it was one of the families who had been here for generations; his English was unaccented.

"I suppose so," said Maddox. "Let's see your driver's license." He handed over a billfold meekly. The address was Sycamore Avenue.

"Come on, let's go pick up the rest of it," said D'Arcy.

Dominguez just said mournfully, "That's one hell of a nice car, that Mercedes. I always wanted a car like that." He didn't try to build up the gambling story. On the way up to Sycamore, he even volunteered some comment. "I just about like to fainted, I saw all those bills—it's like you said, I thought maybe twenty, thirty bucks, and there was all that damn bread—man, I thought I had it made. I mighta known it'd all go wrong."

D'Arcy asked him a few more questions and he opened up without any trouble. He didn't have a job, and his mother was always nagging him to get one, but nobody wanted to hire him, he wasn't much good at anything and life was all kind of a drag, all the dudes he knew from school last year had jobs and were doing all right, could take the chicks out on dates and all. He'd grabbed the purses before, but there usually wasn't much in them, just a few bucks, and his ma would have a fit if she knew about it. "I never been in jail," he said, "you gonna take me to jail?"

"Probably just for a little while," said D'Arcy.

The address on Sycamore was an ancient apartment building. He produced a key and let them in. In the second tiny bedroom he handed over the handbag from a drawer, a big shabby black leather bag, and all the rest of the money was still there, and Miss Alice Green's wallet with her Social Security card in it.

"I'd been looking at that car awhile," he said, "I knew how much it was."

"And how did you expect to explain to your mother and everybody else how you came by it?" asked Maddox.

He shuffled his feet and looked surprised. "I guess I hadn't thought about that. She's gonna be awful mad. I suppose you got to tell her. Yeah, well, she works at a dress factory downtown, my dad's dead." They took him up to the jail and booked him in, told him he could call his mother. It wasn't once in a blue moon they picked up one of the purse snatchers, and of course it wasn't much of a charge, in spite of the amount involved. But in time Miss Green would get back her life savings.

Neither of them had had lunch, and it was after two o'clock. They stopped at the nearest place for a sandwich, and while they waited Maddox said, "The Allway girl."

"I wondered about it," said D'Arcy, "when the family said they didn't know about her dating Peterson. Never heard her mention him. She didn't shoot herself, and by the story he was the only other one there."

"Yes, we go and talk to him," said Maddox.

But neither of them had had anything to do with the case personally, the night watch had seen the start of it, so they went back to the office to go over Stacey's report, look over the details. By the time they digested that it was nearly four o'clock and Bert Peterson would be at his job as one of the bartenders at the Blue Max Restaurant on La Cienega, where the Allway girl had worked too.

It was one of the expensive classy places on that restaurant row, just opening for business when they got there. They asked the hostess for Peterson; of course neither of them had ever seen him; and she took them into the bar at one side of the big open dining room, pointed him out. He was an insignificant-looking young fellow, tall and weedy, with a nondescript narrow face and thin sandy hair.

Maddox showed him the badge and said, "We've got a few more questions for you, Mr. Peterson."

He looked at them nervously. "Oh. About Sandra," he said. "Oh, sure." There wasn't a customer in the bar yet. "I guess it'll be all right if we talk here." He went over and sat down at one of the tables and they joined him. D'Arcy offered him a cigarette and he said he didn't smoke.

"So you and Sandra had been dating quite a bit?" asked D'Arcy. "And then she got mad at you because you'd been dating another girl?"

"That's right," said Peterson.

"It's funny that her family had never heard about you, when they'd heard about everybody else she dated."

Peterson didn't say anything.

"And you say she shot herself after you'd had the fight," said Maddox. "But you see, Peterson, she didn't shoot herself. She couldn't have. We know that now, from the scientific reports. She was shot from at least three feet away. And she hadn't been holding the gun. Have you got anything to say about that?"

Peterson didn't say anything for quite a while, staring down at the tabletop.

"She was shot in the car all right," said D'Arcy, "and you seem to have been the only one there with her, by the story." They watched him. He went on not saying anything, and then unexpectedly and embarrassedly he started to cry. A couple of early customers had come in, and the other bartender was looking concerned. He came over and said, "What's the matter, Bert? Who are these guys?"

Maddox showed the badge and took Peterson by one arm. "I think we'll continue this little talk somewhere else."

Peterson let himself be led out blindly, got into the back seat of the car without protest. He went on crying for a minute and then just sat hunched over in silence. At the station, they took him into one of the cramped interrogation rooms and D'Arcy said, "Is there something you'd like to tell us, Bert?"

Peterson didn't look up at them. He said thickly, "Yes, I got to tell you now. I never meant to do it, I never meant to hurt her, it just happened."

"You hadn't been dating her, had you?"

He shook his head. "I've never dated many girls, I'm not very good with girls, I don't know how to get along with them, do things to make them like me. I don't know why, there are a lot of fellows uglier than me seem to make out all right. But I never meant to hurt Sandra, oh, God, it just happened."

"How?" asked Maddox.

He sat up straighter, and got out a handkerchief and blew his nose. "I'd never dated her before, but she was so pretty, and she'd been friendly to me when she came into the bar to pick up drinks—I'd asked her for a date a couple of times, but she always said she was busy. Until just last week. And then she said okay, she'd go out with me on Friday —I guess I was already in love with her, she was so pretty and sort of sweet—and then it all started going wrong from the first. I was going to take her out to a real nice place, do things right, show her a good time, and maybe she'd go with me steady—and then it went wrong, because my car went on the fritz. I felt kind of silly about it, having to ask her to drive, see, it only went out that afternoon—and I didn't have much in my bank account, just the cash on me, to take her out, I couldn't afford to rent a car, and I called her—and she said that was okay, she'd drive—but that's no way to take a girl on a date. And we went to that Scandinavian place, it was pretty expensive, and I could see she was sort of bored. I just don't know how to talk to girls—and I said what about a movie and she said she was tired, wanted to go home—so I said okay, and when she drove me to my apartment I asked her for another date and she turned me down. And I was feeling just like hell about everything, I knew then I was in love with her, and I begged her to go out with me again, I'd do anything she wanted to get her to like me—" He put both hands to his face. "She was sort of kind at first, she said she didn't think we got along so good, just skip it—and I went on begging her and then she got mad—and I guess embarrassed—and she told me to just skip it, she told me to forget it—and I don't know what got into me but I said I'd kill myself if she wouldn't go out with me, and she said for God's sake stop acting like a kid. She said, you wouldn't have the guts anyway—and I said it again—and she just opened the glove compartment and said sort of contemptuous, well, there's a gun, little man, but I don't believe you—I'd heard she carried a gun in her car for protection—I'd never touched a gun in my life— but I was mad then too and I picked it up and it—it just went off. I never meant to hurt her, I couldn't believe it when she fell over in the seat." And that was easy to say, it just went off, but that had the ring of truth. Just the fluke shot, getting her in the heart. "I didn't believe she was dead. I don't remember going up to the apartment, I just sat there and tried to think about it, about what to do. And after a while I thought if I said we'd been dating and she was jealous, you'd think she'd done it herself."

"But the people at the restaurant would know that wasn't so," said

D'Arcy. "Weren't there any questions asked, when she didn't show up?"

He said, "We got a new manager. I didn't tell any lies about it there. I didn't figure she'd told anybody about the date—I guess it wasn't nothing to brag about. She got along good with the other girls, but they weren't like best friends. I figured the manager'd just think she'd gone off—I suppose he'd have her home phone number but he wouldn't know about her family—and I heard him cussing her, these damn girls, he said—but he couldn't do anything—I'm sorry about it, just so damn sorry. I never meant it. She was so pretty and so nice."

They left him sitting there while Maddox typed that up in a statement, and he signed it apathetically. They ferried him up to the jail and booked him in. The D.A. could decide what to call it, murder two or manslaughter in whatever degree. Either way it wouldn't amount to much. He would spend a little while ir. the joint, probably not long, and everybody except her family would forget about Sandra Allway. And it was past the end of shift again, and they were late leaving, the night watch coming on as they left the station. But this one was cleared away. They would have to waste time on the inquest, the hearing, while other cases came along to work.

* * *

Wednesday was a slow day. The night watch hadn't left them anything new, and they had nearly run out of possible suspects on all the heists. About noon they had a flash from Communications, a new want from the NCIC list automatically relayed to all divisions and departments. There had been a bank job in Phoenix yesterday, and the Feds had been quick on the job, they had put the finger on two men through prints in the get-away car: Ernest Hobson and Arnold Dieter, both with long and bad records of armed robbery. Hobson was originally from the Los Angeles area and was thought to have a wife somewhere here; they could be heading in this direction. There wasn't any make on what they might be driving, but mug shots would be coming through for reproduction. It would be largely Traffic's responsibility to keep an eye out, briefing the squad-car men. And apparently Dieter and Hobson had taken a wad of cash in Phoenix, and might be able to lie low for a while.

Maddox and Rodriguez were sitting talking desultorily, everybody else out on the legwork or goofing off, at two o'clock when another of the stupidities showed up. A call went down to a new heist and they both went out on it. It was a drugstore on Western, and there was only one witness, the manager. It had been a slack time of day, and both the other clerks off on coffee breaks, the pharmacist busy in the back. "There wasn't a customer in," said the manager, "when this guy walks in and looks around, he comes up to the tobacco counter where I'm standing, and puts a gun on me. Broad daylight, the way the crime rate's up is one hell of a thing, and we've never been held up before. Describe him? Well, he was maybe around thirty-five, medium-sized, I might recognize him. He had on a brown suit. He didn't say much, just to hand over the cash, and he got about a hundred bucks, this is the main register. Oh, and he dropped something."

"Dropped something?" said Rodriguez.

"Yeah, when he put the cash in his pocket he pulled his jacket open, he stashed it in his breast pocket, and something fell out of his side pocket. I picked it up after he went out, before I called you." He handed it over and it was a book of matches, nearly full. Printed on the front was *Golden State Motel*, an address on Glendale Boulevard in Atwater. "And," added the manager helpfully, "he was missing part of a finger. About half the forefinger on his left hand, I noticed it when he reached for the bills, he had the gun in his right hand, see."

"Sometimes," said Rodriguez, "this job can be boring."

The manager hadn't tried to follow him out, couldn't say anything about a car, but that had been about forty minutes ago. They got on the freeway and drove up to Atwater, found the Golden State Motel, and went up to the manager's office to ask about any occupant with a missing finger. They didn't have to ask. At the desk the manager was talking to a stocky medium-sized man in a brown suit who was just handing over a little sheaf of bills. "That's correct, Mr. Lyons, thirty-six dollars even, and I hope you've enjoyed your stay with us." The hand holding the cash had half of the forefinger missing.

"Mr. Lyons," said Maddox, and the man turned. He had a rather pleasant round face and friendly blue eyes. "We want you, Mr. Lyons, for the heist you pulled at the drugstore about an hour ago."

The manager looked startled, but Lyons was flabbergasted. He stared at the badge. He asked in naked astonishment, "How in holy hell did you find out about it so fast?"

Maddox showed him the book of matches. "You shouldn't be so careless with your property, Mr. Lyons," he said gravely.

"Oh, for Christ's sake," said Lyons.

They took him back to the jail and asked a few questions in an interrogation room. His name was Robert Lyons and he was from San Francisco, he said. "So you'll be printing me, I might as well come clean with you, you'd find out anyhow. I just got out of Susanville three months ago, I jumped parole up north. My sister lives down here, she's just had a baby and I wanted to see her. Of all the goddamned rotten luck—and I only got a lousy hundred bucks on that job."

At least they had gotten it cleared away before the end of shift, and tomorrow was Maddox's day off.

* * *

On Thursday the night watch had left them another heist, with a good description of the heister, who didn't seem to bear any resemblance to Dapper Dan or anybody else they'd heard of recently. Resignedly, Rodriguez went downtown to consult the computers at R. and I., and gathered the names of a handful of possible suspects. The day men divided them up and went out looking for them, the last known addresses scattered all over the county, leaving D'Arcy to mind the store. They only found three of them to question, and the answers weren't very helpful, but two witnesses thought they would recognize the man, so all three got lodged in jail pending a lineup. They could hold them twenty-four hours without a charge. This time they might make an arrest.

Rodriguez and Feinman had just come in about two-thirty when a new call went down, a homicide, and nobody else was there so they went out to look at it. The address was Oporto Drive up in the hills, and they found the squad-car man, Jowett, listening to two excited middle-aged females. He greeted them with some relief. "I don't suppose it's much for you to work," he said. "The woman's dead"—and his nose wrinkled—"and I guess she's been dead awhile. It could have been a heart attack or something, there's not a mark on her I can see. Her name's Alicia Cummings, this is her house. The other two got worried because she hadn't showed up somewhere they expected her, and came up here looking, broke a window to get in."

The two women came down from the porch to the squad, where he had been talking to Rodriguez and Feinman. "Are you doctors? She couldn't have had a heart attack, she was absolutely fine and only forty-nine—"

The other one said, "I just know somebody murdered her, I had this awful feeling, one of my premonitions—"

Rodriguez got them calmed down. One of them was plump, one scraggly, both expensively and smartly dressed, in their forties. Both of them had been crying. The plump one, Mrs. Sale, seemed to be the more sensible, and Feinman managed to hush up the scraggly one, Mrs. Doty, and they heard a capsule report. "We always meet every Thursday, our bridge club, two tables of us, and Alicia never came today—it was my turn to have the meeting—we just couldn't understand it. She hadn't called me or anybody, the last time I talked to her was last Saturday and she never said a word about not coming, and if something had come up at the last minute she'd have called—and of course we were all talking about it, we were worried, it wasn't like Alicia, and finally Edith and I decided to come up and have a look—we couldn't concentrate on bridge anyway—and her car's in the garage and we had an awful feeling something was wrong, and we broke a window in the back and Edith got in and found her—oh, it's just terrible, her dying here all alone—"

"Did she live here alone?" asked Feinman. It was an old house and a big one, handsome beige stucco, with well-kept landscaping.

"Oh, yes, she's divorced, she got a very good settlement and didn't have to work, and they never had any children. Of course she had a lot of friends and was very active socially—she went out a lot—"

They had opened the front door from inside, and Rodriguez and Feinman went in to a large dark living room. It took a minute for their eyes to adjust to the light, but there was enough smell of death to tell them there had been a body here for a while. Feinman found a switch and flipped on the overhead light. The body was lying on the big couch, stretched full-length. Alicia Cummings had been a good-looking woman for her age, with a trim figure and a round pretty face, dark hair. She was wearing a printed nylon dress and high-heeled shoes, and a good deal of jewelry—earrings, two rings, necklace, bracelet, wristwatch. The living room was open to a large dining area and Rodriguez wandered in there while Feinman contemplated the body. A minute later he called, "Come look at this, Joe."

There was a used cup and saucer on the dining table with dregs of coffee in the cup, an ashtray holding several stubbed-out cigarette butts. Rodriguez had proceeded to the kitchen beyond that and Feinman found him looking at the counter beside the sink.

"Educated guess," said Rodriguez grimly.

"Oh-oh," said Feinman.

There was a skillet in the sink, half full of water, and on the counter a couple of plates and used tableware. The dinner plate held the small remnant of a hamburger patty, four or five french fries, the other plate a spoonful of peas.

"Number nine," said Rodriguez, "will you bet?"

"No bets," said Feinman. "She'd finished dinner—last Saturday night?—and had a couple of cups of coffee, probably taking her time by the cigarette butts. And before she had a chance to start cleaning up the kitchen she began to feel dizzy and faint—what did the doctor say, symptoms coming on in thirty to forty minutes?"

"And," said Rodriguez, "she went in and lay down on the couch until she felt better. She thought. She'd realize in a short time that there was something seriously wrong, but by then she was past calling for help. My God, we'd better catch up to this nut fast."

"How?" asked Feinman, and went out to call the lab and morgue wagon. There wasn't anything else for them to do here. They would need the photographs for the evidence file, when and if they found the lunatic and this got to court, and the coroner's office would tell them how she had died. But it was a good bet that Alicia Cummings had been number nine.

They got the other women's addresses, asked them to come in and make statements on finding the body. The necessary paperwork did pile up. It was nearly the end of another day. At the office, Feinman called the coroner's office and told them they were getting another body, probably in the same series. The lab would be running tests on the leftover food. They would know definitely sometime, but they really didn't have to wait for the autopsy report.

* * *

Johnny McCrea had come on swing shift at four o'clock. He liked the swing shift, except that it interfered with dates. His steady girl friend, Joyce Boucher, worked at a Security Pacific bank as a teller, and she had weekends free but his night off was Wednesday, and it wasn't often they did more than go out to dinner. He was beginning to think seriously about asking her to marry him.

At the briefing, he heard about the wanted ex-cons, Dieter and Hobson, and dutifully studied the mug shots provided for every squad. The first couple of hours of the tour were quiet; he didn't get any calls or write any tickets. Then at six-fifteen he was sent to an address up north on Vermont. It was a block of shabby old little stores, and the address turned out to be a place with a sign over the door that said *Fabrics and Notions.* There were two people standing in front, a man and a woman. McCrea got out of the squad, putting on his cap, and went over to them. "What's the trouble?" he asked genially.

They were a couple in late middle age, the woman a little too fat, the man tall and lean. She was wearing a white uniform smock. The man said, "I'm afraid it's pretty bad, Officer. It's old Mrs. Geiss, it looks as if she's been attacked and maybe robbed. We just found her."

"It's just horrible," the woman said. "She looks awful bad. This is her store here, we're Mr. and Mrs. Hartwig, we got the health-food store next door. It's just terrible, the poor old soul lying there, maybe all last night too—it wasn't until I went out at noon to get some fresh milk at the grocery across the street—I hadn't noticed we were nearly out, we always have lunch in the store—that I noticed she hadn't opened up, the closed sign in the front door—and I wondered about it, but she's an old lady and I thought maybe she wasn't feeling well, just stayed home a day—she's alone in the place—"

Hartwig said, "And she's figuring on retiring and going on Social Security. She's had this place for years and she had a long lease but it's up in July and the rent'd go sky high, she said business has been awful slow—"

"People don't sew much anymore, she did alterations too but I guess it didn't bring in much. She just lives around the corner on Clarissa, she could walk to work—" Mrs. Hartwig was babbling in a scared voice. "She's such a nice old lady—"

"Where is she?" asked McCrea.

"You'll have to come through our store." He followed them into the narrow little shop and she went on babbling. "Like I say, I never thought about it, but when we were getting ready to close up just before six I took the trash out to the alley behind the store and her back door's right beside ours, you can see, and I noticed the screen door hanging open, so I thought about burglars, I went to look, and oh, my dear Lord, there she was—and I called Ed—"

McCrea stepped out to the narrow alley behind the row of shops. About six feet from the rear door was the rear door of the place next door. He switched on his flashlight. There was a screen door hanging open and a solid wooden door inside that, also open, and nearly across the threshold was lying the twisted body of a small thin old woman.

"She's breathing," said Hartwig, "but she looks bad."

She did. And it looked as if she had been struck savagely on the head, there was a good deal of dried crusted blood in her gray hair. He turned the flash beyond her body and the beam caught a length of wood lying just behind her, a piece of rough two-by-four. Automatically his training took over and he thought, preserve the scene for the detectives. He squatted down beside her and felt for a pulse. There was just a thread of one under his thumb. If this had happened after she had closed up last night, she would have been lying helpless here for twenty-four hours. These goddamned punks—

Unexpectedly she stirred under his hand, and in the beam of the flashlight he saw her eyes partly open. He didn't think she realized that anybody was there, that help was coming, but she spoke. She said in a thin voice, but quite clearly, "Serpent's tooth."

McCrea stood up and said to the Hartwigs, "Don't touch anything. There'll be some detectives out to talk to you." He went back to the squad and called an ambulance, relayed the call—assault—to the dispatcher in Communications.

The ambulance came just before Donaldson and Brougham got there, and took the old lady off. McCrea told the detectives all he knew, and Brougham said interestedly, "Serpent's tooth. She said that? That's a funny one."

"It's somewhere in the Bible, I think," said McCrea vaguely.

"Well, we'd better talk to these people, and check with Emergency to see how bad she is. You can get back on tour."

* * *

That was waiting for the day men on Friday morning, and Feinman passed the night report on to Maddox, who had come in a few minutes late. Donaldson had put a police seal on the store, pending the lab examination. The doctor he talked to at the Emergency ward had said Mrs. Geiss was in critical condition, there were skull fractures, loss of blood, pneumonia. In March the days were warm but the nights could be chilly, and if she had been there all night and all day—"My God, these damned savages," said Maddox. He called the Emergency ward at Cedars-Sinai and after being handed around a little finally talked to a doctor who could tell him something.

"Is she likely to regain consciousness?"

"Possibly," said the doctor. "I couldn't say. Sometimes the old people are tougher than you'd expect. But she's on the critical list."

Maddox reflected. "I wonder if it'd be any use to station somebody there just in case she does come to and could answer some questions."

"It's worth a try," said Feinman.

Maddox went across the hall. "You can have a nice quiet day for once," he said to Sue. "Sitting beside an old lady." He told her about it.

She said soberly, "Poor old dear, I hope she can tell us something about who did it. I'll go right over."

Then Feinman told him about the possible number nine, and he did some more swearing.

"If there was any possible lead, any way to look—my God, even any possible way to safeguard the damn markets—a thousand markets all over the damned county—but one thing did occur to me, and I hope to God it occurred to the lab. That Pliofilm on the packages of hamburger. At the Babcocks', she'd evidently thrown the packaging out, and the trash got collected before we suspected the hamburger—at the Hogans', ditto. But we did pick up the package on the two girls, at that apartment, and I sent everything in from the happy patio party at the Boyds'. I should think that Pliofilm would take prints just dandy."

"And then we'll have to get all the butchers' prints to compare," said Feinman, and added hastily, "I know, I know, we've got to find out, however long a job it is."

Maddox got Baker at the lab and put the question to him. Baker said doubtfully, "It's not as good a medium as you might think. We've been working on it, sure. But it's tricky stuff, slick enough but sticky and thin. We haven't picked up any latents off any of that so far. And now there's this new job, we're supposed to give the full treatment to this store on Vermont. Franks brought in some odds and ends from the homicide yesterday, and there was half a pound of raw hamburger from the refrigerator with the Pliofilm still folded around it. Besides the leftovers. We'll have a look, see what we can raise."

"Priority," said Maddox. "We've got to catch up to this one fast, Harry."

"How right you are," said Baker. "My wife usually cooks hamburger at least once a week, but she's sworn off until we get this nut and stash him away. But there's this new one—I'll let Garcia and Franks go out

on it and do some work on this. Probably get back to you this afternoon."

It was Rodriguez' day off. Feinman had arranged for those lineups at
the jail, and he and D'Arcy went to collect the witnesses and attend to
that. It turned out to be a fiasco. The two witnesses were positive that
they would recognize the heister, and they both said he wasn't any of
the three suspects. Annoyed, Feinman and D'Arcy ferried them down
to R. and I. to look at the books of mug shots, after they had let the
suspects go. That was often a waste of time, the wanted men weren't
always listed, and it worked out like that this time. They spent a couple
of hours down there and the witnesses came up with nothing.

When they got back to base about noon, Ellis was talking with
Sergeant Ambrose and Detective Morales of the Narco unit in the door
of the office. They were all looking grim. Ambrose said, "We've got the
word from a snitch, there's a rumble about to begin down around
Manual Arts High."

"So go and have fun with the kiddies," said Feinman.

"It may turn into business for you," said Ambrose.

That was all too true. There were always the street gangs around, it
was a fact of city life, and they were always rambunctious, composed of
the dropouts and addicts and petty criminals drifting around looking
for trouble to get into. They were responsible for most of the purse
snatching, a lot of the muggings that went on day in day out. And they
overflowed onto the school grounds too, dealing in dope, recruiting the
younger kids. That vandalism at the junior high school the other day—
they went in for that too, the senseless violence. And they conducted
open warfare on each other. The two gangs causing the most trouble in
Hollywood these days were the Caballeros and the Dukes, Mexican and
Negro respectively, and every now and then they came to full-scale
battle, usually arranged beforehand. The Narco men collected Sergeant
Ralston from the Juvenile office and went out to see what was going on,
and Feinman and D'Arcy went up to the communal office and sat
down wearily, reflecting on the thanklessness of trying to make bricks
without straw.

They didn't have long to discuss it. Within half an hour, before they
had gone out for lunch, they were called out to a homicide, and it was
going to make a hell of a lot more paperwork and take up a lot of time,
all for nothing, but that was often the way the job went. It was one of
the gay bars down on Santa Monica. One of the fags had gotten into

an argument with another, and they both had been high on too many vodka martinis, and one of them had gotten knifed in the heart. There was nobody in at the lab, to come and take pictures, and Feinman decided it didn't matter much anyway. There were about twenty witnesses, but it was going to be like pulling teeth to get any definite statements from any of them.

The bartender was the one who pointed out the knifer. "I got the shiv away from him after he done it," he said virtuously.

"And plastered your damn prints all over it," said D'Arcy.

"What the hell, you want I should have let him hang on to it? Him as drunk as a skunk, he might have stuck it into somebody else. Not that any of these damn queers'd be any damn loss," said the bartender, scowling. "I'd never of took the job if I'd known it was a queer hangout. By damn, I can remember when this was a nice clean town, and now wherever you look there's hordes of cheap hookers and their pimps and all these goddamned fags—and I guess it's about as bad in any big city, or I'd go back to Chicago."

They couldn't talk to the knifer when he was drunk, and they took him over to the jail to let him sober up. They got names and addresses; the paperwork would start tomorrow. And then they came back to the station to find it packed with the gang members, and the detectives from Narco and Juvenile and a handful of Traffic men trying to keep them in order. There had been quite a melee down by Manual Arts, and one kid was dead of head wounds and three more seriously injured. Some of the gang members were juveniles, some technically adults, and it was going to be one sweet mess to sort out.

Dowling and Nolan came back in the middle of it with a heist suspect to question. They stashed him in an interrogation room for a while, helping to sort out the kids, and when they went to look for him he had sneaked out in the crowd and vanished.

"Where the hell has Maddox got to?" asked Nolan. "We could use another hand."

"I haven't seen him since this morning," said Feinman. "But we've been busy."

* * *

After an early lunch Maddox had gone out to find that Rodney Engel. It was just one place to look, the known nut, and it was a long shot but they had to cover all bets. They had the address from the psychiatrist at Atascadero, and when Maddox found it, it was a very classy address, a big sprawling house in Flintridge with an outsized pool at one side.

He found Mrs. Howard Engel home. She was a tall thin chilly-eyed woman in a stunning purple housecoat, and she was alarmed and annoyed to find police on the doorstep. She answered questions reluctantly, as briefly as possible. It turned out that the husband was a lawyer with an office downtown.

They had pulled Rodney Engel's record; he had two counts of child molestation and had been put away in Atascadero, diagnosed as a schizo, for the last five years. But Maddox hadn't talked to her for ten minutes before he knew they could forget about Rodney Engel as their lunatic. He didn't have a driver's license, had never driven a car, and one thing they knew about their lunatic was that he was mobile. Mrs. Engel told him that there was a male nurse with Rodney all day. Maddox gathered that Rodney had been an embarrassment to the affluent Engels, and no wonder. This had been another waste of time.

On the way back to Hollywood, he was thinking, another weekend coming up, and would the nut be out running around all over the county to a dozen markets, slipping the lethal packages of hamburger into the meat cases? But the warnings had been well publicized, the public should be aware of the danger.

And then, as he caught the light, coming off the freeway at Los Feliz, he thought, but my God, was it? The radio, the TV news—but there were thousands of people in the county who either didn't know much English or habitually use it, who might be blithely unaware of the nut running around with the lethal hamburger.

He was disturbed enough at the idea that he didn't wait to get back to the office; he stopped at the nearest pay phone to call Rodriguez at home. "Listen, César, I've had the damndest thought, and it should have come to all of us before—"

Rodriguez heard about it and laughed. "You can stop worrying, *amigo*. Of course that occurred to me too, and I contacted all the Spanish-language stations."

"Thank God," said Maddox.

"Of course that doesn't take care of all the hordes of Vietnamese and Cambodians in the county—but then I don't think many of them have gotten enough Americanized to eat much hamburger," said Rodriguez.

At the station, Maddox was surprised to run into all the commotion, but it was getting straightened out. Some of the kids had been turned loose, some of the ringleaders had been taken to jail, and most of the rest were down in Juvenile and Narco. The Narco men had confiscated quite a pile of dope, mostly marijuana.

"And where the hell have you been?" asked D'Arcy.

Maddox told him. "We can wash him out."

"And we've now got this new damned thing—" Feinman groaned. "A mile of paperwork, and it'll all come to nothing, the fag hasn't got a pedigree, it's a first count, and the D.A.'s office'll call it involuntary manslaughter and he'll get probation."

"Annoying," agreed Maddox absently; he was still thinking about the nut.

Franks came in, looking tired, and said, "I thought you'd like to know what's going on, God knows when you might get a written report. We've been over to that place on Vermont, and picked up a few latents. Haven't run them yet, and of course a public place like that, they could all belong to innocent customers. I went over to the hospital to get the victim's prints for comparison, she looks pretty bad. There are about half a dozen that don't belong to her, but as I say they could be anybody's, we'll check to see if they're in Records. The cash register was open and empty, and by the tab there should have been about thirty bucks in it."

"Thirty pieces of silver," said Maddox softly.

"What? Oh, yes. There were just her prints on the register. And my God, that piece of two-by-four—" Franks made a clucking sound. "Rough wood like that won't take prints, and it could have come from anywhere. Could have been lying around in that alley. It was the weapon all right, there's blood on it. Type O, which the doctor says is her type."

"In fact, you give us nothing so far. Unless any of the prints show in Records."

Franks grinned at them smugly. "Oh, we've got something for you, boys. On the new homicide yesterday. The leftovers and so on. When you get the autopsy report, it'll tell you she was number nine. The raw hamburger is loaded with the Demerol, and there were traces in the little piece left over. And the raw stuff was still in the original package, and half an hour ago I raised a pretty clear latent on the Pliofilm."

"Oh, frabjous day," said D'Arcy, sitting up with a jerk. "I take it, not the corpse's?"

"No, no, I got those for comparison."

"You haven't had time to check it yet?" asked Maddox.

"I just sent it down to R. and I., but they're usually busy. We'll probably hear tomorrow morning."

*   *   *

Gonzales was just about to head back to the station at a quarter to four, the end of shift coming up, when he got a call to unknown trouble at an address on Detroit, and he uttered a few expletives in Spanish to himself. It had been a nice quiet day, no more pieces of dead bodies showing up.

The address was an old apartment house, and the dispatcher had given him the number; Gonzales climbed stairs to the second floor and pushed the bell. The door was opened by a fat black woman who looked relieved at the sight of the uniform. "Come in, Officer. I'm Mrs. Parker, this is my daughter Mary Lou, we thought the police had ought to hear about it."

"About what, Mrs. Parker?"

"About Benny," said the girl behind her. She was rather a pretty girl, not very dark, with a nice figure; she was about twenty. They were both looking a little worried. "We don't want to make trouble for anybody, but you've got to be honest. You've got to do what's right. We've known the Turners a long time, they're good people—except for Benny —Josie Turner's a good friend of mine. But, well, I better just tell you what happened. Benny, he's got a kind of notion for me, which is just silly, he's been trying to make up to me and hanging around. I never went out with him. Like I say, the Turners are good people, but Benny, he's been in trouble. For stealing. Reason he got fired from his last job, Josie told me. And a couple of days ago, he came around and said he had a present for me. He's asked me to marry him, and that's just silly too." She tossed her sleek black head. "I haven't got any time for Benny Turner, I don't want to get married for a while anyway, I'm taking a secretarial course and I'm going to get a good job and make something of myself."

"That's right," said her mother proudly. "She's a real smart girl," she told Gonzales.

"Anyway, I said I didn't want his presents, but he made me take it, it was in a little box, and I looked at it and I thought it was just cheap stuff, something he'd got for about five bucks at a discount store maybe. But then Mother looked at it and said that was a real diamond, and a pretty big one. And it doesn't look exactly like silver—"

"It's what they call white gold," said her mother. "My Auntie Leda had a pin made of it."

"And if it's a real diamond—well, where would Benny Turner get it? Unless he stole it?" The girl was looking distressed.

"We sure don't want to make any trouble for the Turners, but we know Benny's stolen things before—it was an awful grief to them when he got arrested that time—and Mother and I talked it over—"

"My, I do miss Harvey," said her mother. "My husband," she explained to Gonzales. "He was a real smart man, he always knew just what to do about things. He got killed in an accident two years ago, truck jack-knifed on him."

"Well, anyway, we thought we'd better tell the police," said the girl. "In case Benny did steal them some place, and give them to you so you could give them back." She produced a little box from her sweater pocket and handed it to Gonzales.

He opened it. There was a plain, rather wide wedding ring and another, with a solitaire diamond—it looked like a real diamond—in an old-fashioned-looking raised setting.

"There are initials inside," said the girl.

Gonzales looked, and there were, faintly visible. He couldn't make out what they were. "Well," he said, "the detectives may know something about it. But thanks very much, we always appreciate cooperation from the citizens."

"We don't want to make trouble," said Mary Lou, looking troubled, "but you got to do what's right."

Gonzales was fifteen minutes late handing over the squad to the swing-shift man, and delayed another five minutes telling Maddox in the detective office about Benny Turner.

* * *

Sue came in at a quarter to six, looking tired and subdued. "She died," she said. "She never came to at all again. She looked like a nice old lady." Maddox gave her a cigarette and lit it for her. "I hope we can catch up to whoever did that to her."

"Just another anonymous assault," said D'Arcy somberly. "I don't suppose we will. Unless any of those prints are known to Records."

"The things we see," said Sue.

"Well, there was one funny little thing in Donaldson's report about that," said Maddox, "that may give us somewhere to look."

Sue reached to the ashtray on his desk, and said suddenly, "What's this? Where'd it come from?"

"Oh, that. Gonzales just brought it in. The honest citizens—" And Maddox started to tell her about that, but she interrupted him.

"Mrs. Erwin's mother's wedding set!" she said excitedly. "For heaven's sake, Ivor, it was that assault and robbery last Sunday—of course she could identify them—by the description this has got to be—and the initials, there they are—"

"So, have we cleared away something else?" said Maddox. "Benny Turner—" And he laughed sharply. "The piddling little assault and robbery, while this lunatic is still loose, and no leads—"

CHAPTER SIX

On Saturday morning, as soon as Maddox got in, he checked with the lab about that print off the Pliofilm. "Well, it wasn't in our records," said Baker. "Sorry. They sent it on to the Feds."

Maddox said, "Hell. And of course it could belong to the butcher who did the original packaging." Just being thorough, they would have to find out. He said so to Baker.

"I already thought of that. It came from a Safeway, and you said the one on Sunset nearest to her house. I'll get down there sometime today or tomorrow and ask the butchers for their prints. Honest people are usually cooperative, and they're all wanting to clean this up too."

It was Feinman's day off. And there was all the paperwork to do on the knifing yesterday. At least the night watch hadn't left them anything new, but on the weekend more things might be coming up. And there was this little stupidity about Benny Turner. Sue had taken the rings up to show Mrs. Erwin, and came back at nine-thirty to say, "She identified them all right, I knew she would. Have we got an address for Turner?"

"The honest citizens passed one on to Gonzales. Eden Avenue downtown. I suppose we'd better pick him up."

"Daisy and I can do that, it's not much of a thing."

Maddox said, "You stay off the street and mind the baby." There was this and that to do on the Geiss thing too, but clear Benny out of the way first. Rodriguez and D'Arcy went over to the jail to see if the gay was sober enough to question, and Maddox drove downtown and found the address on Eden Avenue. It was an old single house. There were five Turners at home, including Benny. They all looked dismayed at the badge, and Mrs. Turner said in a grieved voice, "You been getting into more trouble, boy? You ought to be ashamed, disgracing the family, we've always been honest people," and she started to cry. Benny was about twenty-one, gangling and sullen-looking; he was just looking surprised. Maddox didn't think he would pose any danger as a passenger, and took him back to the jail. He was already tired of Benny, and wanted this out of the way, and he sat Benny down in an interrogation room and said abruptly, "All right, you know what it's about, the assault on the old lady last Sunday. Up on Chula Vista. You knocked her down and robbed her." Benny asked for a cigarette and he gave him one.

After a couple of drags Benny said, "I never did nothing like that."

"Come on, the old lady's identified those rings you gave Mary Lou Parker as her property."

"Oh," said Benny. "Oh." He looked sad to think that Mary Lou had snitched on him to the cops. "Well, I never meant to hurt her. I just needed some bread, I been out of work."

"What were you doing up in Hollywood?"

"Well, I was just sort of roaming around, I had my sister's car. And I got a pal does yard work for people up that part of town, he gets paid pretty good, I just thought I'd ask around about it, those are nice houses, people must have money. And then when I got up there, I thought maybe if nobody was home someplace I'd, you know, see if I could get in. I never done nothing like that before," he added hurriedly. "And I don't know what made me do it, I never meant to hurt the old lady but I could see she was all alone—but there wasn't much there anyways. The pawnshop only give me twenty bucks for the rest of the jewelry."

The mindless punks, thought Maddox. He booked him in on the assault charge, after getting the name of the pawnshop. Benny would probably get a six-month suspended sentence and maybe in time to come graduate to heavier charges. In the lobby out in front he ran into Rodriguez and D'Arcy. "What did you get from the fag?"

"Double-talk," said D'Arcy. "He don't know nothing about nothing, he never had a knife, it was two other guys. But that bartender's coming in to make a statement and that'll stand up in court." None of them was much interested in that, it was just a case that had to be worked. They went back to the station separately. An autopsy report had just come in on the body found in the street some days ago; there was nothing in it, the man had died of acute alcoholism. One of the derelicts, and no ID on him. Maddox laid it on his desk and lit a cigarette.

"The lab gives us nothing on that Geiss killing," said D'Arcy. "And it's nothing of an MO to ask Records about."

Maddox agreed. "The violent, anonymous break-ins a dime a dozen. But I think she gave us something herself, boys. In Donaldson's report on it"—he rummaged for that and found it—"she said to the patrolman, 'Serpent's tooth.'"

Rodriguez cocked his head. *"Extraño,"* he said. "Serpent's tooth."

"It's something out of the Bible, isn't it?" said D'Arcy.

Maddox laughed. "People are always confusing the Bible and Shakespeare. 'How sharper than a serpent's tooth it is to have a thankless child.' *King Lear.* It strikes me that the old lady knew what she was saying, if she was just barely conscious. By the first report, she lived alone and there wasn't anybody to notify—I wonder how the funeral will get arranged—but we ought to go and ask some questions, she must have had some friends."

"It was just a break-in," said D'Arcy, "she wouldn't have known him. She wasn't thinking straight."

"I wonder," said Maddox.

Rodriguez brushed his moustache with one finger. "I see what's in your mind."

"Let's go poke around a little, *amigo.*"

They took his new transportation up to that block of stores on Vermont and started by talking to the Hartwigs at the health-food store. They got only general background. The Hartwigs hadn't known Emily Geiss well, just as a neighboring shopkeeper, but they did know she had lived on Clarissa, the apartment at the corner of Dracena. They had talked with her only casually. "But she said once that she was all alone in the world, her husband dead and all her family." They were sorry to hear about her death. Just an awful thing, somebody breaking in and killing her.

There was a little market across the street, other shops along here, shoe repair, women's dresses, a bakery—but nobody in those places had known her at all, just who she was. The people at the market knew her as a regular customer, but not much about her. Parking slots were rare up here; Maddox and Rodriguez walked up the short block of Clarissa Avenue to the next corner. It was an old eight-unit place in this old part of town, and on the door of the left front apartment downstairs was a sign that said *Manageress*. Rodriguez pushed the bell. The woman who opened the door was a comfortable-looking middle-aged woman with suspiciously brown hair, in a blue cotton housedress. She looked at the badge in surprise. Maddox told her about Mrs. Geiss and she was dismayed and grieved. "Oh, my goodness, that's just terrible!" she said. "That poor old woman! Murdered, I can't believe it—I wouldn't see her every day, I never knew she hadn't come home—" She asked them in, to a pleasant shabby little living room, asked them to sit down. "This is just an awful thing."

"We understand she hadn't any family," said Maddox. "There'd be nobody to notify."

She said doubtfully, "Well, in a manner of speaking. I'm Mrs. Munn, by the way, I manage the place, which I guess you already know, it belongs to an old gentleman in a nursing home. My husband's pretty handy so he can do all the repairs. Well, Mrs. Geiss had lived here a long time, she was here when we came, and I knew all about her, she'd come in and chat when she paid the rent. No, she hadn't any family, and I wonder about clearing out the apartment—what to do with her things. But there's Mrs. Gibbons, and I knew she'd kept up with Mrs. Olson, of course—she didn't come here very often, but she's a younger woman, and of course she thought the world of Mrs. Geiss. No, she'd been married a long time back but her husband got killed in an accident and they never had any children. She'd kept that little shop for years and years, I don't suppose she made much but enough to keep herself."

"These friends of hers," said Rodriguez.

"Well, she didn't have many friends, she lived a quiet life, I often thought she must be lonely. She hardly ever went out, except to the store. I guess Mrs. Gibbons was the closest friend she had, and Mrs. Olson next. Mrs. Gibbons, her first name's Florence, she's about Mrs. Geiss's age I guess, they'd known each other a long time. I don't know where she lives, she came to see Mrs. Geiss sometimes and sometimes Mrs. Geiss would go to her place for dinner—she didn't drive, somebody would come to get her, one of Mrs. Gibbons' family. Of course I knew Mrs. Olson better, she used to live here. Oh, you can smoke if you want, here's an ashtray."

"Mrs. Olson doesn't live here now?" asked Maddox.

"No, not for about eight years, she finally got a good job at Bullock's Department Store, in the office there, and it's the one out toward Santa Monica so she moved to be closer. But of course I knew her when she lived here, and that just shows you what a good kind woman Mrs. Geiss was, I don't know anybody else that'd've done what she did for Mrs. Olson."

"What way?" asked Rodriguez.

"Why, her husband left her—that was a good twelve years back, he just left her with hardly a cent to her name, he was sort of shiftless and been out of work, and she didn't know which way to turn. But Mrs. Geiss paid the rent for her and lent her money to live on, till she found a job. The little boy was about eight then, Mrs. Olson's boy, and Mrs. Geiss liked children. She was awful good to them, to the Olsons, and Mrs. Olson thought the world of her."

"You can understand that," said Rodriguez. "I suppose we'd better let them know, and I suppose they might help you in clearing out the apartment."

"I don't know where Mrs. Olson's living now, but there might be something to tell you in Mrs. Geiss's apartment."

"We were going to ask you to let us in there."

"Oh, surely, I'll just get the key." She climbed the stairs ahead of them to the front apartment on the second floor, and unlocked the door. "Oh, dear, it does seem sad to think of her going like that. Well, if there's anything else I can do—I ought to get back to my laundry—"

They looked around the little apartment with its old furniture, the prim small bedroom with the single bed, the neat clean kitchen with just enough space for a tiny table and two chairs. Everything was orderly, her few clothes in closet and drawers. The phone was in the kitchen, and on the counter beside it was a small address book. Rodriguez flipped over the pages. "Doctor, dentist, and here we are, Florence Gibbons." The address was on Asbury in Glassell Park. "And under O, Nancy, Flores Street. That's in West Hollywood. The serpent's tooth?"

"Let's go and look," said Maddox.

They tried Glassell Park first, and found Mrs. Gibbons at home. It was a modest little house in a narrow street. She started to cry when they told her about Mrs. Geiss, and said between sobs, "She was my oldest friend, we knew each other for fifty years, I can't believe she's gone, and such a terrible way—"

They gave her time, and presently she sat up and blew her nose. She was a fat old lady with wavy white hair. "The last time I saw her, we had her to dinner a week ago tonight, Larry went to pick her up, that's my grandson."

"She knew all your family, of course," said Maddox.

"Oh, yes, we all thought the world of Emily, my daughter called her Auntie, and the children—I've got four grandchildren, the three girls and Larry. Emily felt as if they were her own. They'll all be just as grieved to hear about this—"

Maddox was genial, drew her out to talk. Her daughter Linda lived in Burbank, her husband was in construction. Larry was the baby, only nineteen. The name was Fuller.

"Why, surely, her apartment—Linda and I can take care of things, it's little enough to do." She knew about Mrs. Olson, hadn't seen her in years, but knew of Mrs. Geiss's interest in her and her boy. "She did too much for them if you ask me, Emily never had much money but I know she'd helped to buy clothes for the boy, that was years ago, of course. But anything we can do, I've just got the Social Security, but there'll have to be a funeral—"

In the car, Rodriguez said, "Saturday. Olson will be at work. Maybe the kid too. He's what, twenty?"

"We can ask," said Maddox, and switched on the ignition.

The place on Flores Street was a jerry-built garden apartment, nothing very fancy. Olson was listed as number eight, but nobody answered the door. They tried the next apartment across the hall, and a middle-aged woman opened the door to them. "We're looking for young Mr. Olson," said Maddox easily, "I think he lives across the hall with his mother?"

She said, "Yes, that's the name. I don't know them, what's it about?"

"We're insurance adjusters looking into a little accident he had. Do you know where he works?"

She relaxed a trifle. "Oh, he's had another accident, has he? No, I guess he doesn't work anywhere because he's in and out, and besides I heard her kind of nagging him about not having a job, their door was open when I was going out once. He used to have a car, an old piece of junk, but I guess he wrecked it a couple of months ago. I didn't know he'd gotten another one."

"Let's see, it's John, isn't it?"

"Brian," she said. "I don't know his middle name. I don't really know them."

They sat in the car over cigarettes and Rodriguez said, "Larry and Brian. Of course you get the violent punks from any background, but Mrs. Gibbons' family sounds nice and respectable. No serpent's teeth."

"Yes," said Maddox, "but we'd better have a look at Larry anyway. Damn. Saturday, and Saturday night, people tend to be out and about." He started the engine. "Have to look her up at Bullock's and ask about him."

At that big and elegant department store they had to show the badges to get up to the business offices on the top floor. There were cubbyholes of offices down two corridors, and the first one they came to was labeled *Personnel.* The smart young woman at the desk said, "Mrs. Olson? She's in Accounting, four doors down."

There, they were pointed toward one desk among a dozen, where a woman bent over a typewriter. "Mrs. Olson?" said Rodriguez, and she looked up. She was a rather haggard-looking woman in her forties, dark-haired and wearing too much makeup. She looked at the badge expressionlessly. "We're trying to locate your son to ask him a few questions. Do you know where he is?"

She put a hand to her head as if it ached, and said in a tired voice, "Has he been doing something wrong? If he's not at the apartment, I don't know where he is—but he'll probably be home to dinner, unless one of his pals happens to have some money."

"He's not working?" asked Maddox.

She shook her head. "He never holds a job long, when he gets one. Has he done anything real bad?"

"Has he been in any trouble before?"

"Oh, no. I've never had the police asking about him before," and her eyes were fearful and wary.

They didn't tell her about Mrs. Geiss. "Well," said Rodriguez in the corridor, "maybe we're on the right track here. It could be Brian takes after his worthless father."

"And she'd known him as a child," said Maddox. "She wouldn't have been afraid of him. Sorry for the poor boy who couldn't get a job. I wonder if she'd given him money before, if he came asking."

"How do you want to play it?"

"We'll have to find him first," said Maddox. "Meanwhile, just to play safe, let's have a look at Larry."

* * *

D'Arcy and Nolan had fetched in all the witnesses they could locate from that gay bar, and roped Sue and Daisy in on talking to them. The bartender came in and made a statement. None of them was at all eager to talk to the police, and the detectives needed all their patience. Ellis came to help out. In the middle of the afternoon he was called to the phone and was gone a long time. By the time he came back they had let the last of them go and D'Arcy and Nolan were just sitting there talking.

"Where the hell is Ivor?" asked Ellis. He was looking harassed. "That was Captain Lorenzo at Robbery-Homicide down at headquarters. They've been getting a blast from the market managers' association on this goddamned hamburger business. The association wants to set up a joint meeting with the police to talk about it, suggest some way to beef up security at the markets."

"Well, that makes sense," said D'Arcy. "If they know how we read the MO, maybe they can arrange their own safeguards better. Have one of the butchers keeping an eye on the meat cases all the time, or whatever."

"God," said Ellis, "the crowds in every market, I don't know. Anyway, it's set up for tomorrow morning at headquarters. There'll be one hell of a bunch of them, delegates from the association, and it's going to be a session. We'll have to give them chapter and verse on what we've got."

"Which is damn all," said Dowling, beginning to fill his pipe. "But when they know how we figure it's being done, maybe the individual markets can tighten up security, at that."

"Maddox and I'll handle it," said Ellis, "but I don't look forward to it. Lorenzo said their representatives were sounding damn mad at the police, why the hell can't we do something about it. My God, what the hell do they expect us to do, it's a needle in a haystack—one nut, and probably he doesn't look like a nut." He ran a hand through his thinning sandy hair.

D'Arcy said, "They don't wear labels. The markets are blaming us because the sale of hamburger is down—that's par for the course."

Ellis said, "Well, let me know when Ivor gets back."

* * *

Daisy had just finished getting the bartender's statement down, and he had signed it and gone out when a new call came in. The rest of the men were still busy with the other witnesses, and she and Sue went out on it; it didn't sound like much of anything.

It wouldn't make much work for them, it was just another of the things police saw and had to deal with, only in the big city there was more of it.

The address was an ancient ramshackle two-story house on Marathon Street, over past Virgil, one of the oldest sections of town, and the squad was waiting outside it with a woman in the back seat and Cassidy standing beside it. His round good-humored face lit up at the sight of Sue and Daisy. "Say, I'm glad they sent you out on it, not that it's a sight for females. It's just a suicide but one hell of a thing even so, I mean, you feel sorry. And this woman, she's all to pieces over it. I was just thinking maybe we ought to get the priest to come over, not that he could do much, I suppose. Her name's Lillian Ferguson, the woman in the squad. The other one's Audrey Lutz."

Sue got into the front of the squad and Daisy in the back. The woman was sobbing and hiccuping. She was about forty-five, a dumpy woman with graying blond hair, wearing a cotton dress and cardigan; there was a worn brown handbag in her lap.

"Take it easy, Mrs. Ferguson," said Daisy gently. "Would you like to tell us something about this?"

She raised a ravaged face with sagging jowls and reddened eyes. "Miss," she said thickly, "it's Miss Ferguson. I never been married—

it's just, it's all for nothing, all just a waste. She wasn't like me, I never got much education, but she'd had a year in college, her folks had a little money. Only they were the straitlaced kind, and she got into kind of a fast crowd in college, somewhere back East. I kept hoping she'd come back to the church, she was brought up Catholic like me, and Father Donovan, he'd've helped her any way he could, I'd told him about her and he's prayed for her. I wanted her to talk to him, but she wouldn't. She'd got the idea that there was no way God was going to forgive her." She blew her nose and leaned back, looking exhausted. She didn't ask them who they were, just accepted their presence. Her eyes were shut now. "I was a hooker too," she said. "You're young and you think everything's going to last forever and tomorrow's always another day—but it's no kind of life—I was always just on my own, no man ever ran me, but you get tired—and you begin to think what you're doing to yourself—and your immortal soul. I knew Audrey for twenty years and more, she was another one like me—ran off from home and came out here, maybe get in the movies—but it don't happen so easy. And there we both were—cheap hookers in a rooming house, picking up johns at ten or twenty bucks per. And nobody gets any younger. And I got to going to church again, and I got to know Father Sebastian at the Holy Family, and he helped me—I got no education, I never had a regular job in my life, but I was raised to do housework, I can do that, and he got me the job, housekeeper for Father Donovan at St. Mary's. I been off the street for five years and I got a good life now, I'm happy and all right with God. But Audrey, she was still at it, only way she knew how to live, but she was way down. It's no kind of life—I'd kept up with her, Audrey and I were good friends, and I wanted to see her quit the street too, and pull up and get straight like I did. I kept asking her to come to church, let Father Donovan talk to her, but she wouldn't. She wouldn't. And things were bad for her, that kind of life ages you, she'd lost all her looks and a hooker forty-seven years old don't pick up the johns so easy. There are too many pretty young girls that don't know no better running the streets—who wants a hooker forty-seven years old? She'd got right down, there were times I gave her money for the rent here and to eat on, she didn't want to take it but I made her. She'd been looking real bad lately, real sick, she'd lost a lot of weight, she looked awful, but she said she couldn't afford to go to a doctor. The last time I saw her, last week, she looked even worse, and that landlady coming around asking for the rent a day early—I paid her. And then last night Audrey phoned me, she said to come and see her this afternoon—she sounded different, I couldn't say how, and I thought maybe she'd had some luck, or maybe she'd decided to talk to Father Donovan—but when I got here—" She began to cry again.

They got out of the car and Cassidy said, "It's the last door on the left on the second floor." The old house had been cut up into as many rooms as possible, thin partitions in unexpected places. There didn't seem to be anybody around. They climbed rickety stairs; the door to the last room on the left was standing half open and they went in. It was a room about ten feet square, and held just a single bed, a cheap chest of drawers. A few clothes were hung up on nails on one wall; there was a small rag rug on the floor and a torn curtain at the one window.

She was lying on the bed, and there was blood all over her and the bed, long dried. She had cut her wrists with the knife still lying on her chest, and her thin haggard face looked oddly peaceful. There was a piece of paper with writing in pencil on it on the chest, weighed down with a cheap ashtray, and Sue picked it up. The writing was firm and legible. "Dear Lil, I'm sorry you've got to find me like this but you're the only friend I ever had in my life, a real friend I mean. I can't go on anymore like this, and it's best I just go out. You said about the church —well, I don't believe God would ever forgive me all I've done, and now killing myself, that's a mortal sin, but I just don't seem to care anymore. Thanks for all you ever did for me and good-bye. I love you."

Sue passed the note to Daisy in silence. In silence they went down the stairs, and in the tiny entrance hall found a hawk-faced woman ranting at Cassidy. "And who's going to pay to clean up the room, I'd like to know—that little bitch killing herself in my house, and you say there's blood—well, sure I knew she was a hooker, it wasn't no skin off my nose—and I don't suppose she had a dime, and she owes me a week's rent—"

On the sidewalk outside Sue said, "People."

"The things life does to them," said Daisy. She got into the front seat of the squad and used the radio to call the morgue wagon. She asked Lillian Ferguson, "Are you all right to go home, Miss Ferguson? Have you got a car?"

She was sitting up wiping her eyes. "I've got Father Donovan's car, he lets me use it. Yes, I'll have to go home and tell him—he'll say masses for her—and he'll know what to do about the funeral."

* * *

Over in Burbank, Maddox and Rodriguez had taken one look at Larry Fuller and the nice respectable Fuller family and decided to forget about him. The Fullers were too shocked and grieved to hear about Mrs. Geiss to wonder why police were taking the trouble to break the news. There were two older girls, both married, a girl still at home, and Larry, who was going to Pasadena City College. He was a good-looking boy with a frank open manner, obviously shaken up to hear about Aunt Emily.

Rodriguez said, back at the car, "Looks aren't everything, but I think we can write him off."

"You feel like doing a little overtime tonight?" asked Maddox.

"Sure, as it happens I haven't got a date. Try the Olsons' about seven o'clock?"

"On the nose."

They drove back to Hollywood and heard about the fags, and the meeting set up with the market managers' association. Maddox swore, discussing that with Ellis, but said, "You can see their point of view. It must be one hell of a situation for them, George. But all we can tell them is how he's probably doing it, and then if they'd like to hire a security guard to watch the hamburger tray at every market in the county, fine and dandy, I'd be all for it. We'll suggest that to them."

"And I can hear what they'll say," said Ellis. "This is cutting into their profits already, and security guards don't come cheap."

"But," said Maddox sardonically, "think how pleased they'd be if one of the guards should pounce on the nut, which could well happen at that. One in the eye for us, private enterprise triumphant where the police couldn't do a damn thing."

"Suggest that to them," said Ellis wryly.

* * *

Maddox told Sue to expect him when she saw him, and he and Rodriguez went out to an early dinner at a place in West Hollywood. They got back to the Olson apartment at a little after seven. This time they found Brian Olson there. He was a stocky dark young man looking older than his twenty years, with a heavy growth of beard staining his nominally clean-shaven bulldog jaw, and hooded dark eyes. He looked at the badges and said, "Ma said there'd been some cops around." She just sat across the room saying nothing, and looking even more tired. "What the hell about? I haven't done anything to get into cop trouble."

"We've just got a few questions for you," said Maddox. "We'll ask them back at the station." It would just waste time to let Mrs. Olson know about Mrs. Geiss—she'd be hearing soon enough—what they were thinking about it, to delay them with explanations and protests. She watched them out with enigmatic eyes, in silence, and in silence Brian rode back to the station with them. There, they settled him in an interrogation room and Maddox started the ball rolling.

"Did you know that Emily Geiss is dead, Brian?"

He widened his eyes in obvious astonishment. "Aunt Emily? No, I didn't know—gee, that's tough, Ma'll be real sorry to hear about that— I'm real sorry too. Did she have a heart attack or something?"

"Aunt Emily was pretty nice to you and your mother, wasn't she?" said Rodriguez.

"Yes, she sure was, what did she die of? Of course she was pretty old—"

"So it wasn't very nice of you to bash her over the head and clean out her cash register, was it?"

He shied back. "What the hell do you mean? You mean somebody killed her? My God, that's awful. But I wouldn't do a thing like that, I don't know why you think I would."

"Had she given you money before when you asked her?" asked Maddox. "Had you ever asked her for money?"

"No, of course not." His eyes were wary. "She was sure nice to Ma and me when we were down on our luck, but we're doing okay now. I wouldn't have touched a hair of her head. Where'd you get the crazy idea I did?"

"Can you tell us where you were last Thursday night between, say, five and seven?" The doctors thought she had been attacked around then, and probably it had been nearer five, when she would have been getting ready to leave for home.

He licked his lips and his eyes shifted once, and then he said frankly, quickly, "I'd have to think—Thursday, oh, yeah, I was at a disco on the Strip with some pals."

"They'll back you up? Names, please. And addresses."

He recited them glibly. Phil Esperanzo, Tony Adams, Jim Dannenberg, and added addresses. "We were there from about five on, had dinner there, and picked up some chicks." And they could reserve judgment, but the pals would probably back him up, the same type.

"What did you use to pay the check?" asked Rodriguez. "You don't have a job, do you?"

He scowled. "Oh, hell, I'm going to get one, I was just talking to a guy at a gas station today, it's a drag but I can pump gas all right."

"But you'd been short of money lately?"

"I can always get money from Ma," he said shortly. "You guys are way off the beam. I'm not a criminal of any kind."

"We had another thought, Brian," said Maddox. "Aunt Emily had always been nice to you, given your mother money when she needed it—"

"She paid it back."

"And she'd bought clothes for you when you were a kid. Maybe given you money since. Could it be that you got the notion that she had a lot more money than she did, that she acted poor because she was a miser?"

"No," he said.

"And just maybe you went to see her on Thursday night—"

"How'd I do that? I don't have any wheels," he said quickly. "Ma lets me drive her heap but she don't get home till six or after. You're just nuts."

"But one of the pals would have wheels. I'll buy the gas, buddy, I got a hot date, do the same for you sometime. About the time she'd be closing her store," said Maddox deliberately, "and you asked her for more money? And that time she turned you down. So you thought you'd get it anyway. She was closing up the place, she'd probably take the money from the register home with her."

"Where'd you pick up the two-by-four, in that alley out back?" asked Rodriguez conversationally.

"What the hell are you talking about? I wasn't anywhere near that damned place. I don't know anything about it."

"And the back door was unlocked, and she heard you get in and went to investigate. It was probably dark back there, and you thought she wouldn't see it was you—you'd already left by the front door, hadn't you? All the stores along there closing up, nobody noticing anything. But she did recognize you, you know. She knew who'd bashed her on the head—the boy she'd known since he was a little kid."

"That's just a bunch of crap," he said scornfully. "I wasn't there, I'm sorry if she got hit on the head but I never did a thing like that to Aunt Emily."

"No, probably you didn't mean to kill her," said Maddox. "Just put her out of action. But she was a frail old lady, Brian. The nice old lady who'd been so good to your mother—"

"A bunch of crap!" he said, and his voice rose. And if these had been the bad old days, how easy to tell him, but she identified you before she died. But of course they couldn't do that kind of thing now, with the courts so careful of the accused's rights, and in principle that was just fine. The old lady hadn't identified him in any legal sense.

"You got what was in the register, not very much, and I wonder if you thought about breaking into her apartment a block away to see if there was any more hidden away there. But you're just a punk kid, you didn't quite have the nerve for that, did you? Nerve enough to hit the old lady over the head—the old lady you called Aunt, the old lady you'd known for years—that was all. You figured it'd be put down as a casual break-in. But the old lady's dead, and that adds up to homicide, Brian. Murder two, at least."

"I'm sorry she's dead," he said woodenly. "I really am. I liked Aunt Emily a lot. But I'd never do a thing like that. I don't know why the hell you guys think I could have."

They said it all over again, and he said it all over again, and they came to a dead end. There wasn't any evidence on him at all. The cash couldn't be identified as belonging to her, and only her prints had been on the register. There had been other prints in the store, but they couldn't take his prints without his permission unless they charged him, and they couldn't charge him without evidence.

"Have you ever been fingerprinted, Brian?"

He said contemptuously, "Of course not, I've never been arrested for anything, I'm not a criminal! You've got one hell of a nerve to ask all these questions, accuse me of a murder, for God's sake." He was smart enough to know that they'd find a record if he had one.

Maddox went out to the main office and called up a squad to take him home, and he went out with a single backward look of contempt and triumph.

"Cocky," said Maddox. "Too cocky. Like Joe's pint-sized burglar."

"Oh, he's the one did it all right," said Rodriguez, and sighed. "And we'll never be able to charge him on it. The pals—they'll be the same kind, and we know the reasoning of that kind, if you can call it that. He never meant to kill her and she was old and was going to die pretty soon anyway. The pals will back him up, it'd be a waste of time to ask them the questions. There's just that one thing she said—two words. Any reasonably intelligent judge would have the same gut reaction we did, but gut reactions don't count in court. Even the intelligent judge would have to throw it out. She'd have known other children in her lifetime. And she was seriously hurt, maybe confused, not knowing what she was saying, with the skull fractures and loss of blood."

"Damn it to hell," said Maddox softly, "it'll go into pending and Mrs. Geiss will go to her grave and that'll be that. Only one thing consoles me, César."

"And what might that be?" Rodriguez blew a long stream of smoke.

Maddox laughed sharply. "That one," he said, "will go from bad to worse. That kind always does. He's lazy and egotistic and only smart up to a point. He hasn't got a record yet, but he'll be collecting one. And when it came so easy to him to bash an old lady on the head, the woman he'd known for more than half his life, sooner or later he'll kill somebody else, meaning to or not, and maybe that time there'll be the evidence."

"The pattern," said Rodriguez, sounding tired. "You can't win them all. So we call it a night and go home. I suppose there's just a chance one of the pals might snitch on him. Scared enough of cops to say he hadn't been at that disco. Do we spend time on it?"

"Damn it, I'm just stubborn enough to hope for that. We'll haul them in and lean on them. It'll likely be a waste of time all right, but let's go for the long shot."

The night watch was all out on something; they just hoped it wasn't anything to make them more legwork or paperwork.

* * *

What the night watch had left them on Sunday morning was another burglary and another heist.

Feinman, reading the first report, swore mightily and said, "By God, Leach again—he might as well leave his calling card—by God, getting in through a closet window about a foot square—and it's the same damned area, off Laurel Canyon, another big expensive house with the loot to be picked up. And the good security, but who the hell would bother to install bars on a window that size? The people were just out to dinner, home by ten o'clock. By God, that cocky little devil's laughing at us. He's slick and fast and very much a pro, and he knows he's left us no evidence worth the name. I'll lay a month's salary the whole damned haul was turned over to the fence by midnight, and Leach was home in bed with his wife. By God, I'd like to wring the little devil's neck!"

"And the heist," said Maddox, passing over that report, "was Dapper Dan again. All the earmarks too. The same natty polite fellow, same conversation, a liquor store on Wilshire, and he thanked the victim for his trouble in handing over the take. He got nearly four hundred bucks."

Most of the witnesses on that one had given the descriptions that added up, but individually they weren't worth much. None of them had made any mug shots from the books of photographs at R. and I. downtown, and none of them had been willing to try a session with the police artist and the Identikit. "Damnation," said Maddox, looking at his watch, "that meeting downtown. George and I are having a session with the Robbery-Homicide boys first, I'd better get going." He took off in a hurry with Ellis.

The rest of them kicked the new ones around a little, and the liquor-store owner came in to make a statement. Feinman went on fuming about Leach, finally calmed down some; and then last night's burglary victims came in to give them a list of the burglar's haul, and riled him all over again.

Sunday morning in central Hollywood was usually quiet, all the stores and offices closed and not so many people on the streets, but that in itself was opportunity for the mischief, and at ten-thirty there was a purse snatching at a bus stop on Sunset. The victim was an elderly woman on her way to visit her sister, both of them widows minus any families, and she had lost all the money she had left to last for the rest of the month. It had been two young men, or teen-agers, she thought, she hadn't gotten a good look. Just came up behind the bus-stop bench and grabbed her purse. Her name was Harriet Greenspan, and she sat in the chair beside Sue's desk and said, "We're both stubborn, Rosie and me, neither of us wanted to give up our houses and live together, but I guess it'd be the smartest thing to do. Save on the taxes, and I guess I can make out to put up with her being so crazy about gardening if she can put up with my soap operas."

Sue called a squad to take her to the sister's house in Glendale.

At twelve-thirty another woman came in to complain of a purse snatching, and she was furious, and said so in strident tones. "In the church parking lot!" she said. She was a big buxom woman with faded red hair and a forceful jaw. "One of these long-haired louts, I couldn't describe him, they all look alike to me, I suppose he's got a drug habit to support. Attacking the respectable citizens, and on Sunday in the church parking lot! It's St. John's Episcopal Church on Sunset. I was late, the car wouldn't start at first, and I was in a hurry. I parked, and that lock's awfully stiff, I just put my purse down on the hood while I locked the car, and he came running out of nowhere and grabbed it up and ran off—I chased him but he was too fast for me, I'm not as young as I was—when I got out to the street he was just gone. And for heaven's sake, I'd have reported it then but I'm the organist and the service was just about to start—and I must say I didn't much appreciate Mr. Longford's sermon on brotherly love." She'd lost her billfold with all her credit cards and about twenty dollars. All they could do was to tell her to inform the credit-card companies about the theft, and she said crossly she already knew about that.

*　*　*

When a new call went down at one-thirty Bill Nolan went out on it. It was one of the solid old apartment houses up on Los Feliz, and the squad-car man was Jowett. He had a civilian with him, standing in the handsome quiet foyer beside the wall of mailboxes.

"I'm not too clear about what this amounts to," he told Nolan. "I was out for a Code Seven, they had to repeat the call, so I was late on it and the ambulance was already gone when I got here. This is Mr. Siegel, he can tell you all about it."

"Not that I know much," said Siegel. He was a wiry little man with gray hair and bright eyes like an intelligent terrier. "I don't know the man at all, even if he does—did—live across the hall from us. You don't neighbor much in these places, you know. I knew his name, that's about all, and I'd seen him coming and going occasionally. He seemed like a nice young fellow. Don't know what he does or anything about him. And these apartments are pretty well built, soundproof. The only reason I heard her was that I'd just decided to go over to the market for some beer. My wife's away visiting our daughter, and she can't abide the smell of beer so I don't usually keep it around, but it turned kind of warm this morning and I thought a bottle of beer'd go down just right. And when I opened the door to the hall I heard her crying and screaming, the door across was open, and so naturally I went to see what was wrong. And she came running out screaming that he was dead, so—naturally—I went to look."

"Yes, sir. Was he dead?"

"No, but it looked as if he was hurt pretty bad, there was a lot of blood, and so I called an ambulance. Naturally," said Siegel. "And then I called the police. The young lady was in hysterics and the ambulance took her along too. It looked as if he'd shot himself, there's a gun there —though the girl said he'd never do such a thing—"

"Well, let's have a look," said Nolan. "Did you touch the gun?"

"No, no, I left it where it was."

They all went up to the second floor. Siegel stayed outside in the hall. It was a nice apartment, well-furnished and orderly. There was blood on the living-room carpet, quite a puddle of it, but dried. About six feet away there was an old S & W .38 lying on the floor. Nolan looked through the place, but there was no sign of ransacking, everything clean and neat. On the front of the refrigerator in the kitchen was a card stuck up with a magnet, *In Case of Emergency Notify* and a name and phone number. It was an out-of-state prefix. He copied it down. Better find out whether the man was dead or not before he called the lab. He found a bunch of keys on the dresser in the bedroom and locked the door, sent Jowett back on tour, and went back to the office. He got hold of the doctor at Emergency, who said in an annoyed voice, "The gunshot wound just brought in—I couldn't say, for God's sake, we're just getting to him. He's lost some blood, he may live or not, ask us later."

Nolan thought, and came to the conclusion that there would be time to call the lab later. The girl, whoever she was, had said the fellow wouldn't have shot himself, and maybe he hadn't, or maybe he had. But you could say that it amounted to an emergency.

He dialed the long-distance number and broke the news to a man with a quiet slow voice, who took it sensibly, though Nolan could tell he was shocked. The man said they would come down at once.

Nolan sat back and thought, probably the doctors wouldn't know one way or the other for a while.

"Don't tell me, something new to work," said D'Arcy.

Sue Maddox came in with a paper cup of coffee in one hand and said, "Isn't Ivor back yet?"

"Maybe a new homicide," said Nolan. "It seems to be all up in the air. A Ronald Davenport, at an apartment on Los Feliz, he's been shot. Maybe he did it himself."

Sue dropped the cup of coffee and it spilled all over the floor. "Davenport?" she exclaimed. "Ronald Davenport?"

* * *

When she got to the Emergency ward it was a while before she found anybody who could tell her anything. That was always a busy place. Finally she located a nurse who knew something about it. The nurse was a bossy hard-bitten blonde about forty, probably very efficient. "The gunshot wound," she said. "Are you a policewoman?"

"Yes," said Sue, sidestepping all the hours she had spent on getting to be called Detective. "There was a girl brought in with him, in the ambulance. How is she? And is he going to live?"

"I couldn't say," said the nurse. "They're giving him plasma. We don't even know the girl's name—"

"Jill Fenton," said Sue. "How is she?"

The nurse smiled a little grimly. "You just caught me going in to give her a shot. She was in hysterics when she came in, and we got her calmed down, but then she passed out and when she was conscious she was getting hysterical again and the doctor's ordered her sedation. You want to talk to her? I don't know what you could get out of her. You've got two minutes before I come back with a hypo." She took Sue down to one of the little cubicles at the end of the corridor.

But Jill Fenton, sitting up on the narrow hospital bed, wasn't in hysterics now. She was pale as death, and her beautiful hazel eyes were unnaturally wide and fixed, and she recognized Sue. She said, "I'll never go back there. I don't know where I'll go or what I'll do, but I can't ever see her again. My mother. My mother! She's killed Ronald, it was the only way she could keep us apart, she's killed him and I'd like to die but I don't suppose I will. No, I've got to tell you—so you can prove she did it—" Her eyes were enormous, looking blind. "We were going out to the beach this afternoon, Ronald said he'd come by about noon—he had papers to correct—and he didn't come—and she'd been out the night before, she said to see some friend, somebody worked with her at Paramount—I had an essay to write for English literature class. But she doesn't have many friends. And when Ronald didn't come—I knew something was wrong, he would've come—" She was trembling violently. "She said—she said—you see, he doesn't really care anything about you, but that was just silly, because Ronald and I— and I had to find out—and I went there on the bus, his apartment, to find out—and he's dead, she killed him, just because I loved him—"

Then the nurse came in with the hypo.

CHAPTER SEVEN

The doctors weren't saying much one way or the other. It was another situation where a patient on the critical list might be able to answer questions if he was briefly conscious. Sue went back to the station. She was telling Daisy about it when Maddox came in, and said, "That's a queer one all right. You think it was the Fenton woman who shot him?"

"We only met the man once," said Sue, "but he struck me as the last man to commit suicide, Ivor, and he hadn't any reason—they were going to be married, everything fine between them. The only one with any reason to want him dead was that obnoxious woman. I suppose she thought once he was out of the way she'd get the girl right under her thumb again." She was angry about it.

"Leaping to conclusions," said Maddox. "You know better than that."

Daisy said dryly, "Jill leaped to the same conclusion, and so have I."

"Who went out on it?" He got hold of Nolan, and the girls filled in the background for him, and he was interested.

"That's one hell of an offbeat thing. I thought it was early to call the lab out, but we'd better."

"And in case he can tell us anything," said Sue energetically, "better make sure we hear it."

Maddox thought so too, and called Traffic. The watch commander agreed to pull a man off a regular beat to keep vigil by the hospital bed. Only Garcia was at the lab, and Nolan handed over the apartment keys to him. "I was just talking to Davenport's father—they live up in Oregon. He said they'll be right down. Do we go pull in this Mrs. Fenton for questioning?"

"Be your age," said Maddox. "We haven't got any evidence to warrant that yet. If he comes to he can tell us who shot him, and the lab may turn up something at the apartment to put her on the scene."

Sue and Daisy were still angry. "That poor girl," said Sue, "it's just damnable, he's such a nice fellow and they're so much in love. And that greedy bitch just wanting to exploit the girl for what she could get out of her. I hope he isn't going to die."

"Damnable is the word," said Daisy. "And you know if he does, the girl will feel guilty about it for the rest of her life. I'll just say one thing, whether he does or not, I just hope to God we can pin it on her."

"Calm down," said Maddox. "All we've got here is three romantic females having a gut reaction. He may be able to tell us. If that's the way it was, it's surprising she didn't kill him outright at such close range. And it might be a while before we know anything." Sue and Daisy went back to their office and Maddox sat down at his desk and said to Rodriguez and Feinman, "The market managers are in a tizzy. There was a hell of a lot of talk but I don't know what they intend to do. I suggested the idea about the security guards and they just yelled about the cost. But that'd be the only real safety measure they could take."

"And," said Rodriguez, "no more cases since last week, and we'd have heard. We don't even know whether that's because the nut's faded into the woodwork or because the public's stopped buying hamburger."

Maddox leaned back and shut his eyes. "Publicity," he said sleepily. "Get it into the media, how we deduce he's planting it at the markets, get the public involved. Something might turn up from that, with the thousands of citizens keeping an eye out."

Feinman said, "Spreading alarm, but we've had to do that anyway, and that is a thought."

Rodriguez yawned. "Do you still want to talk to Olson's pals?"

"Not today, César. I have had it with the stupid civilians." Feinman asked who Olson was and they told him. Then D'Arcy came back; he had taken the liquor-store owner downtown to look at mug shots.

"He picked one out without being a hundred percent sure, and it turned out that the guy's still in Folsom on a three-to-five since last year."

"Dapper Dan," said Maddox. "The bungling civilians." There weren't many more possible suspects to look for on any of the heists, and on the burglaries no leads at all, as there usually weren't. Feinman was muttering about Leach again.

"If we could put all the fences out of business—but my God, no way to know who and where they are, we don't pick up one once in ten years and when he gets out, after a couple of years in the joint, he starts all over again under another name and front." The job could be discouraging sometimes.

Before they left, Maddox checked with the hospital again. Davenport was still unconscious, with a uniformed man sitting beside him, and the doctors hadn't tried to get the slug out, wouldn't until he got stronger or, of course, died. They were still concentrating on keeping him alive. Everybody else had left when he finished talking to the hospital, and he cursed at the phone when it went off but answered it. "Police," said a high sharp voice. "I want to report my daughter missing. Her name is Jill Fenton, I'm Mrs. Fenton. She hasn't come home and I don't know where she is. She went out to see—a friend—but she hasn't come home and I—"

Maddox was just thankful Sue hadn't taken the call; he knew his Sue's impetuous temper. He said in a neutral tone, "Your daughter's at Cedars-Sinai, Mrs. Fenton. Her friend, I presume you mean Mr. Davenport, has gotten himself shot, and it naturally upset her. She'll be in Emergency probably overnight." There was a moment of heavy breathing at the other end of the line and then she said, "Oh!" and there was nothing but relief in her voice. "Oh, thank you." Maddox thought she had really had a scare about the girl. An insensitive, unimaginative woman: she knew the girl had gone to his apartment, didn't know whether he'd been found yet or not, how had she expected the girl to react? Or hadn't she given it any thought? And he realized he was leaping to the same conclusion as Sue and Daisy.

"Oh," she said rather blankly. "I'm sorry to hear about Mr. Davenport, what happened?"

"He may have shot himself, or he may not," said Maddox. "We really don't know much about it yet."

"Oh. Well, I'm relieved to hear Jill's all right, I'll go right out there to see her. Thank you." There was a click on the line. A stupid woman, he thought, whether she had shot Davenport or not.

* * *

Sunday night was sometimes busy, but tonight the night watch didn't get a call until ten o'clock, a reported assault. Roger Stacey went out to see what it was. The call was to the corner of Sunset and La Brea, and the squad was in a red zone in front of an all-night drugstore. The uniformed man was talking with a woman sitting in the back seat. He straightened from the open door as Stacey came up. "She's been raped by a couple of men, she's pretty shook up. I've called an ambulance."

Stacey got in the car beside her and saw that she was a pretty young black girl, maybe in her early twenties. She'd been crying, and there was blood on her white uniform dress, and she had a nasty little cut on one cheek and she was trembling. You had to be gentle and easy with this kind of thing; Stacey introduced himself and said, "There's an ambulance on the way. Can you tell me your name, miss?"

"Celia," she said. "Celia Jenkins. I don't want to go to the hospital, I want to go home. Will somebody please call my brother? He'll come to get me."

"I'm sorry, Miss Jenkins, but we'd like to have you examined by a doctor first." The ambulance came then, and she protested weakly but the attendants got her on a gurney and took her off. Stacey followed the ambulance back to the hospital, and waited about half an hour until a good-looking intern came out to the waiting room and asked, "You the cop? Well, she's been raped all right, and knocked around a little, and she'd been a virgin, if you're interested. But she isn't much hurt otherwise, she can go home any time. She asked the nurse to call some relative."

She was sitting on the edge of the examination table in one of the small cubicles, and she had stopped shaking. She was dressed again in the torn stained white dress. He asked her if she felt better and she said, "I guess so. Is Jim here yet?"

"We'll find out in a few minutes," said Stacey. "But we'd like to know just what happened, Miss Jenkins, if you feel up to talking about it."

"My mother'll just have a fit, and Jim too," she said. "And Mrs. Asher. And I guess it was my own fault, trying to save money." She managed a small smile. "And if Mother had been with me it probably wouldn't have happened, but she's coming down with the flu, she was fretting about the dinner party at Mrs. Asher's, but I said I could manage everything, not to worry. I'm nearly as good a cook as she is. And her car's in the garage for a new radiator, I'd have to take the bus, we live down on Catalina and they both said—Jim and Mother—I'd better get a taxi home. Jim, he's my brother, he works nights at an all-night gas station on Western. But I could walk from the bus, the Ashers' house is just up on Hemet, only a couple of short blocks from Hollywood Boulevard." That would be up off Laurel Canyon Boulevard, thought Stacey. "And I got there about five o'clock, everything was arranged and the table set, and Mrs. Asher asked about Mother, she's a nice lady, and everything went off fine, there were six people to dinner and the roast came out real well and everything else, and I cleared everything up and got the dishes in the dishwasher—I'd already done one load—I left about nine o'clock. It wasn't really late. I never said anything to Mrs. Asher about not having a car, I thought it was silly to call a taxi, spend all that money when it was just across town on the bus. I walked down to the corner of Hollywood and Fairfax and I was waiting for the bus when they came up in a car—it wasn't really late but there wasn't anybody around on the street—"

"More than one man?" asked Stacey.

"It was two men in a car—they drove up beside the bus stop and one of them leaned out the window and started to talk dirty to me—you know—and I began to get scared, and then he got out and grabbed hold of me, I tried to fight him and he hit me in the face and dragged me into the car. I think they were both doped up on something, they were laughing and acting sort of wild. That one held me down in the back seat and we drove some place, I don't know where, a side street I guess, and then they—you know—raped me, one after the other—I tried to fight them but they were both big and strong—"

"Could you give any kind of a description of them?" asked Stacey.

She said, "Not much, I guess. They were both white men, I could see that by the streetlight, they were maybe twenty-five or so, but when they drove up there, to the bus stop, I just noticed as the car didn't have a California license plate, it was different. I don't know what it was. And in the car—while they were, you know—raping me—this one fellow, he had a gold chain on, round his neck, and it had a kind of charm on it, a zodiac sign I think it was, some fishes. And then they let me out of the car and I didn't know where I was, it was all dark and a street of houses and I walked down to where I could see lights on a main street, and there was that drugstore and the man there called the police for me—Oh, I want to go home! Please, will you see if Jim's here? I asked that nurse to call him—"

"I'll see," said Stacey. At the desk he found a nice-looking young black fellow talking to a nurse, looking very worried. He got the home address and drove back to the station, passed on the story. "Does that ring any bells in your head?"

Donaldson said, "It sure as hell does. A gold charm, a zodiac sign. There was a rape case about six weeks back, I'd have to look up the report, I think her name was Jones or Thompson or something—another colored girl. She was a waitress at a coffee shop on the boulevard, coming off duty late, and got grabbed in a parking lot by two men. That was all she could tell us about them, that they were white men, they got her in a car and drove her up in the hills somewhere and raped her, and shoved her out on a side street. She got a householder to call police. All she noticed was that one of them was wearing a gold necklace with a zodiac charm on it. Hell, a lot of young fellows wear that sort of thing. She never saw the license plate, of course."

"Fish," said Brougham. "That'd be Pisces. Not a hell of a lot to go on. Well, we'll have to get out a report on it."

*   *   *

On Monday morning when Maddox and Sue came in together a little late, Dowling said that Rodriguez had already gone out on something, he didn't know what. Maddox called the hospital. Davenport hadn't been conscious yet but the doctors were more hopeful about him.

"I'm worried about that girl," said Sue. "Where's she going to go? She says she never wants to see her mother again, she won't go home. She's not eighteen yet. I wonder if she's got some friend she could stay with, temporarily anyway—it's a bad situation for her. It'd be impossible to get her into Juvenile Hall, and that's no solution anyway. I think

I'll go over to the hospital and see her, if she's still there—I suppose they'll release her sometime today."

"Well, call in if there's any news," said Maddox. "If I have any bright ideas what to do about the girl, I'll call you."

Sue drove out to the hospital and talked to another nurse about Jill. The nurse was busy and uninterested. "She's all right now, we're releasing her in an hour."

Jill was sitting on the bed in the same cubicle, and she looked better, but still pale, her eyes too bright. She said in a steady voice, "It's all right, I've thought what to do, I can call Marcie, she's my best friend and her mother and father are nice, they'll let me stay awhile, until I can find a job. But I can't do anything until I know about Ronald. If he's going to die. If he does, you'll arrest her, won't you, and I hope she goes to jail for a long, long time. I never want to see her again. She came here, you know, but I wouldn't talk to her." Her voice was too quiet and dull. "Right now I'll just sit here in the waiting room until I know about Ronald. They won't let me see him."

Sue was slightly relieved that she had somewhere to go. She had a word with the uniformed man sitting beside Davenport; he said Davenport hadn't been conscious or said anything, they were still giving him intravenous treatment.

* * *

Rodriguez had gotten chased out on something new as soon as he got in, the first detective to arrive. It was awkward when things happened between shifts; this call had come in a couple of hours before the end of the night Traffic shift, and the two patrolmen had had to hang around waiting for detectives. They were dead on their feet and on overtime when Rodriguez got there. It was a single house on Citrus Avenue, and the body was in the backyard, the body of a big black man in late middle age. He was wearing bright blue nylon pajamas and a blue bathrobe, and there was a pair of bedroom slippers lying beside the body. There was blood on the chest of the pajamas, but Rodriguez couldn't see whether he'd been shot or stabbed.

One patrolman said, "The woman doesn't know anything about it. Their name's Currier. She asked us to call her daughter in Pasadena. Listen, we should've gone in and turned the squads over an hour ago." Rodriguez let them go and started to sort out what had happened here. In the house he found a small fat black woman on the couch in the

living room with a younger woman beside her. They'd both been crying. The house was comfortably furnished, and looked clean and neat.
The older woman said she was Mrs. Currier.

"It just don't seem possible that Dan's dead, all of a sudden like this,
don't seem possible. He was only fifty-two, a big strong man."

The other woman had an arm around her. "Now, Mama. Bob had to
go to work but he said to call if there's anything he can do." She looked
at Rodriguez. "I'm Lydia Ely, I'm their daughter. I'll take care of her."

"What happened here, Mrs. Currier?" asked Rodriguez.

She was rocking back and forth a little, in timeless expression of
grief. "I don't know, I just don't know, but it's got to be something to
do with that no-good trash next door. We always had good neighbors
here, honest people, and old Mrs. Cowan owned the place next door,
she was a quiet old lady, but she died about six months back and since
then the place has been rented. The new people moved in about a
month ago—we don't know them, but they're no-good trash—seems to
be a lot of coming and going, young people, and they're noisy, always
playin' that loud rock music on the phonograph and a lot of yelling and
screaming—them getting drunk and maybe on the dope. It riled Dan,
it'd go on till the middle of the night, and he needs his sleep, got to get
to work early—Oh, I got to call Mr. Healey and tell him, Dan's
boss—"

"Don't worry about it now, Mama. It's Healey's Plumbing," she told
Rodriguez, "Dad had worked there for twenty years."

"He'd gone over there to complain about the noise half a dozen
times, he said the man looked like a mighty mean customer and just
cussed him." The house next door was on the corner, there wouldn't be
neighbors on the other side to complain. "All I know is, it was going on
again last night, real loud, and Dan was mad. We went to bed about
ten o'clock, but he couldn't get to sleep, he was cussing about all the
noise. I'm deaf in one ear and I just turned over on my good ear and
got off to sleep. But when I got up the usual time, about six, Dan
wasn't here. He wasn't anywhere in the house and I couldn't make it
out. I thought maybe he'd gone out to the garage for something and I
went out the back door—and there he was in the yard. Oh, oh—and I
could tell he was dead, there was blood on his nightclothes—I tried to
keep my head, I come in here and called the police—" She sat up and
looked at Rodriguez. Her first shock was past, and her mind was working. "I reckon what must have happened, Dan went over there to

complain again and some one of those no-good trashy people killed him. That must be what happened. The best husband a woman ever had," and she started to cry again.

Rodriguez used the phone to call the lab, and he was thinking he could use some help on this, so he got Dowling to come out. The house next door was quiet enough now. The backyard here had a little lawn, some flower beds, but at the place next door the yard was just bare earth. He looked over the low picket fence. It hadn't rained in two months and the dry dusty soil wouldn't show any marks. He looked at the body. He thought Currier had been shot.

Baker showed up in a mobile van about the time Dowling arrived, and when he'd taken some photographs Rodriguez and Dowling shifted the body to look at the back. There was a fairly large exit wound. "Shot," said Dowling. "That's an entrance wound in the front all right. The slug went right through him." They looked around but couldn't find it. The morgue wagon came for the body.

Rodriguez and Dowling went up to the house next door and rang the bell. After a long interval the door opened and they faced a big heavy black man in underwear with a grimy bathrobe over that. He scowled at the badge. "Did you see your next-door neighbor last night?" asked Rodriguez. "Mr. Currier?" The man shook his head. "You had a party here last night? What's your name?"

"Todd. My name's Henry Todd. We didn't have no party."

"Who lives here?" asked Dowling.

"Just me and my wife and her sister."

"We've heard you've been causing a little disturbance, with the loud music," said Rodriguez.

He scowled again. "We was just playin' a few records, nobody got any call to mind the music."

"Currier had complained before, hadn't he? Didn't he come over to complain again last night?"

"No, he never. I never laid eyes on him." He didn't ask why they were interested. They went back to the yard next door where Baker was still looking for the slug.

"It must be around here somewhere," said Dowling.

"I don't think he was shot here," said Rodriguez. "My guess'd be that the body was moved. It's a damned nuisance that the slug went right through him. If he was shot next door, it'll be there somewhere. I think we'd better ask for a search warrant."

* * *

Sue was just thinking about going out to lunch when her phone rang, and it was the uniformed man sitting at the hospital. His name was Gorman. He said, "He just came to and I've got something for you. He said—"

"I'll be over," said Sue. She wanted to see Jill again, ask if she'd called Marcie.

"And his folks just got here," said Gorman.

And belatedly Sue was wondering how the Davenports might feel about Jill. She looked into the detective office to tell Maddox about this development, and drove out to the hospital. Gorman was waiting for her in the lobby. He was just past the rookie stage, a rawboned young man with an ingenuous smile and shrewd eyes. "He came to about half an hour ago, just for a minute," he said to Sue, "and he said—I wrote it down for you—he said, sounding kind of surprised, the old bitch shot me. And I asked him, who shot you, Mr. Davenport, and he said, Jill's mother, where's Jill—and then he passed out again."

Sue was gratified. "That's fine," she said. "That's good."

"You want me to stay here any longer?"

"No, you got what we were after, thanks."

"His folks just got here," said Gorman. "They look like nice people. Okay, I'll get back to the station."

Sue went up to Emergency, looking for some late news on Davenport, and talked to an intern. He said, "We can say he's going to make it now, he's doing a lot better. We'll probably try to get the bullet out sometime today."

"Oh, that's good." Sue looked around for Jill and had just spotted her, hunched on one of the benches in the little waiting room, when a couple came down the corridor to the nurses' station. Sue said tentatively, "Mr. Davenport?"

He was tall and broad-shouldered, with a shock of thick gray hair, and she decided instantly that he was a teacher too, maybe a professor. But the woman, trim-figured and dark-haired, had the same steady blue eyes and wide mouth as her son. They looked at the badge, and Sue said quickly, "We're so glad he's going to be all right. We know who shot him now."

Mrs. Davenport asked quietly, "Was it that girl's mother?"

Sue was surprised. "Oh, you've heard about Jill—"

"Well, of course. Where is she, do you know? We want to see her."

Her voice didn't offer a clue as to how she felt and Sue was tempted to bypass that one but said, "Well, she's there in the waiting room." The Davenports went in there, up to the girl huddled on the bench.

"My dear," said Mrs. Davenport quietly, "we're Ronnie's parents. You're Jill, aren't you? Isn't it wonderful that he's going to be all right?"

Jill looked up at them slowly. Her auburn hair was disheveled and her clothes dirty and wrinkled. Her eyes filled with tears and she said brokenly, "Oh, Mrs. Davenport, I'm so ashamed—so ashamed—because she hurt Ronald—you'll never forgive me, if he'd never met me all this wouldn't have happened—"

The man said in a quiet voice, "My child, you mustn't think that way—" But Mrs. Davenport sat down beside her and put an arm around her.

"Now that's not so," she said in a warm voice. "We've heard all about you, my dear, and we've just seen Ronnie—I think he knew we were there—and he's going to be fine."

Jill said chokingly, "But I thought you'd hate me."

"That's silly, darling, you're Ronnie's girl and you're both going to be very happy."

"Oh, Mrs. Davenport, I'll take care of him until he's well again—I'll take care of him all his life—"

"Of course you will, but right now I think you'd better come back to the hotel with us and rest. And as soon as Ronnie's out of the hospital we're taking you both back to Portland with us."

"But," said Jill wildly, "he wants me to g-g-g-graduate from high school before we get married—"

"Well, there's no reason you can't do that in Portland," said Mrs. Davenport sensibly. Jill took one look at her kind eyes and buried her face in the other woman's shoulder and sobbed. Her future mother-in-law patted her soothingly.

Jill and Ronnie, thought Sue, were going to be all right. She started for the elevator feeling a relieved warmth in her heart. But there was now Mrs. Enid Fenton to deal with, and good riddance.

* * *

Maddox had thought twice about tackling Brian Olson's pals. It was very unlikely that Brian had told them about the break-in, and in asking them to back up the alibi about the disco—which he'd have done by now—he'd have told the auspicious tale of some chick's husband jealous, maybe sniffing around and even telling lies to the cops— something like that. It would be a waste of time.

Rodriguez and Dowling came in and Rodriguez put in the request for the search warrant while Dowling told Maddox about the new homicide.

"I don't think Todd's bright enough to think about that slug," said Rodriguez, "but we left Franks there to keep an eye out anyway." They sat around waiting for the warrant and it came through just after Sue had left for the hospital. Rodriguez and Dowling started back for the homicide scene, probably stopping for a sandwich on the way, and then Maddox went out for lunch with Feinman.

When they got back Sue was waiting impatiently. She told them what had gone on at the hospital. "So we've got her nailed. And, oh, Ivor, I'm so relieved about Jill, his parents are wonderful people and they'll look after her. But that damned woman—"

"Have you had lunch?" asked Maddox.

"I forgot all about it."

"Well, you go and have something to eat, you're eating for two, remember. There's time enough to pick her up." He saw her off and called the lab. "Has anybody had a look at the gun picked up in that apartment yesterday?"

"It's an old S & W .38," said Garcia. "One slug fired, and it was fully loaded. There weren't any prints on it."

Yes, a stupid woman, thought Maddox. She'd wiped off her prints, or used gloves, but she might have had the sense to get his prints on the gun. "The kickback just came in from the Feds, on that print we got off the Pliofilm," said Garcia. "They don't know it. And I don't think Harry's got to those butchers yet."

"Were there any prints besides Davenport's in the apartment? I trust you got his at the hospital."

"Yep. There weren't. The place was clean as a whistle."

"Well, it doesn't matter," said Maddox. The woman was a film cutter at Paramount, he remembered. She'd be back from lunch by now. He collected Nolan and went out to get her.

*   *   *

Todd looked at the formal search warrant suspiciously and uncomprehendingly. Rodriguez had to spell it out for him, that the judge had given the police permission to search the premises.

Todd grunted. "What ya lookin' for?"

"That's our business," said Rodriguez. "Just don't interfere, Mr. Todd."

He let them in grudgingly. There were two women in the bare dirty living room, a big stereo, and a lot of LP records stacked around, a minimum of furniture. One of the women was fat and one thinner, both very black. One of them held a tumbler filled with cheap red wine, by the smell. The three men passed them in silence, went through the kitchen, where dirty dishes were stacked all over, and out to the backyard.

These were generous-sized lots, the subdivision being made a long time ago when the city had more space to spare. The backyard was about fifty by fifty feet.

"It could be somewhere in the house," said Dowling. "And if it hit a wall or the floor, he'd likely have noticed it and dug it out."

"I don't think so," said Rodriguez tersely. "Currier wouldn't have gone inside the house. He was in nightclothes. The way I read it, he stepped over the fence and came to the back door here to complain about the noise. He'd have had to wait until the rock music stopped temporarily to make himself heard. He was annoyed, with good reason, and he wouldn't have been very diplomatic. And there was an argument, and he got shot. Maybe Todd was a little high and just brought out the gun on impulse—or it could have been one of the women, who knows? Then they realized they were saddled with a corpse, so they dropped him back over the fence into his own backyard." He was irritated at the stupidity of the whole thing.

At least there wasn't much cover here, and they started looking around at every square inch of the yard. Forty minutes later Dowling spotted the slug, lying half covered with loose dusty soil at the end of the lot. "Don't touch it," said Baker sharply. He edged it into an evidence bag tenderly. "On a direct line with the back door, you notice. Very nice."

They went back to the house and Rodriguez asked Todd, "Have you got a gun of any kind?"

"Why do you want to know?"

"Come on," said Rodriguez, "you've got a gun here, haven't you?

We've just found a fresh slug in your backyard, and it hasn't been there long."

"Oh," said Todd. "Oh. Well, I guess that must be from when I shot a rat out there the other day. The wife said there was rats in the garage —and I went to look—and I seen one runnin' out, so I shot it, but I guess I missed it though."

"Let's see the gun," said Dowling.

Reluctantly he produced it. It was a Colt .32 revolver, and it still had five slugs in the chamber. "You gonna take my gun? A guy needs a gun for protection these days. Dammit, does that paper say you can take my gun? Am I gonna get it back?"

"That depends," said Rodriguez. "We'll be letting you know."

When the slug hadn't been in the body, they couldn't connect it on the evidence that it had been fired from that gun belonging to Todd, but the lab could sometimes do small miracles with the microscopes.

* * *

Maddox and Nolan got past the security guards at that old studio lot in the middle of town, and were eventually directed to the upper floor of one of the permanent buildings. Paramount had had a disastrous fire recently, and there was a big bare space of land, still looking scorched, where some of the old sets had burned, just adjacent to this building.

They found Enid Fenton in a hall outside one of the cutting rooms, drinking a cup of coffee and talking to another woman. Maddox showed her the badge for form's sake and said, "You're under arrest, Mrs. Fenton. You have the right to call your attorney before you say anything to us."

The other woman's mouth fell open and she gave a little squeal of alarm and surprise. Enid Fenton said, "What on earth for? You can't arrest me—I haven't done anything wrong."

"I'm afraid we can, Mrs. Fenton. The warrant will be coming through sometime this afternoon. We'll have to ask you to come along with us now."

"You're crazy," she said. "What am I supposed to have done?"

"The charge is attempted homicide," said Nolan, "on Ronald Davenport. It was last Saturday night, wasn't it?"

She said instantly, "I don't know anything about it. I deny the charge absolutely."

"Well, let's go and talk it over at the station," said Maddox. The other woman watched him take Enid Fenton's arm with her eyes full of mingled shock and avid curiosity.

At the station they took her into the office across the hall and gave her the chair beside Sue's desk. It was Daisy's day off. They asked her formally if she wanted to call an attorney, and she said, "I don't need a lawyer. This is just crazy."

Maddox offered her a cigarette and she bent to his lighter. "Would you like to tell us about it, Mrs. Fenton?" asked Sue coldly.

"There's nothing to tell," she said coolly. "I don't know anything about it."

"But he told us, you see," said Maddox gently. "He told us you shot him, Mrs. Fenton. He's going to recover and he'll be testifying about it. You thought if he was out of the way, you could go on managing your daughter's life just as you always had, didn't you? That was why. Where did you get the gun?"

She sat quite still for a moment, the cigarette in one upraised hand, and then startlingly she came out with a string of vicious obscenities.

"It doesn't matter whether you say anything or not," said Maddox. "Wouldn't you like to call an attorney?"

She took a long drag on the cigarette and laid it down in the ashtray. Her haggard face suddenly looked ten years older. She said bitterly, "When I think of all the sacrifices I made and the money I've laid out on that damned stupid girl—all the plans Al Bernstein and I had for her—he had to work like hell to arrange that screen test, you know, it isn't so easy these days. And she'd have made it, nothing in pants could resist those eyes and that figure—she'd have made it big, right to the top—and she's ready to throw it all away because she's in love—in love, my God! She'll find out there's no damned man on top of the earth counts more than money—money—money!" That was savage. "Ten years from now she'll know what I was talking about, and what a goddamned fool she was. Ungrateful little brat, never thinking about me, about all she could do for me—after all the years I've sweated at that job! And now it's all gone down the drain." She was bursting out with all of it in one vindictive flood. "I never wanted a kid at all, a messy baby to take care of, but Howie was a sentimental idiot and back then you couldn't get an abortion so easy. And then when she got to be about ten, she started to blossom out—all those looks, those eyes and all—and I began to see the potential—she could go right to the top, be a big star—all the money—and I worked like a dog to get her ready for it, give her what she'd have to have. And now it's all gone down the drain, all for nothing—and I wind up in jail." She looked from one to the other of them and she said flatly, "All right, that's exactly what I thought, if that damned fool teacher was out of the picture she'd come to her senses, and if he had to be put out of the way with a gun, that was the way it had to be. I had the gun, it belonged to Howie, and he left it when he deserted me. That damned no-good shiftless bum—I had enough of men with that one! Sure I knew where lover boy lived, he's in the phone book, and when he opened the door I just walked in and shot him. So I couldn't even do that right, and he isn't going to die." Her tone was resentful. "I thought he was dead. I thought if I left the gun everybody'd think he'd done it himself or some thief had killed him."

"It wasn't a very smart setup," said Nolan, "but it doesn't matter now."

"So he wins the last throw. Goddamn him. I just hope that damned stupid girl wakes up someday and realizes what she missed."

"We'll take you down to jail now," said Maddox. She never said another word on the way down to the Sybil Brand Institute, the women's jail downtown.

* * *

They had gotten on to the media again, and there would be fuller articles in the papers, on the TV news, about the lunatic, how the police thought he was planting the parcels of hamburger. But there hadn't been any more cases since the death of Alicia Cummings—that autopsy report was due in, but they knew what would be in it—and it was possible that the lunatic had gotten his little kicks and retired satisfied.

On Tuesday morning Maddox came in a little late, and he hadn't had time to take the night report from Feinman when the phone rang on his desk, and he said resignedly, "Here we go," and picked it up. "Sergeant Maddox."

It was a sheriff's deputy out at their Valley station; his name was Shapiro. "We thought you'd like to know there's been another one," he said genially. "The hamburger nut strikes again. Oh, she's okay, they got to her in time, but it was a damn lucky thing her husband got home when he did. She's kind of a cute little old lady, Maddox, I got a kick out of her. Their name is Blodgett—Marion and Fred Blodgett—and they live on the outskirts of North Hollywood. Her husband's retired, worked for the city as an electrician. He was out playing golf yesterday afternoon, and when he came home about three o'clock he found her passed out on the kitchen floor, so he called the paramedics. They pumped her stomach out, and it was the hospital called us. She'd had the hamburger for lunch."

"Oh, for God's sake," said Maddox. "Are people still buying the stuff? After all the warnings we've sent out—"

"Well, I asked her that," said Shapiro. "I saw her at the hospital yesterday evening, and I asked her, hadn't they heard all the warnings about the spiked hamburger? And she said, land sakes, neither she nor Fred ever watches TV or listens to the radio, it's a waste of time, and they don't read the news in the paper because it's always bad news. When the weather's bad and she can't work in the garden she's reading mysteries from the library, and Fred likes to work crossword puzzles when he isn't playing golf, which he usually does alone because he's so deaf it's no pleasure to try to talk to people."

"Oh, my God," said Maddox.

"They hadn't heard a thing about it, heaven help us. The way you can try to get the word out on a thing like this, and what a hell of a thing it is, and then good old human nature throws the monkey wrench into the works."

"Say it again. Where did it come from? Not that it matters."

"A Ralph's Market on Sherman Way. They'd bought it on Saturday."

"Weekends again," said Maddox. "You've got the doctor's statement, the lab report, I suppose. In case we ever drop on the nut and this comes to trial."

"Oh, yes, it's all down in black and white," said Shapiro. "My God, haven't you got any leads on it at all?"

Maddox told him why they hadn't, about the market managers' association. "I don't know if they're trying to set up any security measures, they ought to, of course. One thing I do know, I've told my wife and mother-in-law to stay away from hamburger while this is going on—and they used to give it to the dog too, and he's a valuable dog—and I don't know but what it's put me off it for life." Shapiro laughed. "And if the nut gets bored and quits, we'll never know who he was."

"Possible," said Shapiro. "You never know what a nut will do. We just thought you'd like to hear about the latest one."

And Maddox suddenly thought, putting down the phone, that one thing hadn't occurred to them. It just occurred to him now. All the incidents with the hamburger had been, you could put it, private. There hadn't been any deaths or illnesses from the hamburger at the fast-food chains or restaurants. And that made some sense, of course. Those places would have their own direct sources of supply, they wouldn't be depending on retail markets.

He looked up at Feinman and asked, "What did the night watch leave, anything to work?"

"A hit-run. This woman killed crossing Sunset about the middle of the evening. The car ran a light and the witnesses think the driver was drunk, it was weaving all over the place. We've got them coming in to make statements. Damn it, these drunks," said Feinman. "She was only about twenty-five, she'd worked late at a market and stopped to do an errand on the way home."

"Don't mention markets to me," said Maddox. And he had to be in court at ten, to cover an indictment.

*   *   *

The witnesses, of course, gave them not enough and too much. There were six of them, and they didn't agree on much. They said the car was green, blue, off-white, beige. It was a sedan, but they couldn't say whether it was two-door or four-door. They did agree that it was a medium-sized car, something like a Chevy or a Dodge or a Buick. And the way it was weaving all over the street, there was something wrong with the driver.

It was nothing they could do anything about.

An autopsy came up about noon and Feinman handed it to Daisy. "I guess you were on this. Not that it's a case, you'll just file it away." It was the autopsy report on Audrey Lutz, and of course it was short and blunt.

"That one," said Sue. "I wonder if Father Donovan arranged a funeral for her. But when they think suicide's a mortal sin, they don't bury them in a Catholic cemetery, do they? That'd be another grief to poor Miss Ferguson."

"I don't know, Sue," said Daisy soberly, "all the answers, I mean. But if God's really infallible He must have known from the start how fallible humanity would turn out to be."

*   *   *

At five o'clock that afternoon, with the end of shift coming up, everybody swore when a new call came in, but the citizens wandering around making trouble for the cops didn't know or care anything about cops' regular working hours. D'Arcy and Feinman took the call.

It was the pillowcase heisters again, and this time there had been four of them. It was the first time they'd hit a bar this early, but it was a slightly different bar than they'd hit before. It was a place called The Projection Room on Santa Monica Boulevard, a discreetly handsome high-class place about half a block from the old Goldwyn Studios. In fact, if it had been half a block farther west it would have been in county territory and the job would belong to the sheriff's boys. It was a place where a good many studio people gathered at odd times of day.

D'Arcy and Feinman started to talk to the witnesses, and heard what they'd heard before, the one tall man, good-looking, nothing much about the other three, the guns, the demand for cash only. One of the difficulties on this caper, of course, was that bars were usually under-lighted and the witnesses hadn't had a very good look at the heisters. The bartender had been temporarily absent in the men's washroom during the whole heist.

About all they could do now was get names and addresses, ask the witnesses to come in and make statements. It was six o'clock by then and they'd all be wanting to get home.

The fourth man D'Arcy talked to was a Gilbert Brant, a fair-haired big fellow about thirty-five, who said, "Sure, I'll come in. They got thirty bucks off me, the bastards. I can give you a good description of one of them, the one who took around the bag. I'm a commercial artist, I've got a good eye for faces, and I was sitting right under the spotlight by the side door."

D'Arcy's interest quickened. "You might be able to give a better description, being an artist, Mr. Brant. Would you be willing to see a police artist, try to come up with a composite sketch?"

"Sure," said Brant. "The Identikit thing? I'd be interested to see how that works. Sure, I'll do that."

"We'll set up an appointment for tomorrow morning," said D'Arcy. "The sooner you get to it, the better chance you'll get an accurate sketch. We'll get back to you first thing in the morning."

* * *

When the phone rang on Maddox's desk at nine-thirty on Wednesday morning, he suffered a sudden foreboding that somebody was going to tell him about another victim of the lunatic. But it was a hearty baritone voice announcing itself as Lieutenant Humbert of Hollenbeck division. "We've had a little general gossip come through that you've been coming across bits and pieces of a dismembered corpse, Sergeant."

"Oh, my God, yes."

"Well, it's possible we can give you another piece. A head," said Humbert. "It turned up about forty minutes ago, up in Griffith Park." Since the Hollywood division's caseload had gotten so heavy, Hollenbeck division had been policing that big piece of real estate.

"That might be a big help, if it belongs to the same corpse. Where did it turn up?"

"Now, we don't get the cut-up corpses just so often," said Humbert. "It was a funny sort of fluke, Maddox. You know a lot of the park is pretty wild, underbrush and bushes, and in the ordinary way the damned thing might have stayed there for years, never been found at all. It looks as if it was tossed off the road down a hillside—it was in a paper bag, by the way—"

"For God's sake."

"—but it ended up a couple of feet from one of the sprinkler heads." There were automatic sprinklers throughout the park, to keep it looking like a park and cut the danger of fire through Southern California's long dry season. "And one of the Parks and Recreation men was up there cleaning out the sprinkler heads, and picked up the bag to keep the place looking neat and clean, and it was heavier than he expected so he looked inside."

Maddox laughed. "Little surprise."

"I'll say. Likely he'll never get over the shock. Well, I thought about your little problem, and dropped it off at the coroner's office. If it's part of your corpse, you can take it from there."

"Thank you so much," said Maddox.

He went right down there to look at it. Bergner and Whitman had it on an examination table and were interested. "Well, it's part of the same body," said Bergner, "look at the saw marks on the neck—they match—and the features match too, you could say. We've come to the conclusion it's an Hispanic male between thirty and forty, no scars or marks, say six feet, a hundred and eighty pounds."

"Yes," said Maddox.

"But something damned offbeat," said Bergner. "It's been frozen. The head. It's just starting to thaw out now."

"What?" said Maddox.

"That's right. It's been in a freezer up till around twenty-four hours ago."

"Now, I will be goddamned," said Maddox. He looked at the head again reluctantly. It was certainly fairly well preserved. The features were regular, even handsome: a wide brow, straight nose, something of a lantern jaw, a fine line of small moustache. This was part of the same body, the doctors said so, and he'd been dead about three weeks, but he didn't look like it. "By God, I wonder if we could get a usable photograph," said Maddox ruminatively.

CHAPTER EIGHT

"At any rate," said Bergner, "there's your cause of death," and he turned the grisly specimen over and laid his spatulate surgeon's hands on the left rear side. "Massive contusion, and there'll be a fracture under it that drove the bone into the brain."

Maddox didn't look at the thing any longer than he had to. He went out and called the lab, and Franks came out with the camera equipment. He took one look at the head and said, "Christ. Well, if we can get a decent close-up I can block out anything that shows of the hacked neck. Maybe if I use a black backdrop—you might get the newspapers to run it, can but try." He set up the camera and started to fiddle with it. In the end he got a couple of shots that didn't look too gruesome, and sent prints up to the detective office by noon.

"Gah," said Rodriguez, looking at them. "What a nasty thing, I don't think the papers would print it. Did you say the damn thing had been frozen, for God's sake?"

"That's what Bergner said. The damndest thing—but anybody who'd cut up a corpse might do anything. If the papers won't run it we can get one of the artists to make up a sketch, they'd run that." He took the prints to the *Times* and *Herald* himself, and Rodriguez took some more to a couple of the Spanish-language papers. The *Times* man looked dubious and said this was a family newspaper but he'd see what the city desk said. "Public service," said Maddox. "We'd like to get him identified."

"Well, in any case it's too late to run it in the final edition. Maybe tomorrow, if we run it at all."

There had been a new heist on Tuesday night, at a drugstore, and the two witnesses had come in that morning. They gave good descriptions of the two heisters, both young; there hadn't been much cash in the register, as the manager had already bagged it for the bank night deposit, and it was locked in his car, but they'd gotten a big haul of drugs from the pharmacy that would net them a profit on the street. The witnesses agreed to look at mug shots and Dowling took them downtown to R. and I.

D'Arcy was already there, sitting in with the police artist and Gilbert Brant. Within an hour, working with the Identikit, they had come up with a composite drawing and Brant said confidently, "That's him all right, you've got him down just fine. I got a good look at him, and it's a kind of distinctive face, isn't it? Not very pretty, but you'd remember it. That's him, the one who carried the pillowcase around to collect the cash."

The sketch showed a light-skinned Negro in his mid-twenties, with a loose-lipped mouth, wide-apart eyes, big ears, a sloping weak jaw. "We'll get it in production," said the artist. "I suppose you want copies for the next Traffic briefing." D'Arcy said they'd be obliged and thanked Brant.

Out in the hall he found Dowling puffing on his pipe and talking to a pretty policewoman while he waited to see if the witnesses picked out any mug shots. D'Arcy had to wait for those copies anyway, and joined him.

The witnesses finally agreed on one mug shot, and the man they picked had the right record for the job. He was one Eugene Glass and he had a short pedigree for petty theft and a longer one for armed robbery, and was a known addict. He was just out from his second sentence and still on parole. The last known address was Magnolia

Avenue downtown but that could be checked with his parole officer. Dowling did that and the Welfare and Rehab man said he was still there, and he had a job with a gardening service. Dowling tried there and the boss told him Glass had walked off the job, the lazy bum. Dowling sighed and started downtown to look for him at that address.

D'Arcy took the stack of copies of the sketch back to the station. The rest of them would be distributed to the other divisions from headquarters, and put up on bulletin boards, placed in all the squad cars. At least nothing new had gone down. Maddox and Rodriguez were still out talking to newspapers and TV studios. The autopsy report on Alicia Cummings had come in.

*   *   *

Rodriguez got back to the station about four o'clock. The papers had all agreed to run the picture of the head, but the TV stations had balked. Too gruesome for family viewing, they said. Thinking about the latest victim of the lunatic, Rodriguez hoped gloomily that they'd run the damned picture on the front page; considering the price of newspapers, it was queer how many people hardly looked beyond that, or just took out the sports section. He had done a lot of running around and was glad to sit down for a while. Maddox was still out, and when D'Arcy came back after dropping off the copies at the watch commander's office he said Dowling had just brought in a suspect for questioning. On that heist last night. The witnesses had made a mug shot.

"Don't tell me we're going to find one of those we can arrest," said Rodriguez. But now and again they got enough to lay a charge on one of the heisters. He was just going out to the coffee machine in the hall when the phone rang on his desk.

Baker was on the other end, and he said, sounding pleased with himself, "I've got something for you. That slug we picked up in the backyard of that place on Monday. You remember the gun you collected was a .32 Colt—"

"I remember," said Rodriguez. "Have you done us any good?"

"Well, the slug was fired from that gun," said Baker.

"And nothing to say it was the same slug that went through Currier, I suppose. Well, it was a long chance." He laughed. "Todd saying he'd been shooting rats—that's not the classiest section of town but it's a long way from a slum, and I doubt there'd be any rats around, but that's the story we're stuck with."

"Why don't you wait for it?" said Baker. "If he shot a rat the rat was wearing blue nylon pajamas just like Currier. You couldn't see it with the naked eye, of course, but it showed up under the microscope, just enough of a scrap to match. That's the slug that went through Currier."

"Maravilloso!" said Rodriguez. "I will be damned."

"It's funny what a bullet will pick up sometimes. It's enough to nail Todd for it. Or whoever was holding the gun, you'll have to sort that out."

Rodriguez began to laugh. "Of all the damn queer things—thanks, Harry."

"Pleasure," said Baker, and hung up.

Rodriguez took D'Arcy with him to see if Todd was home. That somebody was home was evident from the blaring rock music audible down the block. "You can see how Currier felt," said Rodriguez. They had to wait until that record came to an end to push the doorbell. In a minute Henry Todd opened the door to them. "Mr. Todd," said Rodriguez, "we want to talk to you. Was it you or one of the women who shot Mr. Currier? Come on, let us in."

Todd stepped back unwillingly. "I don't know what you mean, man. Nobody shot nobody." The two women were in the bare living room and there were a lot of LP records on the floor beside the big stereo. The women just stared.

Rodriguez said, "I gather you haven't got a job, Mr. Todd. You can afford just to sit around and play records all day and night to annoy the neighbors?"

He said, scowling, "We got the welfare money."

D'Arcy said dispassionately, "And you know, César, even if we spell it out for him he'll never understand how he got fingered. The bullet that killed Currier came out of your gun, Todd. It went right through the body but it took a little scrap of his pajamas with it, and the scientific detectives found it, so that's how we know one of you here shot him. Was it you?"

One of the women gave a little yelp and said, "Goddamn it, Henry, I said you was a damn fool to do that. Now look what a mess you got landed in!"

"Shut up," said Todd, but the harm had been done, and Rodriguez laughed.

"So now we know who had the gun. We can guess what happened."

They could see Todd thinking it over slowly as it dawned on him that they knew.

He said, "I was drunk. I didn't know what I was doin'. No, I guess I thought it was a burglar, tryin' to get in the back door."

"Oh, for God's sake," said D'Arcy.

"You can decide which story to tell the judge while you sit in jail, Todd," said Rodriguez. "We're taking you in now."

He began to swear, but he didn't try to put up a fight. They ferried him up to the jail and booked him in. He had about five dollars on him, a pocket knife, a pack of cigarettes in one pocket and half a dozen marijuana cigarettes in another.

Rodriguez said, "Of course, on the welfare money. *Dios.* Doing what comes naturally, and just the Curriers' bad luck that Todd and his harem happened to move in next door."

There wasn't any point in wasting time to talk to him, or even get statements from the women. The definite lab evidence was all they needed.

D'Arcy said, "The hell of it is, he won't serve much time."

"No, they'll call it manslaughter and he'll get a one-to-three, and be out in a year. While the productive hardworking citizen molders in his grave."

But they weren't running the system. On the way back to the office Rodriguez asked, "How are you coming with the Spanish?"

"Oh, fine, I think." D'Arcy didn't add anything about the Spanish teacher, and Rodriguez wondered about that. In his time D'Arcy had taken up with some unlikely girls, but the Spanish teacher—*extraño*, thought Rodriguez to himself.

* * *

If they often didn't get enough evidence, and had to leave things up in the air, again the stupid punks made things so easy that it set them wondering about the state of human intelligence. Dowling picked up Eugene Glass at the cheap apartment on Magnolia and brought him in, and he and Nolan talked to him in an interrogation room.

"You couldn't even wait to get off parole to pull another job?" said Dowling. "That drugstore last night. Who was with you on it?"

Glass was a fat young fellow with bad skin and little piggy eyes. He said stupidly, "What do you mean?"

"Two witnesses picked your mug shot," said Nolan, "out of the book. You pulled that heist. Who was with you on it?"

Glass thought that over and said, "Oh, hell. Goddamn it."

"Your parole officer got you a job with a gardening service. You were doing all right for eating money."

"Oh, hell," he said. "That crummy job, it was too hard work, pushin' a lawn mower and all. I got tired of it."

"There were two of you on the heist," said Nolan. "Who was the other one?"

Glass said sullenly, "Oh, hell, it was Mario Hernandez, we met up in the joint last year. You got me, you better damn well get him too."

"Where does he live?" asked Nolan. This kind of thing made them feel tired.

"Somewhere down on Twelfth," said Glass.

This would make some more paperwork, and there were things they had to do to spell it out for the court. They booked him into the jail, applied for a search warrant for his cheap apartment, and went out to find Hernandez. Eventually, in the apartment they found most of the haul of drugs from the pharmacy. Hernandez did a lot of swearing and wouldn't give them the time of day, but that didn't matter. By the time they booked him in it was the end of the shift.

*   *   *

The *Times* and the *Herald* ran the shot of the head on Thursday, as did one of the Spanish-language papers. But nobody had called in to identify it immediately, and it was just a chance that anybody ever would. He could have been a drifter without any friends. That night was quiet, with no new cases showing up to work. The composite sketch of the pillowcase heister had been sent to all the squad cars in the metropolitan area, and maybe somebody would spot him. Or maybe not. Maddox was talking with Rodriguez and D'Arcy in the office at four o'clock when an assault was called in, and he went out with Rodriguez to look at it.

The squad-car man was talking to a fat woman at the corner of Romaine and Western. He said the ambulance had just left. She said indignantly, "It makes you wonder what the world's coming to these days, the little kids turning into criminals. I'm the one called the police, least I could do, and I ought to be home fixing dinner but you've got to cooperate with the police."

"What happened?" asked Maddox.

"I was just coming home from the market on the corner, when I saw this one kid stabbing another kid, and he saw me and run off down the block. I don't know how bad the kid was hurt, but I went back to the pay phone on the corner and called the cops."

That was all she knew, so they went out to the Emergency ward to find out about the kid. He was just getting patched up, and the doctor said he was lucky, the knife had just missed his heart and he'd just lost a little blood. "You can talk to him, he'll be released in the morning."

He was a thin dark boy about fourteen, and he told them his name was Juan Espinosa. "Somebody better call my grandfather and my mama, they'll be worried when I don't come home. It was that Manuel Leandro, and he got my grandfather's money—a ten-dollar bill—" He was tearful about that. "I just got home from school and my grandfather said to go up to the store and get some milk and bread and eggs—my mama wasn't home yet, she works—and that Manuel came up to me and said give him all the money I got, I told him, I asked him please not to take my grandfather's money, but he stuck a knife in me and stole it anyway."

"Do you know where he lives?" asked Rodriguez.

"I just know him at school. No, I don't know. My grandfather'll be mad to lose all that money."

In the hall, Maddox said, "Some of them do get started early."

"I wonder if there's anybody still at the school," said Rodriguez.

It was the same junior high school that had gotten vandalized a while ago. They found a couple of secretaries still there and one of them looked up Manuel Leandro's address for them, Ardmore Avenue. Before they went to look for him they went to break the news to Juan's grandfather. Juan's father was dead and he and his mother lived with the old man, who was on Social Security.

At the apartment on Ardmore they found Manuel's mother at home. She was a fat blowsy woman with dyed red hair, and she was halfway drunk. The place was filthy and there was a little girl about three playing with a stuffed toy on the floor and a baby yelling in the background. "I don't know where Manuel's got to," she said, "or when he be home."

Maddox said, "Leave a note for the night watch. It's Juvenile business anyway." But Sergeant Ralston had already left when they got back to the office.

* * *

On Friday morning Maddox had just gotten in when he had a call from Valley division, a Lieutenant Conrad. "We've just had these two women come in to say they recognize that picture in the paper, I didn't know what they were talking about until they showed it to me. The picture of a corpse, I take it, and the case seems to belong to you."

"How very gratifying," said Maddox. "Shoot them over."

"Oh, I did," said Conrad, "I just thought I'd better tell you to expect them. That's not a very pretty photo, and there was something funny about it, he didn't seem to have a neck."

"Oh, it was there," said Maddox, "only not much of it."

The night watch hadn't located that Manuel Leandro, and D'Arcy went over to the school with Ralston to look for him. There had been another mugging on the street last night and that was all.

The two women burst in on Maddox at about nine-thirty. The older one was Maria Ramirez, the younger, Elena Mendoza. Mrs. Ramirez had been weeping; the other one looked more excited than anything else. They both spoke only slightly accented English. Maddox pulled up chairs for them and Sue came in to offer moral support.

"Like we told the other cop up at home," said Mrs. Mendoza, "that's Tony!" She put the newspaper on the desk, a Spanish-language paper. The photograph of the head was in the lower left-hand corner of the front page. "I don't see this regular, we don't take it, but I just got to work this morning, I work at a Denny's coffee shop on Saticoy, when a customer in for early breakfast left it and I picked it up to throw it out and saw that picture, and it's Tony!"

Mrs. Ramirez said, "My Tony—and it says he's dead—but how could he be dead, he's just young, he'll be thirty-two in July—"

"And I just told the boss I had to leave, I went right up and told Mama and showed her, and we went to the police station. How could Tony be dead? We'd been worried about him, he always called Mama at least once a week, and he hadn't in a while and we couldn't get hold of him on the phone—but how could he be dead? He said he was going to Las Vegas, that was about three weeks ago, but he don't usually stay there more than a couple of days—"

"Let's take it from the beginning," said Maddox. "Tony who?"

"Well, Tony Ramirez, of course—my brother Tony. He lives in Hollywood, his job's here, he worked for a Safeway market—a Safeway market on Vine, only they just closed it to move somewhere else and he was sort of between jobs, he was supposed to start at the new place next week, it's on Western."

"Where did he live?" asked Maddox.

"He's got an apartment on Hobart."

Mrs. Ramirez said mournfully, "We thought maybe he'd got married, decided to marry that girl. I always wanted Tony to marry a nice girl and have a family—and he ought to have did it in the church, but Tony's got right away from the church, it was a grief to me—"

"What girl?" asked Maddox.

"Oh, we'd never met her," said Mrs. Mendoza, "we live out in Van Nuys and we're all kind of busy. I got two kids and my husband drives a truck all day, he don't like to go out at night. But Tony'd been going with her a couple of months or more, her name's Teresa Alvarez. She works at some nursing home."

"When did you hear from him last, Mrs. Ramirez?" asked Maddox.

"We tried to think on the way over here," said Elena. "He phoned Mama three weeks ago today."

Mrs. Ramirez's ample bosom heaved. "That's right—oh, my Tony dead—he was the oldest—he phoned me about four o'clock that afternoon, he sounded just fine, joking and laughing, he said he was going over to Las Vegas the next day—"

"He's a great one for cards and gambling, but he never gets in over his head, loses money he hasn't got."

"Did he say anything else, Mrs. Ramirez?"

"He said he was going to that girl's apartment for dinner—she was a pretty good cook but not as good as me—it was a joke—and I told him to have a good time in Las Vegas—we just talked, he sounded fine, just the same as always—oh, oh, the paper said he's dead—"

Maddox reflected that that sounded very damned close to the estimated time of death. The legs and lower torso had shown up the next morning. "Do you know where the girl lives?"

"It wasn't far from his place, it was St. Francis Avenue I think, he met her when she came into the market and they sort of hit it off," said Elena.

"Oh, I want to see him, I want to see my Tony—where is he?"

Maddox said, "I don't think you'd better do that, Mrs. Ramirez."

"Did somebody murder him?" asked Elena. "That'd be crazy, unless it was some robber, Tony got along good with everybody, nobody'd want to hurt Tony."

"Well, this is very helpful information," said Maddox, "thanks very much."

"But there's got to be a funeral!" wailed Mrs. Ramirez. "Where is he, where's my Tony?"

"Your husband had better contact the coroner's office," said Maddox, and she heaved and wailed again.

"My husband's dead—"

Maddox said to Elena, "Then maybe your husband had better attend to it, make arrangements."

She looked a little pale now, taking the implication that the body was in poor shape. "All right, where do we go?" He told her. She helped her mother up. "Come on, Mama, there's nothing more we can do for Tony now."

Maddox watched them out and Sue said, "He was going to dinner at the girl's apartment, and that night was about the time the doctors thought he died, wasn't it?"

"It was indeed. I think we'll have to locate Miss Teresa Alvarez. St. Francis Avenue," and he got out the *County Guide*. "It's only about a block long, just the other side of the freeway from Hobart."

"Had you thought to look in the phone book?" asked Sue, and he grinned at her.

"I was just about to." He looked and she was there, at least a T. Alvarez.

"Do you want company?"

"Not at the moment."

The apartment building on St. Francis was an old one, here since the twenties, but looking reasonably well maintained, with a palm tree at one side of the narrow front yard. In the row of mail slots Alvarez was listed at apartment eight upstairs. Getting no answer there, Maddox went downstairs to the door labeled *Manager*. A stocky pear-shaped man answered his ring.

"I'm trying to locate Miss Alvarez," said Maddox, "would you know where she works?"

"Oh, number eight. I was just about to go up there, she's been complaining there's something wrong with her sink or garbage disposal, it's stopped up."

"Is that so?" said Maddox. "Do you know where she works?"

"At the Sunset Nursing Home, it's somewhere down on Larchmont, I think." Maddox thanked him. "I hope there's nothing much wrong up there," said the manager. "The company owns this place is always damned slow to fix things that need more fixing than I can do."

Maddox looked up the address at the nearest pay phone. The nursing home was one of the older ones, taking up half a block with a little parking lot at one side. In the narrow lobby were two old people in wheelchairs staring vacant-eyed out the front window, and a receptionist in nurses' uniform was behind a high counter.

"Does a Miss Teresa Alvarez work here?" asked Maddox.

She was a thin blond woman, rummaging through some papers. "Oh, yes, Teresa's one of our cooks."

"I'd like to talk to her."

"Well, I'm afraid she'll be busy now, it's nearly time for the midmorning snacks to be taken around."

Maddox debated. "What time does she get off work?"

She was uninterested in him. "Well, we keep to the nurses' hours, the second staff comes on at three."

Maddox found a coffee shop up the block and had a cup of coffee. He wondered just what was wrong with Teresa Alvarez's sink and then told himself he was woolgathering. A girl couldn't have managed that messy, bloody business, and why should she want to? Tony Ramirez sounded like an amiable young fellow, gregarious and likable. But he'd been intending to go to her apartment for dinner that night, before his legs and lower torso had come to light.

At three o'clock he was back at the nursing home with D'Arcy. He asked the receptionist to produce Miss Alvarez and she was annoyed. "I'm just leaving and I have an appointment. What do you want to see her for? Don't you know what she looks like? Well, you can't miss her, she's a very big woman with braids." She bustled out before they could ask her any more questions.

"Braids?" said D'Arcy. But a minute later they spotted her as she came into the lobby; by the description it had to be her. She was at least five-ten, taller than Maddox, and she had a fine deep-bosomed figure, a little generous but well-proportioned. She had long glossy black hair in braids wound around her head. She was wearing a white uniform and a blue cardigan over it, and a shoulder bag swung from one arm. She had a bunch of keys in one hand. "Miss Alvarez?" said Maddox, and showed her the badge.

She looked surprised and suddenly wary. "Yes?"

"We've got a few questions to ask you," said Maddox, "about Tony Ramirez." She didn't say anything at first.

"What—about him?"

"You'd been dating him recently, hadn't you? At least that's what his mother and sister say."

"Well, yeah, some. I haven't seen him in a while, it wasn't anything serious. Why are the police asking about Tony?"

"He was supposed to be going to your apartment for dinner, three weeks ago tonight, we know that. Did he come?" She looked confused and wary. "You must remember," said Maddox. "It's not so long ago."

"Oh, yeah," she said slowly. "Yeah, he did. But he left early. I guess that's the last time I saw him."

"Did he say where he was going from there?" asked D'Arcy.

She shook her head. "I don't know any of his friends," she said hurriedly, and there was fear in her eyes; she wanted to get away from them. "I don't know where he went, I haven't seen him since."

"But he did come to dinner," said Maddox.

"Yeah, but he left about eight, I guess it was." She didn't ask again why they wanted to know. When neither of them asked her any more she headed for the door rapidly, and the keys trembled in her hand.

D'Arcy said to Maddox, "Are you thinking what I'm thinking? But it's impossible."

"She's a big strong girl, isn't she? Tony seems to have been a nice fellow, and good-looking, by what you could still tell. Maybe she's got another boy friend who's the jealous type. And the first body parts were found about a block and a half from her apartment. And her sink's stopped up."

D'Arcy made an incredulous sound. "It's impossible. A girl. She looks about twenty-five."

"It's too late to get a search warrant through today, but we can get one by tomorrow morning."

"But, Ivor, we must be seeing things—no girl would let somebody use her apartment for a thing like that."

"She knows something about it," said Maddox. "I think a lot about it. She was scared."

"She was," agreed D'Arcy, "but I still say it's impossible."

"Well," said Maddox placidly, "the lab will tell us."

* * *

Patrolman Jeff Stoner came on swing shift just before four o'clock, and sat yawning through the briefing in the watch commander's office. Sometimes he got fed up with this job. It could get damn boring, riding a squad for eight hours. Civilians might think it was an exciting job, but any uniformed cop could tell them different. It was just a job, the drunks and muggers and heisters between the traffic tickets. His wife worried about it, with the crime rate up; she didn't know how deadly dull it was most days. He'd been riding a squad for eight years, and he'd only fired his gun once on the job, at that escaped lunatic holding a knife on a girl. All the expensive ammunition got fired on the range, you had to keep up a certain score.

He went out to the parking lot with the rest of the men, and took over the squad from Gonzales. The squad was about due for a tune-up, it had been running a little rough lately. He started out cruising the beat. An hour later traffic began to build up as offices closed and people started home. He spotted an old Buick taking a chance, making a light on the amber at Sunset and Highland, but it wasn't worth a ticket. The traffic thinned out by six-thirty and at seven o'clock he called in a Code Seven; as usual he was starving. He went to a coffee shop on the boulevard and wished he could have a drink before dinner. He was back on the street by seven-thirty, radioing in that he was available.

At eight-forty he was cruising up Franklin on his routine way to take a run up Outpost Drive, when just as he was approaching Beachwood Drive a car came bucketing down there and swung wide onto Franklin burning rubber. It was doing at least fifty-five, and Stoner swore after it and switched on his red light and siren. The damn fool, this narrow old street and not many streetlights—it was an old Chevy, and in ten seconds after the siren went off behind it it slowed abruptly to about twenty. Stoner pulled up alongside it and motioned the driver into the curb. The Chevy pulled over obediently and Stoner parked behind it, got out, and put on his cap. He walked up to the driver's door and said, "You were exceeding the speed limit, sir, I'm afraid I'll have to write you a ticket."

"Oh," said the driver. He was alone in the car. There was one of the few streetlights here, and Stoner got a good look at him and thought, I've seen this guy someplace before. He got out his book of tickets, thinking—and just as he opened his mouth to ask for the driver's license it hit him. About thirty-five, short brown hair, flat ears with no lobes, a little squint in the left eye—It hit him all of a sudden. The two ex-cons wanted for a bank job over in Phoenix, Dieter and Hobson, and this was Dieter. It was a recent mug shot, the picture was back in the squad. And the word was, armed and dangerous. Stoner put the book away and slid the gun out of the holster. "Get out of the car," he said. "Keep your hands where I can see them—get out nice and slow and put your hands on your head."

"Say, what is this?" said the man in a pleasant voice. He opened the door and started to get out. Then he ducked down behind the door and suddenly there was a gun in his hand and he fired twice. Stoner felt the slug hit him, high on the left shoulder, and it was a big one and knocked him off balance. Dieter slammed the door and took off fast; he hadn't killed the engine. Stoner, on his knees, got off four shots at the car before it turned up Delmar. He said aloud, "ECP seven eleven," and he was bleeding all over the uniform but he crawled back into the squad and before he picked up the mike he wrote that down in his notebook.

Forty minutes later he was saying it to Stacey, at the Emergency ward at the hospital. "ECP seven one one, one of the old plates, and I'm positive it was Dieter."

"Okay," said Stacey, "we'll get on it. You're going to be okay, he just winged you."

"And my wife's going to start worrying harder after this," said Stoner. "And I'll probably have to buy a new uniform, damn it."

* * *

The DMV in Sacramento told them that the Chevy was registered to a Wilma Tandy at an address in South Pasadena. Rodriguez and Nolan got over there by nine o'clock on Saturday morning. It was an old court; the address was one of the rear units, and there didn't seem to be anybody home. They tried next door, and a pretty young woman in shorts holding a fretful baby said helpfully, "Oh, Wilma, well, I don't know where they are. No, she lives alone but she's had company lately, her sister and her husband and a friend of his. They probably went someplace to relax, it being Saturday, I think she said something about the beach."

"Hell," said Rodriguez in the car, "we'll have to stake it out, and they may not come back till all hours."

* * *

The search warrant for Teresa Alvarez's apartment was waiting on Maddox's desk at nine o'clock, and he collected Baker and Garcia from the lab; the van followed Maddox and D'Arcy up to St. Francis Avenue.

The pear-shaped manager peered at the warrant in bewilderment. "But what's it all about? You're police? What do you want with Miss Alvarez? She's a nice quiet tenant, seems like a nice girl."

"We'd be obliged to you if you don't mention this to her," said Maddox. "We'll probably be finished here before she comes home. There may not be anything in it at all. By the way, did you get around to looking at her drainpipes?"

"No, I never. I wasn't feeling so hot yesterday. But what are you looking for, what's the matter?"

They didn't tell him. He let them into the apartment, grumbling, and Maddox and D'Arcy watched the lab men start to work. Baker got the drainpipe under the sink dismantled while Garcia had a look at the bathtub. The cleaning up could look very thorough on the surface, but there were usually traces to be found by the scientific examination. Baker said, "There's a buildup of lime here, but some other gunk too, we'll run tests." He took samples of the anonymous residue.

Garcia looked in and said, "I'm trying the infrared on the tub, it won't take long."

The place was orderly enough, and Maddox was chiefly interested in the lab work, but he and D'Arcy looked through the apartment desultorily. She didn't seem to have many clothes. There was an address book by the phone and Maddox flipped through it. It didn't list many names, and only one male name, Carlos Alvarez, an address on Mariposa only about six blocks away.

They'd about decided to leave the place to the lab men and go back to base when they heard Baker say in naked astonishment, "Well, I'll be good and goddamned!"

They went back to the kitchen. He'd taken the garbage disposal apart and was standing there looking at something on the kitchen counter. "I don't believe it," he said. "The things people do—just look at that."

The little object on the counter was the top half of a finger, the nail still intact, about an inch of it. "My good Christ," said Maddox.

"From the garbage disposal, for God's sake," said Baker. "Did you ever see such a hell of a thing? Somebody put the hands down the garbage disposal."

"But the rest of him wasn't so easy to cut up small enough," said Maddox. "Did you say impossible, D'Arcy? By that address book she hasn't got another boy friend. Carlos will be a relative. Let's go get her."

At the nursing home the receptionist said, "You again. What do you want with Teresa? I'm afraid she's busy now, it's nearly time for the lunch trays to go around."

"That's just too bad," said Maddox, and showed her the badge.

"Police!" she said. "What on earth do the police want with Teresa?"

"Never mind," said D'Arcy, "just go and get her out here."

She came into the lobby slowly and looked at them without saying anything. "Tony didn't leave your apartment early that night, did he, Miss Alvarez?" said Maddox. "In fact, he didn't leave it at all. Somehow he got himself killed there. And then somebody cut up the corpse, somebody who didn't know much about anatomy, and scattered the pieces around here and there. What do you know about it?"

She went a curious sickly green color, and sweat stood out on her forehead. She said thinly, "That's not so, I don't know where you got that idea, why you think that?"

"We don't think, we know," said Maddox. "There are traces of blood in your bathtub drain, and the lab will tell us it's his type. And when the hands went down the garbage disposal, the top of one finger didn't get chewed up. It gave the lab a dandy fingerprint. Somebody got cut up in your apartment, Miss Alvarez. And we've only had one dismembered body showing up in the last three weeks, just the three weeks Tony Ramirez hasn't been around or seen his family."

"Oh, Mother of God," she said, and she collapsed onto the bench along the wall. "Mother of God. A fingerprint, and he did a hitch in the Army, they'll have his fingerprints."

"Thank you so much," said Maddox, "that's a shortcut. We'd like you to come back to the station and answer some questions now."

She went out ahead of them blindly and rode back to the station in numb silence. Maddox put her into the chair by his desk; nobody else was in the office. Sue and Daisy came over to listen in. Maddox told her punctiliously that she was entitled to call an attorney before talking to them, and she said, "I don't know any lawyers. I guess it don't matter."

"Would you like to tell us what happened, Miss Alvarez?" asked D'Arcy.

"I guess I got to. I just lost my temper, I got so mad at him—and then—"

"Why?" asked Daisy interestedly.

Teresa turned her head and looked at the two other women. "Maybe a woman'd understand it better, how I felt. See, I don't know many people here yet. When Ma died I came down here from the farm because my brother and his wife were here. Uncle Cris was taking over the farm and there wasn't no place for me. And," she said painfully, "a lot of young fellows, they don't go for a girl as big as me. Tony was the only fellow here who'd asked me out, and he was a real nice guy, I liked Tony a lot. I hoped he was going to ask me to marry him. And I'm a good cook, I liked to show him how good. That was the third time I'd asked him over for dinner. And I fixed everything real nice, I even had flowers on the table, and I fixed his favorite, beef tournedos, and made a salad and hot rolls and baked potatoes with sour cream, and I made a cake for dessert. And—and we had dinner." She stopped.

"Go on," said Maddox quietly.

"Oh, I was so mad at him!" she said in sudden remembered passion. "He said he was going to Las Vegas—and he knew I had a week's vacation coming up, and he was off work too, I'd thought we'd be going out a lot, the beach maybe and movies, maybe a nice restaurant. He didn't have to go right then, he could have stayed around for my vacation! And then, just as he finished his cake—the doorbell rang— and it was Mr. Price from across the hall—there are just two young guys live there together, I don't even know the other one's name, I just heard they both worked for Sears. And he said they'd set up a little poker party and one of the guys supposed to come hadn't showed up, and they were looking for somebody who'd maybe like to sit in—and Tony said sure, and went right with him—and he never came back until midnight! I'd expected we'd have a nice evening, maybe go out to a movie or just watch TV—and he ate my dinner and walked off and left me alone, stayed over there all that time just playing cards! I was just so mad at him I couldn't see straight—and then when he came back he never even apologized! I was in the kitchen when he came back—I hadn't cleaned up the dishes, but finally I thought I better—

and I was cleaning the skillet, Mama's old cast-iron one, and when he'd just said good night and started to go out, I just gave him a big bash on the head with it. I was so mad!"

"So that's how it happened," said Maddox. "And then you found you'd killed him."

She shuddered just once. "Oh, I was scared then," and for the first time she gave a little sob. "I was scared—I never meant anything like that! Yes, he was dead. I lived on a farm long enough to know the feel of something dead, and he was. And it was me who'd done it, even if I never meant to, and I'd go to jail for it."

"So you got the idea of getting rid of the body," said D'Arcy, fascinated against his will.

"I thought—if nobody ever found out who he was—nobody could ever connect him with me. People would think he'd just gone off somewhere."

"That was quite a job for a girl," said Maddox. "How did you manage it?"

"It was a terrible job, it took a long time."

"How did you do it?" asked D'Arcy.

"I knew I'd need a saw, and I know where Carlos keeps one in his garage. I went over there and got it, it was about one o'clock in the morning then. I put it back—afterwards—and he's never said nothing about missing it. And I did it—I cut him up. I'm pretty strong, and I've helped with the butchering on the farm. But it took a long while. I did it in the bathtub. And by the time I'd finished I was just awful tired, but then I had to get rid of the pieces some way. I put some of them in a big sack, and I've got one of those baskets on two wheels for carrying groceries in, I put the sack in that and dragged it down the street a couple of blocks and left it in a trash can. It was just starting to get light then. And I couldn't go to work that day, I was so tired and felt so awful." She sobbed once again. "The rest of it was still in the tub. What I really minded was—was the head. I just couldn't stand to look at it—it seemed to be sort of watching me—and I got a big market bag and put it in that and put it in the freezer."

"In God's name, why the freezer?" asked D'Arcy.

"I don't know," she said vaguely. "I don't use the freezer much. It was out of sight, right then. It wasn't until a couple of days later I got rid of the rest of it, at that cemetery."

"And the head was still in the freezer?" asked Daisy expressionlessly.

"Yes, but it kept bothering me that it was there, and I knew I ought to put it someplace it'd never get found, so finally I drove up to that big wild park and threw it down a hill under a lot of bushes." She added miserably, "I put the clothes in a Goodwill dumpster. There was only twenty bucks in his wallet, and I still got his wristwatch."

Maddox drew a long breath. "Well, that's all very interesting, Miss Alvarez."

"I suppose you're gonna take me to jail now. I'm sorry about Tony, I just lost my temper."

And inevitably, he thought, *Nor hell a fury like a woman scorned.* As she started out obediently ahead of them, he heard Sue say to Daisy in a faint voice, "My God, in the freezer—and the garbage disposal—and he was a real nice guy—honestly!"

* * *

Rodriguez and Nolan had spent a boring day taking turns on the stakeout, spelling each other sitting in Rodriguez' car parked outside the court in South Pasadena. It was after five when the old Chevy pulled up to the curb just ahead, and four people got out of it, two men and two women. Rodriguez and Nolan gave them time to reach the cement walk down the middle of the court, and followed them quietly. Ten feet behind them Rodriguez said, "Mr. Dieter!" One man spun around. Rodriguez and Nolan both had their guns out. The other man was Hobson, as expected. One of the women started to cry.

"I wouldn't advise either of you to go for the equalizer," said Nolan. He got the cuffs on both of them in twenty seconds.

"Back to the car, buddy boys," said Rodriguez. "You're heading for the slammer again. All because one of you forgot the laws when a squad car was watching."

* * *

There was usually some business for the night watch on Saturday night, but there was also that juvenile wanted for assault. "A fourteen-year-old kid," said Brougham. "They start younger and younger." He and Donaldson tried the address on Ardmore again; the kid hadn't come home last night, the blowsy woman had said, disinterested. This time he was home, if you could call it that, and they took him in. He was tall for his age but thin—probably most of the welfare money went for cheap wine. They only talked to him a few minutes.

He said, "Oh, hell, I needed some bread for the reefers, I owed

Eduardo five bucks for those joints and he said I don't pay up he'd turn his big brother on me, he's pretty high up in the Caballeros and a tough hombre. I didn't hurt that other kid much."

"How long have you been smoking joints?" asked Donaldson.

"I dunno, everybody does, but they cost. Ma'd spent all the welfare and there wasn't anything to snitch out of her purse."

They took him down to Juvenile Hall, and they didn't spend much time talking about Manuel. It was the kind of thing they saw too much of, and there wasn't anything to say about it. And then they got a call to a mugging out on Beverly, and later on another heist at a drugstore.

* * *

At least in March the weather was usually nice, not too hot or too cold. There would be about three months of it, and then would begin the foretaste of hell that was Southern California in summer and fall, and often it went on through most of October. Gonzales sometimes wondered why he'd come back here after his spell in the service, but the family was here and it was home.

He took over the squad at eight o'clock. The damned thing needed a tune-up job and he'd say something to the garage at the end of shift. He rode around for nearly three hours without getting any business, and then he was sent up to an address on Hillside Avenue off Outpost, unknown trouble.

These were nice houses up there, an old section but good. There was a couple waiting for him on the sidewalk, a Mr. and Mrs. Gaddis. They were middle-aged, agitated, and anxious but coherent.

"It's the Pollards next door," said the woman, "Greg and Louise Pollard. We're afraid something's happened to them—we've been neighbors here for twenty years, they're such nice people—they've been away on a trip, it was a big family reunion in Iowa, Greg took two weeks off from the bank, he's the manager of a Security Pacific bank in West Hollywood—"

"Now don't panic, Elly," said the man. "Let's tell it in order—"

"I am! They'd been back there two weeks, their daughter moved to Iowa when she got married—and we knew they were getting home yesterday, we'd had a postcard, and I saw them drive in about five o'clock and waved to them—and I went over about nine, I'd made a cake for Louise, but the house was all dark and nobody answered the bell, and I thought, well, they're tired after the long trip, went to bed early—but this morning—Oh, something must be terribly wrong—I couldn't get an answer to the bell, and I was worried, and I said to my husband—"

"Look, Officer," said the man, "we went and looked in the glass door from the patio and Louise is there on the floor, as if she's passed out— they're not drinkers, respectable ordinary people—and no sign of Greg —but the car's in the garage, and there's something wrong there and we thought the police—"

Gonzales had a look, and through the glass door he could see the woman's body on the floor of the kitchen, and he said, "Does anybody you know here have a key to the house? Well, it doesn't matter—" And he thought, they'd been gone for a couple of weeks. Out of state. They wouldn't have heard the warnings. He would bet on what the front-office boys and the doctors would find.

CHAPTER NINE

Maddox listened to what Bergner had to say, at four o'clock on Sunday afternoon, and in all the time he had been a detective he had never felt more helpless or impotent. Whatever kind of case there was on hand, there was somewhere to look, things to do, but here there was just nothing. It might be a ghost, faceless and anonymous, drifting invisibly around and leaving the lethal packages behind. Both the Pollards had died of the overdose of Demerol, Bergner had gone right for it and it showed up as soon as the tests were run. They had been out of the state for two weeks, wouldn't have heard anything about the case, the warnings to the public, and coming home after the long drive, they had probably stopped to pick up a few basic supplies, and got the hamburger as the easiest dinner to prepare.

"Sometime last night," said Bergner, "before midnight, I'd say.

They had both had a meal roughly five hours before death. My God, Maddox, how long is this going on? Eleven people dead now."

"Yes," said Maddox, "and not one damn thing we can do about it, doctor. There are nearly eleven million people in the LA area, and our lunatic might be any one of them. Well, thanks." He put the phone down. He was alone in the office, everybody else out hunting the heisters from the drugstore, who'd been a little drunk and taken a shot at the store manager. He sat staring out the window at the parking lot. Baker had finally gotten around to seeing the butchers at that Safeway, and they had agreed to be printed; none of them had made the print picked up on that Pliofilm wrapping. There was just nowhere to go on this damnable thing, nowhere to hunt.

D'Arcy and Rodriguez came in and he passed on the information. Rodriguez said, "Just as we expected, and not one damn thing to do about it. God."

"I suppose the neighbors there called the relatives to break the bad news," said Maddox. They were still sitting there not talking much when the dispatcher called to report a new homicide, and Maddox and Rodriguez got up tiredly.

When they got there it was a big sprawling lavish house on Crestview off Nichols Canyon Road, that haunt of the more than affluent. It was expensive gray brick with half timbering, with a lot of lawn in front, and a circular drive, professional landscaping. There were several cars in the drive, and only one looked as if it belonged to the house, a bright red Mercedes sports model. The others were older and humbler. The squad car was parked alongside the Mercedes, and the patrolman was Day, waiting for them on the low front porch. He said, "These damn stupid people, you'd think they'd have some respect for their own lives at least. And my wife likes that show. Says the girl was a pretty good actress."

"What's the setup?" asked Rodriguez.

"It's that newest TV star, Karen Bishop. She rented this place. She's dead in there and by the little I had from that crowd it's an accidental OD. What a crew, most of them had probably been taking this and that too, or more likely just smoking joints, but when they found she was dead they called us. There was a party here this afternoon and in the middle of it she passed out and after a while they realized she was dead."

In the huge living room filled with pretentious furniture about a dozen people were just standing around, one of the girls huddled on the couch sobbing loudly. They were all vaguely scruffy people, the casual sloppy clothes, a couple of men with beards. There was a big dining room off to one side with a wet bar. Day said behind them, "She's in the den down the hall. They thought she'd passed out from the drinks at first."

The body was lying on a big leather couch there, the body of a beautiful blond girl with a lovely figure, which they could see because she was wearing a bikini with just a short beach coat over it. Neither Maddox nor Rodriguez was much of a TV fan but she looked a little familiar, they'd have seen her pictures in the papers here and there. Day said, "She'd just made the big time in the last year or so, that show got some top ratings, and the damn little fool was in the money probably for the first time in her life. And then she throws it all away. The people out there admit she'd been taking pills along with the drinks."

"I suppose this'll be making the headlines," said Maddox. "We'd better get somebody out to take pictures." It was, of course, nearly the end of the day's shift.

The people in the dining room were eager to talk, up to a point. "Karen, she was a damn good kid," said one of the bearded men, "she didn't forget the friends she had before she made it to the top. We'd all known her from the time she was waiting on tables hoping for calls from central casting. She had us here to a bash every so often." Maddox gathered that they were all on the bottom rung of show business, of various types. The other bearded man was clutching a fancy guitar. The girl was still sobbing.

"She'd been taking pills of some kind?" asked Rodriguez.

"Yeah, I guess she'd been popping a few of the uppers, she usually did at a party."

"What about the rest of you?"

"Man, I don't mess with that stuff, no, sir, I don't know what anybody else maybe had, I just had a few drinks. Some of the girls and Karen had gone in the pool while the rest of us listened to some music. People were kind of wandering around, know what I mean, and Karen had a couple of servants coming in later to fix dinner. It wasn't until about an hour ago we missed her, and went looking and found her passed out, and Ken realized she wasn't breathing—" It was another stupidity, and the place might be harboring quite a lot of dope. By the smell in the room, there had been marijuana smoked; they would have gotten rid of the evidence before calling the cops. Baker came up to take pictures. They got names and addresses and eventually let the partyers go. When the caterers showed up they sent them away. Nobody could tell them anything about her family, except that she'd come from back East somewhere.

"She'd have had an agent," said Rodriguez. "He'll know all that." The morgue wagon came for the body. They found a little horde of cocaine in one of the bathrooms, a lot of reefers, and prescription pills in her bedroom. "Quaaludes," said Rodriguez. "If she'd been mixing these with alcohol, good-bye. You'd think anybody'd know better. But they never think it can happen to them. You can't even feel sorry for her, she was just a damn fool." Too many of the people in show business were on the drug scene; probably not the serious ones, the really talented ones; but the gaudy world of TV with its fantastically high salaries, its feverish atmosphere where a star today was forgotten tomorrow, wasn't conducive to stability of any kind.

Rodriguez found the name of the agent in her address book, both office and home phone numbers, and called him at home. His name was Bernie Erdman and he was upset and annoyed to hear the news. "My God," he said, "I told the little fool to lay off that damned stuff, but she thought it was the in thing to do. And just as they were going to start filming the episodes for next season too, dammit. I suppose I'm stuck for arranging the funeral and settling all her bills. I don't think she'd made a will. No, I don't know anything about any relations."

"There'll be an autopsy, and the coroner's office will let you know when the body can be released."

"Yeah, yeah," he said dispiritedly.

It was after seven then. Maddox dropped Rodriguez in the parking lot at the station and went home. Hearing about it, Sue said, "I picked up that program once, I thought it was pretty silly, but it's evidently been popular. I just hope we don't get reporters cluttering up the station."

"It'll die down in a couple of days," said Maddox. "I think I need a drink before dinner."

"It's keeping warm in the oven," said Margaret. "Bourbon and soda?"

"Fine."

*   *   *

They got the reporters on Monday, of course, and probably the coroner's office did too, but there wasn't much to tell them and they didn't hang around long. The night watch had left another heist and another burglary. Maddox said, reading that report, "At least this doesn't seem to have been Leach again, to send Joe's blood pressure up. Just a break-in while the people were at a movie, and not much missing."

The victims came in in the middle of the morning to give them a list, and on the chance that it had been an amateur job that was added to the hot list for the pawnbrokers. They now had two new heisters to look for, with fairly good descriptions, and Rodriguez was downtown with the latest victim to see if he could make a mug shot.

Maddox hadn't asked for priority on the autopsy but at the end of the afternoon Dr. Whitman called him from the coroner's office. "We got to the Bishop girl right away, we had the press around and wanted it out of our hair. My God, these stupid kids. It was the combination of Quaaludes and alcohol, she was loaded."

"What we figured," said Maddox. "They never think it can happen to them."

There were headlines in the final editions that night, but the press didn't show up again on Tuesday morning. She hadn't been a really big star, and by next week nearly everybody would have forgotten Karen Bishop.

Nearly as soon as they got in Sue and Daisy were called out on a child molestation, and were gone all morning. When they came back about twelve-thirty Sue looked into the communal office and said, "You can take me to lunch. What a thing. We've been down at Juvenile Hall since nine o'clock, and talking to the head-doctors. The little girl wasn't hurt much, thank God. It was an eleven-year-old retarded boy, lived on the same block. Now we know he likes to play with the little girls, I trust they'll tuck him away somewhere safe where he can't get at them."

The witness picked out a mug shot so they had somewhere definite to look for that heister, but he was off parole and they couldn't locate him.

Rodriguez was just back in the middle of the afternoon when they had a call to a new body, and they both went out to look. The address was Norton Avenue, a shabby, old, small single house needing a paint job, and the body was the body of a big heavy man in grimy undershirt and shorts. He was lying on his back on the living-room floor, and there was a butcher knife in his chest. The uniformed man said, "His name's Murphy, William Murphy, about all I got from her." Across the room a little terrified-looking woman was crouched in a chair watching them and shaking all over. "Mrs. Murphy?" said Rodriguez, and she nodded jerkily. "What happened here?"

"You leave her alone," said a fierce voice, and they looked up. A boy was standing in the door to the kitchen off this room. He was a boy about fifteen, stocky and dark. "She didn't do it, I did."

"Oh, Eddie," she said weakly.

He said defiantly, "I said I'd kill him someday, the way he treated Mom—you're cops, I'll tell you all about it. I don't care what you do to me for it, it don't matter. He was just an old bum"—his face twisted in anguish—"he was always getting drunk and beating Mom and me too—"

"Oh, Eddie," she was crying. There was a bruise on her face, and she had the beginning of a black eye.

"I don't care, he done it once too much—he took all the money Mom had left, and he went out and got drunk again, and I'd just got home from school when he came back and started beating on her, and I just couldn't stand it no more, I got that knife and stuck it in him and I'm glad I did!"

"Oh, Eddie, they'll put you in jail—"

"I don't care what they do, anyways he won't beat you up again," said the boy fiercely.

She raised wet pitiful eyes to the men. "It's true enough, he's been like that ever since I married him, he was always knockin' me around and he never kept a job, he'd get drunk and get fired, ever since Eddie was a baby I had to go out to work to earn money for groceries to keep us alive, and he'd get hold of it when he could to buy more liquor—oh, please, don't be hard on Eddie, he's only a boy and he was thinking of me when he did it—"

"I'm glad I did it," said the boy hoarsely. "I called the cops because I had to tell you why I did it."

Maddox said, "Why didn't you leave him, Mrs. Murphy?"

She looked at him as uncomprehendingly as if he'd said it in a foreign language. "Why, I was married to him. I couldn't do that, we were married in the church and you can't get out of the promises you make to God." The uniformed man said something under his breath. "You won't be hard on Eddie, mister?"

Rodriguez said, "We'll have to take him in, down to Juvenile Hall, Mrs. Murphy. Eventually there'll be a hearing before a judge. I don't think he'll go to jail."

"Oh," she said, relieved.

"I don't care," said the boy miserably, "I always said someday I'd kill him for the way he treated Mom."

They sent the boy down to Juvenile Hall, and of course there would be the paperwork on this. At the station Maddox handed the rest of the responsibility over to Ralston; it was Juvenile business.

At the end of shift Sue looked in and said, "You won't be late?"

"Right behind you," said Maddox.

She grimaced. "That woman, that poor silly woman, staying by a brute like that. I took down her statement. What gets into some women—"

"Well, nothing much will happen to Eddie, he'll be put on probation until he's eighteen."

"I know," said Sue, "but if she'd had the common sense to get away from him it needn't have happened at all."

"Take care on the freeway," said Maddox.

*   *   *

Nobody had caught up to any of the suspected heisters yet, but they were still out looking. On Wednesday afternoon Maddox and Dowling had just brought one in to question and were shepherding him toward an interrogation room when a tall thin old lady hesitated in the door of the office and asked, "Are you the detectives? The man at the desk out in front said to come back here and see the detectives."

Maddox took her across the hall and said, "You can talk to Sergeant Hoffman and Detective Maddox."

She looked slightly relieved at the sight of two other women, and said, "Oh, thank you."

Sue offered her a chair. "How can we help you?"

She sat down and looked at them consideringly. She was a nice-looking old lady, smartly dressed in a gray suit. She said, "My name's Holland, Claudia Holland. And I don't know that I ought to be here at all, I don't know what the police could do about it, if anything, and I feel it's going behind Grace's back, and we've been friends for forty-five

years, since we were both young married women. If Adam was still here
he'd know what to do—my husband—but he died last year, it's been
lonely, and of course Dave died the year before, that's Grace's husband,
Dave King." They were listening to her patiently. "It's difficult when
you've been used to having a man around," she said ruefully. "But
that's just it—the reason I'm here. Because Adam always talked to me
sensibly about money, he took it for granted I had common sense, but
Dave wasn't like that. He always managed everything, Grace never
knew a thing about his affairs, and she's always been a little flighty, if
you know what I mean. He just handed money over to her and told her
what she could spend and that was that. Well, I'm sorry if I'm being
long-winded but I wanted to explain the background."

"Yes, take your time," said Daisy.

She drew a breath. "Well, when Dave died it was all of a sudden, he
died of a heart attack, he was only sixty-four—and Adam and I were
both surprised that he didn't leave all the money tied up, in trust or
something. But he didn't, it all came to Grace unconditionally."

"Excuse me," said Sue, "but is there much money?"

"Well, I should think so, quite a lot, Dave inherited a lot from his
father and he was pretty shrewd about investing. He had a Buick
agency in West Hollywood. And at the time, of course, there was the
stockbroker he'd always dealt with to look after it, it's all in stocks and
bonds—Mr. Wade at Hammond and Forsythe downtown, he and Dave
were friends for years, but he was older than Dave and died about six
months later. And you see, that young stockbroker looking after the
estate now, Grace is just another client to him, he doesn't know her,
doesn't know that she hasn't, well, much sense about money. If she
told him to sell some stock he'd just do it for her, do whatever she said
for the commission."

Sue was enlightened. "You think your friend's acting foolishly and
investing in the wrong things? But, Mrs. Holland—"

She said bluntly, "I think she's being swindled, if somebody can't
stop it. She was telling me all about it yesterday, and it worried me, I've
been thinking about it ever since and I made up my mind to tell the
police about it, even if Grace will be furious about that. I don't know
much about the stock market—Adam was a doctor, on the staff of
Hollywood Presbyterian—but I do know it goes up and down, and
evidently it's been down lately, and Grace hadn't been getting in as
much money as usual, she was worried about it. And I had lunch with

her yesterday and she was telling me all about this, how she was going to make a wonderful new investment and get a high profit on it. She'd seen this ad in the paper under 'Business Opportunities,' and answered it, and the more she told me about it the less I liked it, and I told her so. It sounds like a swindle to me and I told her that, and she just laughed and said I was a suspicious old lady and Mr. Wainwright and Mr. Austin were very nice gentlemen and sounded as if they knew a lot about business."

"Mr. Wainwright and Mr. Austin," said Daisy.

"That's right, she'd met them just the night before, they'd arranged an appointment with her on the phone and come to see her. It's something to do with an investment in South Africa, some big agricultural project, and they told her she'd make a thirty percent profit on the investment in six months, but they wanted a cashier's check because the actual investing had to be through a Swiss bank and they'd only take cash."

Daisy sat up. "Fishy," she said.

"Well, I thought so. As far as I know Swiss banks would take a check like any other bank. And if she gives them a cashier's check—she was talking about thirty thousand dollars—they could just walk off with it and disappear. I told her she ought to discuss it with Mr. Fox, he's the new young broker, but she just said there wasn't any need, she'd just tell him to sell off some stock that hadn't been paying and he'd do it. And I suppose he will," said Mrs. Holland. "If she told him what she was doing I suppose he'd realize there was something funny about it, and maybe she'd listen to him, but he'll just think she wants the money for some other kind of investment, he doesn't know what a fool she is about money. And I don't know what the police could do about it. I mean, there isn't any proof that these two men are crooks, and I don't know how you could find out."

Sue and Daisy looked at each other. "When is she going to meet them again, do you know?" asked Sue.

"I don't know, she was going to call Fox this morning. I don't know how long it might take to get the money. And I don't suppose she'd listen to the police either, even if you say they sound like crooks."

"That's the difficulty," said Sue. She got up. "Wait a minute, I'd like to pass this on to Ivor." She went across the hall. Maddox had just come back and she crooked a finger at him. "We've got a story I'd like you to listen to." He followed her to the other office and Mrs. Holland told the story all over again. He heard her out, massaging his jaw absently, and asked, "When did Mrs. King first contact these men?"

She thought. "Last Saturday, I believe. She called the number in the ad and talked to the Wainwright man and he set up an appointment for Monday evening at Grace's house."

"Has she told them she's going to invest the money?"

"She said she'd think about it and let them know. Think about it! One day she takes to think about it, and decides to hand over thirty thousand dollars to two complete strangers! I expect she called them last night to say she would."

"What do you think about it, Ivor? There's really nothing we can do about it, fishy as it sounds. The woman's an adult and has control over her own money."

"The only thing that occurs to me," said Maddox, "is that they seem to be in one hell of a hurry to lay hands on the money. And no telling how many other gullible people answered the ad—I wonder how long it had been running—"

"Oh, I can tell you that," said Mrs. Holland. "Grace had been reading that column lately and she said it was in for the first time on Saturday."

"Do tell," said Maddox. "But however many other suckers they attracted, there wouldn't be many with thirty thousand to invest. That's going to be a windfall for them."

"Oh, that was another thing I forgot to tell you, when you said 'hurry' it reminded me. They told her she'd have to act quickly because the investment was only being offered in this country for the rest of this month."

Maddox said, "Two very persuasive gentlemen. I'll bet they're gentlemanly and put up a nice front. Did she say what they looked like, what age they are?"

"She just said they were nice and knew what they were talking about, I couldn't tell you that."

"Well," said Maddox, "we know the MO. It just occurs to me, when they seem to be in a hurry to get hold of the money, they may be one step ahead of the law somewhere else and figuring to get a little stake and lie low in Mexico or somewhere for a while."

"NCIC," said Daisy.

Mrs. Holland looked uncomprehending. "Well, we can have a look and see if there are any suggestive wants," said Maddox.

The National Crime Information Center, based in Washington, was in contact with every police force in the nation on a daily basis. It dealt only with current crimes and criminals of the most serious kind, and when a case was cleared or filed it came off the NCIC list. Sue went down to Communications with Maddox, and he asked one of the girls to run it off for him, settled at a viewer to look at the microfilm. It was a long list, and Sue kept asking, "Have you spotted anything?" until he told her to go away and stop nagging him.

At ten minutes to six he came into the office where Sue and Daisy were still talking with Mrs. Holland and said, "There's a possible make. Two jokers wanted for a bunco scheme in Pittsburgh, since about three weeks ago. There's a warrant out. Arthur Dawson and Joel Biddle."

"That's not much to say these are the same men," said Mrs. Holland. "Was it the same kind of swindle?"

Maddox smiled at her. "I don't know, the details don't get onto that list, just names and types of crimes. I sent off a teletype to the Pittsburgh force, and we should know something by tonight or tomorrow morning."

"But she's going to get the money as soon as she can, and hand it right over!"

"Take it easy," said Maddox. "If it looks as if there's any connection, there are things we can do."

"Well, I certainly hope so. Will you let me know?"

Sue said, "Of course you're concerned about your friend. We'll let you know what happens." She had already given her her address and gave Daisy the other one; the flighty Mrs. King lived in West Hollywood.

* * *

The night watch had just drifted in and Stacey had some more snapshots of his kids to pass around. The middle of the week was usually slow and they were surprised when the phone rang so early. Stacey answered it.

"Sergeant Canfield, Bunco, Pittsburgh," said a pleasant tenor voice. "We had a query from your office about an hour ago, I just got back from a call and found it. On Biddle and Dawson, don't tell me you've picked them up?"

"I don't know what you're talking about," said Stacey. "It must have been the day watch." He put a hand over the phone and asked, "Anybody know about contacting the Pittsburgh boys on something?" Donaldson had just found Maddox's note, and passed it over. Stacey scanned it rapidly and said into the phone, "Okay, I'm with it, we'd like to know the details of what they're wanted for. There's a possibility that they may be here."

"That'd be a step in the right direction," said Canfield. "They're a pair of slick con men, they've both served time for it, one count apiece in New York, and Dawson one here in our state pen. We don't know how many suckers they took here, they were promising a thirty percent profit on some investment overseas, and asking for cashier's checks on the tale that that's all the Swiss banks would accept. It was the old Ponzi racket. By their records, they'd hang around one place for six months or so, paying over just enough money in the supposed dividends to keep the suckers sweet, and acting as advertisements to rope more in, and then they'd quietly fade away to happier hunting grounds. We got onto them by way of a smart old lady who spotted it as a con game and told us, and we planted a couple of men at the next meeting with them acting like more suckers, and we collected Biddle's prints from a coffee table—"

"That's a no-no," said Stacey, "it wouldn't hold in court," and Canfield laughed.

"Too right, but it was one hell of a fluke. Sometimes Providence looks after the hardworking cops. That very night the old lady had a burglary, so those boys were printing the place, and ran that one through records and there was Biddle, the Feds had his prints. We got his mug shot from New York and found out he and Dawson worked together. The old lady had been roped in by a friend who'd handed over ten grand to them. Hence the warrant."

"Oh, so thanks very much," said Stacey. "We'll get back to you if anything comes of it." Maddox had asked for any information to be relayed, so Stacey called him at home.

"That's very nice," said Maddox. "I think we may do Pittsburgh some good."

* * *

He got to the brokerage downtown when it opened its doors at ten o'clock on Thursday morning, and saw Fox, who was red-haired and friendly. "We know these men are wanted for the same con game back East." The mug shots had been wired, and they'd see what Grace King said about them. "We thought you should know about it for your client's protection."

Fox was incredulous. "The King woman fell for a thing like that? My God! She called me yesterday and told me to sell off some mutual funds that had been down, I didn't think much about it."

"Have you sold them yet?"

"No, I thought they might go up a few points in the next couple of days. You want me to stall on it? Yes, I see. My God, these damn-fool females."

"You may not have to," said Maddox. It was his day off and he should have turned it over to somebody else but he was interested in this, and he went up to West Hollywood to see if Grace King was home.

She was a little round woman with fluffy hair professionally dyed a discreet pale blond, and she'd once been very pretty. She looked at the badge, asked him in to an attractive living room, and he showed her the mug shots. "Would these be Mr. Wainwright and Mr. Dawson?"

She was amazed. "Why, yes, where did you get their pictures?" Both the men were good-looking; he could imagine that in natty clothes they'd make an excellent appearance, and con men were always smooth talkers. He told her about them in words of one syllable and she stared at him.

"You mean they're criminals? I can't believe it, they seem to be so knowledgeable about investments, they were so nice! You mean they were going to steal my money? Claudia said she thought something was queer about it, but it sounded just fine to me—"

"There are a lot of characters around up to games like this, Mrs. King, and they aim at people with money to invest. You ought to consult your broker before you make any changes."

She was looking subdued now. "Oh, yes, I see. Are you going to arrest them?"

"That's right," said Maddox. He drove back to the office and handed the mug shots to Rodriguez. "It's all yours, she identified them. I'm going home to enjoy the rest of my day off."

Rodriguez said, "And not even our case, just to oblige Pittsburgh." Mrs. King had given Maddox the phone number she had called and Rodriguez got hold of a supervisor at the phone company, identified himself, and asked for the address attached to it. Correctly she called back to be sure she was really talking to police, and said, "It'll take a little while, sir."

"I know," said Rodriguez. Half an hour later she called to say that the number belonged to a unit of the Sierra Vista Motel on Allesandro Street. Rodriguez looked to see who was in, and D'Arcy was brooding over a report at his desk. They drove out to the motel, found the manager, and showed him the mug shots. "Mr. Wainwright and Mr. Dawson," he said. "They're salesmen on a business trip from Atlanta."

"Salesmen all right," said Rodriguez. "Which unit are they in?"

"Number four, but why are the police asking? You don't mean they're criminals of some kind? My God, I can't believe it—well, I think they're in, they don't usually go out early—they've been here about three weeks—"

Rodriguez knocked on the door of number four, and the man who opened it was Joel Biddle, freshly shaven and genial. Rodriguez showed him the badge and said, "In." In the little motel room with the twin beds, other neutral furniture, Dawson was just coming out of the bathroom. They had both been getting ready to go out, probably to call on another sucker, and they both looked like a million dollars, in tailored business suits with crisp white shirts and conservative dark ties, well-polished shoes. They looked like a pair of high-class stockbrokers about to attend a meeting of the board, and a lot of people would trust them on sight.

"It's the fuzz," said Biddle. "I didn't think they were that close behind, dammit."

"Oh, hell and damnation," said Dawson. He just sounded disgusted. "How the hell did you know we were here? We haven't been in California in five years."

"We have our methods," said D'Arcy. "They don't call it the long arm of the law for nothing, Mr. Dawson. You're both under arrest."

The con men never had any tendency to violence, and they were old hands, knew when they were licked. "Give us ten minutes to pack the damn suitcases," said Biddle.

"Let's have a look at them first," said D'Arcy. In the side pocket of one suitcase was fourteen thousand dollars in cash, and an additional ten thousand in the other one. "You've been doing fairly well, but you were looking forward to Mrs. King's thirty grand."

Dawson looked immensely surprised. "Now you're not going to tell me it was the King woman who blew the whistle on us? I don't believe it, she's heaven's gift to anybody wants to take her in. She'd swallow anything."

"We'll let you wonder about it," said Rodriguez.

Biddle said mournfully, "So we get sent back to Pennsylvania, and that damned joint's been there about a hundred years and the beds are like rocks and the food lousy—I'd settle for one of your nice new pens."

D'Arcy laughed. "Sorry, Pennsylvania's got priority on you, gents."

When they delivered them to the jail and booked them in, Rodriguez called Canfield in Pittsburgh. "We've got your two con men all safely stashed away. Will somebody be out to fetch them or do you want us to ferry them back? We're a little busy here."

"So are we," said Canfield, "God knows, but somebody'll be out to get them. Probably tomorrow or next day. I might come myself, I've never been in California, not that I'd have a chance to see much of it on an errand like that. We'll let you know."

* * *

In the middle of Friday afternoon a burglary call came in and Feinman took it. The address was on Outpost Circle, a big old two-story place, and the uniformed man was Gonzales. He said, annoyed, "I don't know why these things have to happen when the end of the shift's coming up. There's not much to it, just another break-in. This is Detective Feinman, Mr. Lukens."

The householder was a heavy-set man about fifty, with a bald head and a pugnacious jaw. He said, "The bastard might have killed me." He had a nasty-looking gash on the top of his bald head that had been bleeding freely.

Feinman said, "You'd better have that seen to, sir."

"Oh, I will, I will. My wife'll see to that, and she's going to have a fit, her mink stole and all her jewelry and the new portable TV—" He was nearly ready to have a fit himself.

"What happened?" asked Feinman.

"I'll tell you what happened all right," said Lukens. "My God, these punks walking in to rob a place when somebody's home in broad daylight—but it could be he didn't know anybody was here, because my car's in for a tune-up and my wife's out in hers, so the garage is empty. I'm just getting over the flu, I've been off work all week, and I was taking a nap upstairs. The first I heard was him coming up the stairs, I was only half awake, I thought it was Marion at first but I hadn't expected her back so early—"

"Was the house locked?" asked Feinman.

"In the middle of the afternoon with me here? No. I got up and put on my shoes and went out to the hall, and here's this punk just going down toward the back bedrooms, cool as be damned, and I cussed at him and I tackled him—he jumped around and we tangled." He was patting the cut with his handkerchief. "But like I say I was only half awake, and he was a lot younger than me—I hope I did him some damage, but he got in a lucky hit and knocked me clean out, I figure I fell against the table up there and that's how I got this. I don't think I was out long, but long enough for him to grab Marion's things and get away."

"Could you describe him?" asked Feinman.

"Well, he was a hefty young guy," said Lukens. "Maybe twenty-five, long brown hair, about all I can say. At least I broke his glasses for him."

"Glasses?"

"Yeah, when I came to I found them on the floor there. I seem to remember knocking them off his face, and when I came to look, I guess they'd hit the mirror on the wall, anyway they're broke all to hell and he didn't pick up the pieces."

"Let's have a look," said Feinman.

Upstairs in the front hall he surveyed the broken glasses. The frames were still there, unbroken, ordinary dark brown frames, and the lenses were in a number of pieces but not crushed. He wondered if anything could be done with them. There had been a rash of these daylight burglaries, and it could be that a number of young punks were just wandering around doing what came naturally, but it also could be that it was just one young punk. He went downstairs and called the lab.

"I may have a funny kind of job for you," he said to Baker. "Come look at it and tell me what you think."

Baker came up in a van and Gonzales went back to the squad just as the Traffic shift would be changing. Baker looked at the broken glasses and rubbed his jaw. "I see what you mean," he said. "Hell, Feinman, how many people in this city wear glasses?"

"If they're prescription lenses," said Feinman, "I suppose they could be identified eventually."

"Eventually!" said Baker. "Do you have any idea how many optome-

trists and ophthalmologists and eye clinics there are in the whole L.A.
area? . . . Neither have I. And they'll all be busy, they'll all have a lot
of clients. And these lenses might have been prescribed for somebody
five years back—those places will only keep records so long—or by
some doctor who's quit practice."

"Don't set up roadblocks," said Feinman. "Have you got one of
those machines that reads eyeglass prescriptions right off the bat?"

"No," said Baker. "But they've got one at the big lab downtown."
He began to pick up the pieces carefully and stow them in an evidence
bag. "Like working a jigsaw puzzle yet," he grumbled. "Fit all these
pieces together. But I suppose we'll have to give it a try."

*   *   *

As Maddox had predicted, the headlines about the big important
TV starlet dying of drugs had occupied the papers for only a couple of
days. There had been a lavish funeral up at Forest Lawn, and the other
actors and actresses on that popular show had shown up to make the
emotional statements for the press—she had a great career ahead of her
—a terrible tragedy—she was such a warm sincere girl, and a gifted
actress—and then it was over. It was in the cards, thought Maddox
cynically, that all those people would have forgotten her in a week's
time. The producers would find some other rising young starlet to fill in
on the show.

Very likely, the only people who would really miss her were the
impecunious old friends she hadn't forgotten, had invited to the bashes
with free food and drinks and reefers and a little coke for whoever
wanted it.

He wondered if her agent had ever located any relatives. If she
hadn't made a will, the state would come in for whatever she left, but
even considering the money she'd been earning, she'd been throwing it
around and there might not be much after all.

And then he forgot about her too.

*   *   *

As usual the night watch was busy on Saturday night, the wild ones
out roaming the streets. Quite early in the evening there was a heist at
a small independent market on Third, and it was a Mexican place
which catered to that population with a lot of imported items from
below the border, and the man had about four words of English. They
communicated with him hardly at all, he kept shrugging his shoulders

and saying, *"No sé, no sé,"* and in the end an exasperated Brougham said, "Oh, for God's sake, let Rodriguez talk to him in the morning."

"Or D'Arcy can start practicing what he's been learning," said Stacey. "Dammit, you'd think they'd learn the language if they want to live here."

There was a mugging on Vine, with the victim hurt badly enough to end up in Emergency. Then things quieted down until ten o'clock, when another heist got called in, a liquor store on Melrose. Stacey went out on it with Donaldson.

The owner was talking nineteen to the dozen to the uniformed man, repeating what he had probably said before, and a diffident-looking young fellow was standing in the background. "Yes, sir," the patrolman was saying patiently, "you told me that. These are the detectives, sir, you can tell them—"

"But, Mr. Jacobs—"

The owner started to tell the new audience all about it. "He came in just as I was clearing the register, getting ready to close at ten—and I'll be damned but he looked like a real gent, you wouldn't look at him twice except that he had such good clothes and even a hat, he looked like a customer who'd be good for a bigger sale than average, and he came up to the counter and I said what can I do for you and he brings out this gun, Jesus Christ, last thing I expected—"

"But, Mr. Jacobs—"

"And he took all the cash out of the register, made me hand it over, it must have been around six hundred bucks in cash—Saturday's always a good day—and I'll be damned but he thanked me for it! And he goes out like he had all the time in the world—Frank here didn't see a thing, he was in the back, but—"

"Listen," said the other one in a louder voice, "I've been trying to tell you, Mr. Jacobs. I can help the cops get him—I got his plate number for you!"

Jacobs dried up and they all stared at the clerk, a thin blond young man. "What?" said Stacey.

"That's right. Like Mr. Jacobs said, I was in the stock room, but I heard him say, 'Lift 'em,' to Mr. Jacobs and I knew it was a holdup, and I just sneaked a look to see what clothes he had on and I went out the back way and onto the street, and when he came out I followed him, it was easy, there were people around and he didn't notice. He got into a car in the parking lot half a block up, and it's pretty well lighted

and I memorized the plate number and wrote it down for the cops."
He handed over a page torn out of a notebook.

"Well, I will be eternally damned!" said Donaldson. "Don't tell me
we're about to catch up to Dapper Dan!"

* * *

They shot the plate number up to the DMV in Sacramento, and in
five minutes the answer came back: the car was a Dodge registered to
Chester Cook at an address on Rosewood Street in Hollywood. They all
went over there. It was the usual old apartment building in that old
part of town, but they couldn't get an answer to the bell. They left
Donaldson to stake it out, but Cook hadn't shown by the end of the
shift. When Donaldson came back to report that Stacey grunted.

"The day men are going to be interested in this one."

* * *

They were interested. Maddox and Rodriguez shot over to Rosewood
Street at eight-thirty, and they got an answer to the doorbell at that
apartment. The man who opened the door was a nice-looking fellow
about thirty-five; he was medium-sized, with brown hair and intelligent
eyes. He looked at the badge in Maddox's hand impassively.

"Mr. Cook? We've got some questions to ask you about the robbery
of a liquor store last night. We'd like you to come in to answer some
questions."

"Oh, really?" he said in an urbane pleasant voice.

"Does anybody else ever drive your car?"

He looked surprised. "Why, no, I'm unmarried and I live alone."

"We have some evidence that your car was used on this robbery.
We're taking you in to answer some questions."

He came with them quietly, and in the interrogation room at the
station he accepted a cigarette from Rodriguez, and said gravely,
"Thank you. May I ask what your evidence is?"

They had the admittal about the car, Maddox told him. "The store
owner seems to be positive that he'd recognize the man, and the clerk
can swear to the plate number. Would you like to try to explain it away,
Mr. Cook?"

He sat quietly for a moment, looking oddly relaxed in the uncomfort-
able hard chair, smoking meditatively. Then he gave them an engaging
grin and said, "I was just figuring the odds, and they're still in my
favor."

"What do you mean by that?" asked Rodriguez, taken aback.

Cook laughed. "I decided a long time ago that I don't like to work eight hours a day," he said frankly. "I'm a loner. I've never had many friends or wanted any. I like to read. I'm a passable bookkeeper and I took an accounting course once, I could get a decent job, but I just don't like to work that hard. I don't ask much of life—I've never cared for the expensive amusements, I'll take a drink before dinner but that's about all. I like a decent place to live, it doesn't have to be fancy, and enough to eat, and a few nice clothes, that's all. And a while back I figured it out that this is the best way to have it all, without slaving in an office." He looked at them calmly. "You'll be taking my prints, so you'll find out that I've done two stretches for armed robbery. But just look at the odds, gentlemen. The first time I was picked up—by a fluke —it was after I'd pulled at least a hundred and fifty jobs, enough to live on for a long time. Then I had a nice room all to myself up at Folsom, and pretty good food at the state's expense, and the prison library got me whatever I wanted to read, and that was only two years. I've never worried about women much, and I was brought up in an orphanage, there's no family to feel disgraced by me." He laughed. "So you drop on me again. The reason you missed me last night—oh, I know your techniques, you had that plate number right away—was that after that job I went to a movie, one of the all-night places was running an old one I wanted to see." His intelligent eyes were amused. "The second time I got dropped on, I couldn't count the jobs I'd done, six years' worth of nice quiet living. And it used to be the courts handed out the stiffer sentences if you'd been in before, but they don't do that now. I've been out this time for five years, and that's maybe four, five hundred heists—some of them up in the San Francisco area, Bakersfield, Ventura, before I came down here. I've never hurt anybody and I never would. Those places are all insured. And so now I'll spend another couple of years in the joint—at the state's expense—maybe even three, but that's all right with me. I figure the odds are all in my favor. It's one hell of an easy way to make it through life."

CHAPTER TEN

On Tuesday morning, Baker called Feinman and said, "That was one hell of a job you handed us, the jigsaw puzzle, but we got all the pieces together finally and I got the prescription from the lab downtown. We'll be sending it out to every eye doctor in the county, but it'll be a while before we hear anything, if ever. You realize those glasses might have been made by any optical company in the country, don't you?"

"Yes, it's a long shot maybe but something to try." They now had another heist to work, since Sunday night, and it looked like the same man of the week before, who had been drunk and taken a shot at the drugstore manager. And just how stupid could you get, wondered Feinman. You'd think a man would want all his wits about him, pulling a heist, and if they didn't catch up to this one he might end up by killing somebody. There were indictments and arraignments coming up in court this week to waste a little time too. But when in midafternoon there was another daylight burglary, he looked back over the reports and began to think seriously that all of those had been the work of one man. They only had one vague description but he seemed to have hit at about the same time of day, from what they could deduce in most of the cases. Feinman was going to be interested to see if any eye doctor could identify that prescription and attach a name to it.

* * *

It was a discouraging job, finding the possible suspects and bringing them in to question, and the only reason they went on doing it was that sometimes it paid off. At least, Maddox was reflecting on Wednesday afternoon, nothing new had been heard from the lunatic, apparently nobody had gotten any of the lethal hamburger over the weekend, and on the whole the current caseload was a little less heavy than usual. D'Arcy had just brought in a new suspect to question and he and

Dowling had shepherded him down the hall to an interrogation room. Rodriguez was typing a report and across the hall Sue and Daisy were talking to a woman who just had her purse snatched half an hour ago. Maddox wandered down the hall to the coffee machine and found a serviceman on his knees beside it with its back off. He looked up at Maddox with a cheerful grin. "Have it back working for you in a jiffy," he said. He was a clean-cut young fellow with freckles and sandy hair. Maddox went back to his desk and lit a cigarette.

"At least we haven't heard any more from the lunatic," said Rodriguez.

"No, and if he's had all the fun he wants we may never hear of him again," said Maddox. "I wonder if that witness will make a mug shot for us." Nolan was downtown with that one. Rodriguez finished the report and separated the triplicate copies, took one over to Ellis' office, and filed the others. He came back and sat down and after a while Nolan came in and said the witness hadn't picked out any mug shots.

"And he doesn't give us a very good description. I think we may as well forget about this one."

"Hell," said Maddox unemphatically.

"You can't win 'em all. Just one of those things. And I haven't done a report on it yet." Nolan rummaged for report forms and attacked the typewriter.

"Say," said a voice from the door, "can I talk to one of you for a minute?"

They looked up. It was the young fellow who had been servicing the coffee machine. "Sure," said Maddox. "What's on your mind?"

He came in and stood beside the desk. "I've got your machine all ready to go again, but I just spotted something and I thought I better mention it. That bulletin board you've got out in the lobby. I just glanced at it as I came by when I came in, but something just sort of rang a bell and I was thinking about it while I worked on the machine. I took another look just now and it came to me. That drawing of the guy up on the board, I've seen him, I know him, sort of."

Maddox sat up. There was only one composite sketch up on the bulletin board, the sketch of one of the pillowcase heisters. "Are you sure?"

"Yeah, I knew I'd seen him somewhere before and when I took a second look at it, it came to me. He used to do yard work for my mother and father, I usually go to see them sometime on Saturday and

I'd seen him there mowing the lawn. He's sure no movie star but it's a face you'd remember."

"I'll be damned," said Rodriguez. "Do you know his name?"

"I never heard that, but probably Dad would know, he'd have paid him. They've got somebody else now, they fired that one."

Maddox asked him for his parents' address and he wrote it down. Their name was Chapman and they lived on Tuxedo Drive up in the hills. "Say," said Chapman, "it says on that picture that he's wanted for armed robbery, can you tie that? I'm glad to know he's not working for them anymore. Oh, I'm positive it's the same guy. I hope you catch up to him." He went out with a cheerful salute.

Maddox said, "Well, you never know when you're going to get a break. Let's see if they know his name." Just to make sure, they took the sketch with them. At a pleasant-looking bungalow up there they found Mrs. Chapman home, a motherly-faced gray-haired woman, who took a look at the sketch and said, "Why, yes, that's Mike. You say my son recognized him—good heavens, it says here he's wanted for armed robbery! I never thought he was very smart but you wouldn't take him for a crook."

"Mike who?" asked Rodriguez.

"Mike Leonard, he did our yard work for a while like Bob told you but he wasn't very reliable and my husband finally fired him."

"Do you know where he lives?"

"Heavens, no, we got him through an ad in the paper."

"Well, thanks very much." At least it was something to go on. They went down to the R. and I. office at headquarters and asked if they had a package on him. In five minutes the cute blond policewoman produced it. "Sometimes we earn our salaries," said Maddox. "How very pretty." Mike Leonard was twenty-six now and had done one stretch for burglary. There were also a couple of counts of possession. The last known address was Elmo Street downtown, and he had been off parole for only four months.

They tried there and talked to his landlady; it was a single house and he rented a bedroom there. She was a respectable-looking black woman with gold-rimmed glasses, and she said, "I've told him to leave at the end of the month, he's been late with the rent lately and besides I need the room, my daughter's getting a divorce and coming home. Well, it could be at this time of day you'd find him up at the pool hall on

Venice, that's another thing, he's been out of a job, and my neighbor Mr. Robinson says he's seen him hanging around there."

Mike Leonard had just finished a game of pool when Maddox and Rodriguez got there, and he was surprised to see the fuzz. He certainly didn't look like the world's greatest brain, but he was scared of cops and rode back to the station meekly. In the cramped interrogation room Maddox said, "Okay, Leonard, we know you're one of the heisters who've been hitting all those bars, collecting the take in a pillowcase. Suppose you tell us the names of your pals on the caper with you?"

He blustered feebly, "I don't know nothin' about no holdups."

"Don't waste our time," said Rodriguez. "You've been identified, you're the one who takes around the pillowcase, we know that. Do you want to take the rap for it alone?" He thought that over painfully. "Come on," said Rodriguez, "we've got you nailed for it, tell us who the other three are. See the pretty picture we got from the description —that's you, isn't it?"

It was a good composite, Leonard to the life, and he looked at it and said, "Yeah, I guess that's me all right. I ain't goin' to do no time in the slammer if them dudes don't too. Anyway, it was Joe's idea."

"That's a good boy," said Maddox. "Joe who?"

"Joe Jackson," he said sullenly, "and the other two are Leo Culver and Al Bell, only sometimes we did jobs without him."

"So let's hear where they all live," said Rodriguez. Leonard supplied addresses for the first two but didn't know where Bell hung out, they used to meet him at a pool hall or a bar some place. It was the end of the day by then, so they booked him into jail and went home, after Maddox had applied for the warrant, and left it to the night watch.

Overnight Stacey and Donaldson picked up Culver and Jackson, and on Thursday morning Rodriguez got the package on Bell, who had a little pedigree of assault, but he'd vanished from the last known address. Three out of four wasn't bad, reflected Rodriguez philosophically, and went back to the office to type the final report on it. It was funny how the breaks came sometimes.

* * *

And they had spoken too soon. At three o'clock that afternoon a doctor at the Emergency ward at Cedars-Sinai called to report another one, a woman brought in with an OD of Demerol. Considering her general type, and knowing about all the other cases, they had suspected it was in the same series. Rodriguez and D'Arcy swore. "At least they got to her in time," said D'Arcy. The woman was conscious again and in good condition after treatment, if not ready for release.

She was a stout woman with white hair, in her sixties, and her name was Ada Klein. She looked up at them wanly from the hospital bed and said, "I just thank God my husband wasn't home, he's got a bad heart and it might've killed him. Thank God he wasn't home, he can't play golf anymore but he'd gone to the country club to have lunch with Bill Gunther. I never gave it a thought, there hasn't been any more in the papers about it and it was a couple of weeks since anybody had got poisoned. I fixed a hamburger patty for lunch—and then when I started to feel dizzy, I got scared, and I managed to call Emergency before I passed right out—"

So the lunatic was still with them.

* * *

There were no leads on the drunken heister, and on Saturday night he surfaced again, at an all-night pharmacy on Cahuenga. There had been two pharmacists on duty, and they both were still shaken up when the detectives talked to them.

"He came in waving this gun around, he had it in his hand when he came in, yes, sir, he was drunk but not falling-down drunk and he could have aimed the gun all right—and he was talking kind of slurred, but he knew what he was doing all right, he said to open the register and hand everything over."

"Could you give a description of him?" asked Stacey wearily.

"Yes, sir, he was maybe about thirty, maybe five-ten, kind of thin, he had bushy eyebrows and a long nose—yes, he was a white man."

"Do you think you might recognize him from a picture?"

They both agreed that they might, were willing to look at the mug shots tomorrow. "Did he take anything except the cash?"

"No, he just grabbed the money and went out, he was sort of staggering—he still had the gun in his hand—"

The other one said, "I think I saw him put it in his pocket as he went out—"

Something a little offbeat to this in addition to the drunkenness, thought Stacey; usually the heister at a pharmacy took all the available drugs too. He just hoped these two could make a mug shot, but of course the heister might not be on record. That was the chance they took.

* * *

Maddox and Rodriguez had been chased out on a new call that afternoon, and it looked like something to give them a lot of paperwork and legwork. It was the daughter who had called in, a Mrs. Janet Fleming, and she was oddly calm, talking to them in the big expensive house off Nichols Canyon Road, not far from where Karen Bishop had killed herself. The body was in the so-called family room off the living room, the body of a woman, and it wasn't anything nice to look at. She had had a figure more skeletal than slim, clawlike little hands with purple polish on the nails, and her expensive strawberry blond wig had fallen off as she fell, and her false teeth were partially out of her mouth, and the plastering of makeup on the dead face was grotesque—green eyeshadow, black mascara, purple lipstick on the open gaping mouth. It looked as if she'd been beaten to death with the poker from the fire set at the hearth in the living room. Her name had been Marcia Reisinger.

The daughter was in her forties, a little plump, brown-haired, and sensible. She said to Maddox and Rodriguez, "I had a key to the house in case of emergency, she didn't want to give it to me but my husband insisted. The patrolman said I shouldn't touch anything, or I'd have tried to call him, he's out playing golf. She usually called me about once a week, and I hadn't heard from her, I was a little worried. Rich said not to fuss, probably she was all right, just on a shopping spree or out with some of the riffraff she ran with." She smiled faintly. "They don't —didn't—get along. But I thought I'd better check."

"Could you tell us something about her friends, Mrs. Fleming?" asked Maddox.

She shrugged. "Not much. I'd better explain, I must sound pretty unnatural—she was my mother after all. But you see, I'd never lived with her much. She put me in an expensive boarding school as soon as I was old enough, and I was only—home—on holidays, if the current husband didn't mind kids around. The latest one was her sixth, and each one had more money than the one she'd just shed, and she always got a big settlement after the divorces. Well, you can see by the house that she was wealthy."

"I gather you didn't share many friends?"

She said unexpectedly, "I felt so sorry for her, you know. All her interests were so shallow, all she thought about was herself, her looks, and clothes, and she couldn't admit she was getting old. She was sixty-nine, I was about the only one who knew that. She'd had her face lifted a couple of times, and plastic surgery, and she was so afraid she might gain weight and lose her figure she starved herself. She didn't have any friends of her own age that I know of. She liked to be around young people, she said old people were dull. You can look in her address book to see the people she knew. There was a time, after the latest divorce, she took up the theater in a big way, she'd gotten to know some acting coach and she was raving about all these talented young people, such a privilege to know people who were going to be famous in the future. But she'd gone off that lately, from what I'd heard the last month or so she's taken up art, she was taking painting lessons from somebody named Markoudian, and he'd told her she had great talent and should have studied before, and of course she was pleased about that. I suppose she'd met more of the bright young people through him."

"Would she have been giving any of these people money?" asked Maddox.

"I wouldn't be at all surprised, I think she probably had, I wouldn't know how much. So naturally they flattered her and that pleased her all the more. I suppose we mustn't judge," she said sadly. "She'd been a very beautiful woman, and spoiled all her life—by her father, and all the husbands. I was a disappointment to her, I'm afraid, I didn't turn out to be beautiful or glamorous and I never had any ambition to be rich or famous. Rich and I have been married for twenty years, we've got three children—she didn't care for them because they were grand-children, you see, and she wouldn't admit she was old enough to have any."

It was a type, and one like that was indeed apt to pick up with anyone who flattered her vanity. God knew how many people she'd known, and people she would have admitted to the house without question.

"You could talk to her cleaning woman, Mrs. Camacho, she'll proba-bly be in the address book, Mother had had her for a couple of years. She didn't like live-in servants, liked the house to herself, but she had this woman come in several days a week, she was fastidious about having everything just so. Oh, and when she gave parties she had caterers, usually the same one, Brockway Catering Service."

"Well, thanks very much, Mrs. Fleming, if you think of anything else we'd be grateful if you'd call us."

She said quietly, "It was a terrible way for her to die. She enjoyed life so much, what she called 'the good things of life.' " She got up. "You don't want me here any longer? I'd better go and find Rich." They got her address in Studio City and let her go. As she pulled away from the curb the mobile lab van was just arriving.

Garcia and Franks had a look around and Garcia grimaced at the corpse. "That won't make pretty photographs. And it's going to take a while to dust this place."

"You might start with the poker," said Rodriguez dryly.

"That's right, teach me my job." Garcia started to set up the camera.

Maddox said, "Somebody she knew, César."

"Oh, yes, I saw it," said Rodriguez. This big room wasn't as formally furnished as the living room; there was a big white couch and matching chairs, a big color TV in one corner. On the long coffee table in front of the couch were two used glasses holding the remainder of drinks. There was an elaborate wet bar in the corner opposite the TV.

"She was sitting here talking to somebody," said Maddox, "having a drink with somebody, and maybe he'd asked her for money and she'd turned him down—it's early to say anything, but it looks suggestive."

From behind the camera Garcia said, "I don't think we'll pick up any prints from that poker, it's rough black steel. Pity it wasn't a nice shiny brass fire set. But we'll have a look at the glasses next."

There was an address book on the ornate little French desk in the living room; they got Franks to dust that first and there weren't any liftable prints on it so Maddox looked through it. It was crammed with names, scrawled in a generous sprawling hand. He found the Markoudian Art Gallery out on Sunset. They were going to be talking to a lot of people on this one. They left the lab men to do their work and started back to the office. There wasn't much they could do about this until they knew the approximate time of death, heard what the lab men would pick up.

As they came into the lobby, Ambrose and Morales of Narco were just towing in a couple of characters for questioning. Ambrose nodded at Maddox and said brusquely, "In here, boys." Nobody else was in the big office. Rodriguez sat down at his desk and lit a cigarette. "This is going to be one hell of a thing to work," he said. Maddox didn't say anything. "Whoever did it might not be listed in that address book, she evidently took up with new people all the time." Maddox was silent, staring at the opposite wall looking abstracted. "Something hit you?" asked Rodriguez.

"I don't know, I'm trying to think," said Maddox. "It was something in a night report, I seem to remember—I can't quite—Oh. Oh, that was it." He got up and went down the hall to the Narco office, Rodriguez trailing him curiously. The door was half open and Maddox looked in and beckoned Ambrose, who came out to the hall. "Who are your friends?"

"Two punks we just picked up for dealing, why?"

"I think I'd like to ask them a few questions," said Maddox. "Of course it's just a piddling little thing and the young dudes go in for that kind of decoration, but you never know."

Ambrose said, surprised, "Be our guest. They've only been here a couple of months, they're from Florida, I guess what you'd call Florida crackers, at least I don't think they're representative of your average Florida citizen. They don't think much of California, by a few things we've heard. A street snitch blew the whistle on them, and we think they may have gotten across somebody, maybe cutting in on another seller's territory."

"Oh," said Maddox. He went into the Narco office ahead of the rest of them. The two characters were sitting side by side in straight chairs under Morales' eye. They were in their mid-twenties, in the usual jeans and T-shirts, one dark-haired and one sandy, one with a long hooked nose, one with a round pug face. The one with the long nose was wearing a gold necklace with a zodiac charm suspended from it, the fish sign of Pisces. Maddox stood over them. "I'd like to ask you some questions about a rape," he said. "Rather two rapes. By the description we had, it could have been you two on those."

It had just been a random thought, but if he had hoped to take them off guard he succeeded. The one wearing the charm gaped up at him foolishly. "Two young colored girls," said Maddox, "grabbed off the street and raped. They gave us a description of two men—"

The pug-nosed one said in amazement, "Man, you gonna tell us two nigger girls told the police? That's just wild, nigger girls don't pay no never-mind to nothin' like that! All of 'em run with all kinds of bucks alla time—"

Maddox said, pleased, "So you were that pair." And that had been the longest shot he had ever tried.

The one with the charm looked at his buddy. "Man, this California place is something else—a mighty strange place." He looked at Maddox, and he was still feeling incredulous. "Nigger girls—we never did nothing like that before, no, man, we got our own chicks back home—but what in hell did it matter? Jeez, we only come out here till the heat was off in Lauderdale, and I'm right sorry we ever left home."

* * *

Mr. and Mrs. Gerald Maxwell arrived home at four o'clock on Monday afternoon. They had been up in San Francisco since Thursday, attending the prenuptial festivities and then the formal wedding of their son Gerald Junior, and they were tired. They were rather social people, belonging to the Opera Association and several clubs; Mr. Maxwell was an attorney with an office in West Hollywood. They were pleased with their son's new bride and her family, and looked forward to a couple of grandchildren in time to come. But after the change in routine, the emotional excitement of the last five days, it would be good to be home.

They hadn't had the least qualm about leaving the house empty, because their security measures were more than adequate. There were excellent dead-bolt locks on all the doors, and steel bars fitted over all the windows, even the tiny ones in the closets and second bathroom.

As they turned onto the side street off Laurel Canyon Boulevard, Mr. Maxwell uttered a vexed sound and said, "Look there, Gladys, the TV antenna's come down."

"Oh, dear," said Mrs. Maxwell, "there must have been more of those high winds since we've been gone." On one side of the roof of their sprawling ranch house the TV antenna was lying on its side. "Well, there's nothing on tonight we wanted to watch anyway, and we can get somebody up to fix it tomorrow."

Mr. Maxwell pulled into the drive and they got out. She unlocked the back door while he got the suitcases out of the trunk. He carried them down the hall toward the bedroom, and she called to him from the kitchen, "I'll just go out to the freezer in the garage to get out those chops—mercy, what's that?"

A strange muffled wailing sounded somewhere above their heads. "Help—get me out—help—"

Mrs. Maxwell fled down the hall and clutched her husband's arm in panic. "It's a ghost!"

"Don't be silly," said Mr. Maxwell. "It's coming from the living room, I think." He went in there and called, "Who are you?"

"Help—get me out—chimney—" came the muffled strange wail. Mr. Maxwell bent to the hearth and peered up it, and saw the soles of a pair of shoes about halfway up the chimney.

"My God," he said, and being a practical man of action went to call the fire department.

They had quite a time extricating the man from the chimney. He had tied a rope around the TV antenna and started down, only to find that the chimney was too narrow to accommodate even his slim build. He'd tried to haul himself out, which was when the antenna broke in two below the rope, and he'd gotten wedged tight, unable to raise his arms or push himself farther down. In the end the firemen, finding it impossible to reach him from above, had to manhandle him from inside, and pulled him down into the hearth in a great shower of soot. He was a little thin man with a rather handsome face under all the dirt, and he mumbled, "Thanks—been there—since Saturday night—" before he passed out on the Maxwells' new living-room carpet.

* * *

Feinman said tearfully, "Oh, dear, oh, dear, I haven't had a laugh like that in years! Oh, my God, you should have seen him—he was a mess! He was starving and dehydrated, the hospital's going to keep him a couple of days."

"It was Leach, then?" asked Maddox, amused.

"Oh, yes, and he isn't acting so cocky, believe me." Feinman sat up and wiped his eyes. "That house is pretty damned impregnable, but he'd seen a note on the society page about the Maxwells being away, and he knew there'd be some loot there, they're loaded. Only even Leach wasn't quite thin enough for that chimney. My God, that was a beautiful thing to see, boys. And his wife"—Feinman started laughing again—"she didn't know where he'd gone, and she was fit to be tied worrying when he didn't come home. And I think I've got something even more beautiful—" He waved a slip of paper at them. "Leach was in his working clothes, dark shirt and pants and gloves, he hadn't a damn thing on him but this." The scrap of paper bore a scrawled telephone number in ballpoint. "I'll lay you any money it's the fence's number," said Feinman. "Leach's car was parked right in front of the house. By God, I wonder if he'll lose his nerve for pulling the slick pro burglaries after this!"

* * *

They got the address attached to the phone number from the telephone company, and it was an antique store in Santa Monica. They descended on it with the search warrant and found a lot of the loot from the burglaries stashed in the back room. There was loot from other burglaries in other places than Hollywood, and they had to rope in the boys from Santa Monica and Beverly Hills.

Feinman hadn't heard anything yet about those prescription glasses, but he was feeling philosophical about it; it would come or it wouldn't.

* * *

Johnny McCrea had a pleasant day off. He slept later than usual and watched a little TV, and went out to the firing range in the afternoon to get in some practice. He picked up Joyce Boucher at six o'clock and took her to a nice place for dinner. He was really thinking seriously about asking her to marry him.

She was interested in his job, and over coffee she asked, "Do the detectives know any more about this lunatic poisoning the hamburger?"

"I don't know," said McCrea. "I don't know how they're working it."

She laughed. "I've got a funny story to tell you about it. I was talking to Marge on the phone last night and she told me about this customer." Marge was her best friend, and worked at a market as a checkout clerk. "This regular customer was in the other day and when she was checking out his groceries she noticed he had a package of hamburger, and she asked him if he wasn't afraid to buy it, it might be poisoned, and he just said, 'Oh, no, my dear, there's no poison in this and in any case it wouldn't matter. If there were, God would not let me be harmed, only evil people can be harmed by poison.' Did you ever hear anything so crazy?"

McCrea laughed. "Putting a lot of faith in God," he said. "Who was this guy?"

"Oh, some old fellow who shops there all the time, he runs a pharmacy up from the market." And then they started to talk about what movie they might go to see.

But later on, McCrea got to thinking about that. All the eight hours he was riding the squad next day on swing shift he thought about it off and on, and at first he thought, just some religious nut, and then he wondered if there could be any more to it, and he thought, the front-office boys might think he was a little crazy too, making a mountain out of a molehill, but the most they could do was call him an eager beaver. And on Friday he went in early and went back to the detective office. Maddox and Rodriguez were there alone.

McCrea said diffidently, "Could I talk to you for a minute?"

"Sure, what's on your mind?" asked Maddox.

"Well," said McCrea, "I was out with my girl on Wednesday night and she's got this friend who works at a market—" He told them the funny little story. "I guess I'm just woolgathering, to think it's anything important, sir, it just sounds nutty, but I thought I'd tell you, you might be interested."

Maddox said slowly, "Well, we're looking for a nut, aren't we? Thanks, McCrea, you thought right. A pharmacy up from this market? Which market?"

McCrea had checked that with Joyce last night. "It's a Ralph's on Rossmoor down from Melrose."

"Well, thanks," said Maddox again.

"It's probably just nothing. And I'd better get on to the briefing," said McCrea.

Maddox and Rodriguez looked at each other. "It's just a queer little story," said Rodriguez.

"Well, you never know. In a business like this we're grasping at straws. I think I'd like a look at this fellow."

It was a very shabby small pharmacy, too poorly stocked to be called a drugstore, on the corner of that old street. At first they thought there wasn't anybody in the place. They walked up to the counter at the back. The framed pharmacist's license was hung on the wall there; the name on it was James Cameron Purcell. All around it were religious texts—*Thou God Seest Me—This Night Shall Thy Soul Be Required of Thee—God Is Near—Repent Before It Is Too Late—Jesus Is Coming Soon*.

The man came out from the back room suddenly and stood behind the counter. He was a tall bony old man with a scaly bald scalp and myopic eyes behind thick lenses. "Yes, gentlemen?"

"Mr. Purcell?" said Maddox.

"Yes, that's right. It's nice to have customers, business is very bad, but I mustn't complain, perhaps that is part of God's purpose. I must wait to see."

"Mr. Purcell, you said something the other day to one of the checkers at the market that we're rather wondering about. That only evil people could be harmed by poison. How did you come by that idea?"

Purcell's pebble-gray eyes brightened with interest. "Ah, that's interesting, that you should mention that."

"You told her that you knew the package of meat you'd bought wasn't poisoned. How did you know that?"

Purcell regarded them with growing interest. Suddenly he leaned across the counter and said, "I believe you know something. Talking about it. Of course I knew. I have wondered—sometimes God sends revelations to more than one of His servants at the same time." He stared at them avidly. "Are you messengers? Messengers from God?"

"We're police, Mr. Purcell." Maddox reached for the badge.

Purcell peered at it and the excitement sharpened in his eyes. He said wonderingly, "Police—why, that's strange, it never occurred to me until this moment that of course the police would be interested in the experiment, of course it would be of great value to the police, I can see that. Why, it would be the most magnificent weapon the law has ever had!"

"The experiment," said Rodriguez softly.

"You do know something," said Purcell. "Others have had the revelation too."

"Would the experiment have anything to do with the packages of meat, Mr. Purcell?" asked Maddox.

He looked at them keenly. "You do know. I wonder how, but God works in mysterious ways. I have not discussed it with anyone—I was sorely tempted to tell the minister, Mr. Dunbar—he's a very godly man —but an inner voice told me to keep silent. After all, the experiment has not proceeded very far. But the police—it's curious that I never thought how interested you would be, what a marvelous scientific weapon it would be for you in fighting evil."

"That's what we'd like to talk to you about," said Maddox. "There are some other people who'd like to discuss it with you too."

"How very interesting and gratifying," said Purcell. "I have badly wanted to talk about it with some godly men who will understand the importance of my revelation."

"Can you come with us now?" asked Rodriguez.

"Oh, certainly, certainly, I know it's of vital importance. It won't matter about closing the store, business is so very bad. Just let me get my jacket." He was back in twenty seconds, his white smock exchanged for a shabby jacket. "This is a red-letter day in my life, gentlemen, I understand now that others have been given the revelation at the same time as myself, and I will be pleased to discuss it with other godly men."

* * *

He sat in the office of the chief psychiatrist at the hospital, beaming around at them. "Did I get your name correctly, it's Dr. Simon? I'm very pleased to know you, doctor."

The doctor said in a quiet voice, "We'd be interested to know how this revelation came to you, Mr. Purcell, and exactly what it was."

"Oh, certainly, it may have come to others in a different way. It began with the rattlesnakes. I had been reading the most interesting article in a religious magazine about a Christian sect which uses rattlesnakes at their service, to prove that God will not allow His own to be harmed. And of course that is true. I thought about it more deeply than I ever had before, and one night—I had just been saying my prayers—it was like a great burst of light—it was revealed to me what a powerful tool it would be, to separate God's own from the evil people. Do you see? It may even be that this is God's plan to cleanse the world anew, through His righteous servants. To introduce a potentially fatal drug into the whole population—if the experiment were carried out properly, but I have not been able to do a great deal—and only the evil ones would die, God would protect all the righteous. Think how we could improve the entire world—why, it could be carried out under the auspices of the United Nations! If it was properly organized—" He was red with excitement and enthusiasm. "I have only been able to do a little, working on my own. Of course we could only prove the true value of the experiment by working in Christian nations—naturally God wishes all the unbelievers to be preserved, in order that they may be converted to the true belief when Jesus Christ comes again, which will be very soon now."

"Did the revelation show you just how to conduct the test?" asked Simon.

"Oh, no, that was Mrs. Carrillo." The anticlimax was almost ludicrous. "She had a prescription for that particular brand of meperidene, I'd never had a call for it before, and as I was transferring the tablets to the new bottle I noticed the color and it struck me they were just the color of raw hamburger, and at once I saw how to conduct the test. And the very little way I have gone with the experiment"—he was triumphant now—"and so far as I have been able to determine from the newspapers and TV, it has been eminently successful. Some have died and some have lived, as God withheld protection from the evil ones. It has been very, very interesting."

"It certainly has, Mr. Purcell," said Dr. Simon. "There are some other people who'd like to discuss it with you, if you don't mind coming along with me now."

"Oh, certainly, certainly, I'll be glad to."

* * *

"Religious mania," said Simon, "give it the lay term. He said something about his wife dying—I think you'll find that he hasn't any friends, has been driven into himself, as it were, and he's been brooding over this idea for some time. Poor devil, he's very happy about his experiment. Of course as a licensed pharmacist he could buy as much Demerol as he liked, no questions asked. And the way he came apart, it's likely he'd have given himself away, that somebody might have suspected he was going off his rocker before now, but the probability is that he talked to very few people. And he'd have gone on with it, you know. I'm just glad you caught up to him."

Maddox said, "And that was the longest shot of all, doctor."

* * *

There were headlines about it, for a day or so. Purcell would, thought Maddox, probably settle down quite happily at Atascadero, as long as they let him have all the religious books he wanted.

The usual early heat wave arrived that next week, a foretaste of what was to come. The lab turned up absolutely nothing useful on the Reisinger case, and it was taking a lot of time to find and talk to everybody she had known. The drunken heister was still wandering around, and they had two more heists to work.

Maddox was late getting away from the office on Wednesday night. He had been out on the legwork all day, and he was tired. On the drive home he found himself yawning repeatedly. He wondered if those latest witnesses were going to make any mug shots for them. He wondered how D'Arcy was doing with the Spanish teacher, of all girls. That was a funny one.

At the house on Starview Terrace he went in the back door and Tama uttered an amiable woof. "I've kept your dinner warm," said Margaret, smiling at him. "You get yourself a drink and unwind." Carrying the drink, Maddox went down to the living room and Sue said, "Better late than never. You look beat. Thank heaven we're both off tomorrow, and thank heaven I've only got a week to go before I can stay home and wait for the baby." The baby was very visible now. "Honestly, the things we see on this thankless job—"

Maddox leaned back in the big armchair. He took a grateful swallow of the drink and grinned at her. "Well," he said, "it's a living."

ABOUT THE AUTHOR

Elizabeth Linington has written more than fifty novels. Among her previous novels featuring Ivor and Sue Maddox are *Skeletons in the Closet, Consequence of Crime,* and *No Villain Need Be.*